MISSION: BUTTERFLY

MARCH OF MANKIND
BOOK 1

SIMONE GEORGES

This book is dedicated to all those who have been injured by the experimental mRNA injection you were coerced into taking. May you heal and see better days.

To my mother who taught me to value truth and integrity and salvation through faith in Jesus, I thank you with all my heart for the clarity of vision you gave me and the path to salvation you showed me.

Dease Lake
Meziadin Junction
Revillagigedo Island
Hazelton Two Mile
Gitanyow
Kitwanga
Smithers

British
Columbia
Burns Lake
Prince
George
97

Preface

The COVID 'pandemic' changed the world in so many ways. I knew it was coming, but it was much worse than I expected. I didn't know it was about totalitarian control. I didn't know they would force ridiculous mandates. I didn't know the government would lie to me day after day. I didn't know they would shun me and kick me out of public spaces if I didn't take an experimental mRNA injection.

I also would never have believed so many people would buy into the lies and the manufactured panic.

But they did.

So, I began to write this book because I wanted to expose these things.

I am Canadian and I am a Christian. As a Canadian, I believe this to be the most beautiful country in the world with its mountains and lakes, canyons and badlands, tundra and grasslands. As a Christian, I fear for this country with its antiquated Westminster parliamentary system that has been thoroughly hijacked by Marxism masquerading as globalism.

Why do I fear Marxism? Well, beyond the fact that is it founded on godlessness, it is based on promises of future utopia if only we turn over our sovereignty to the ruling powers – because they know what is best for us.

The interesting point about this is that I once espoused a fairly Marxist ideology. I read Pierre Valières book *Les Nègres blancs d'Amérique* and became a socialist and a Quebec separatist.

I then moved to Ontario for university where I encountered the "green" ideology, joined the Green Party and acted as treasurer for my local riding. Of course, back then the Green Party didn't espouse most of the self-immolating beliefs it does now, but I was fully sold on saving the planet.

What changed?

In 2011, I was sitting in an apartment in downtown Damascus, Syria, watching CNN. A broadcast came on claiming bombs had been dropped on the city in the night *with bombing footage*. The thing is, I was *in* downtown Damascus. I had been out on the town until 2 a.m. enjoying the Eid celebrations and drinking coffee with happy family groups. It was a scene of conviviality and peace *with no bombs all night*.

It was all a lie by the media. What other lies were they telling? What other lies was I believing?

I looked for truth about the world.

I found it and it was shocking.

It was not the planet I needed to save; it was freedom.

This book was written for all those who have not fully grasped the psy-op that is our current unreality.

I woke up, and you can, too.

Contents

The Gods of the Copybook Headings

Rudyard Kipling (1919)

As I pass through my incarnations in every age and race,
I make my proper prostrations to the Gods of the Market
*   Place.*
Peering through reverent fingers I watch them flourish and
*   fall,*
And the Gods of the Copybook Headings, I notice, outlast
*   them all.*

We were living in trees when they met us. They showed us
*   each in turn*
That Water would certainly wet us, as Fire would certainly
*   burn:*
But we found them lacking in Uplift, Vision and Breadth of
*   Mind,*
So we left them to teach the Gorillas while we followed the
*   March of Mankind.*

We moved as the Spirit listed. They never altered their pace,
Being neither cloud nor wind-borne like the Gods of the
*   Market Place,*
But they always caught up with our progress, and presently
*   word would come*
That a tribe had been wiped off its icefield, or the lights had
*   gone out in Rome.*

With the Hopes that our World is built on they were utterly
     out of touch,
They denied that the Moon was Stilton; they denied she was
     even Dutch;
They denied that Wishes were Horses; they denied that a
     Pig had Wings;
So we worshipped the Gods of the Market Who promised
     these beautiful things.

When the Cambrian measures were forming, They
     promised perpetual peace.
They swore, if we gave them our weapons, that the wars of
     the tribes would cease.
But when we disarmed They sold us and delivered us bound
     to our foe,
And the Gods of the Copybook Headings said: "Stick to the
     Devil you know."

On the first Feminian Sandstones we were promised the
     Fuller Life
(Which started by loving our neighbour and ended by
     loving his wife)
Till our women had no more children and the men lost
     reason and faith,
And the Gods of the Copybook Headings said: "The Wages
     of Sin is Death."

In the Carboniferous Epoch we were promised abundance
     for all,
By robbing selected Peter to pay for collective Paul;
But, though we had plenty of money, there was nothing our
     money could buy,
And the Gods of the Copybook Headings said: "If you don't
     work you die."

Then the Gods of the Market tumbled, and their smooth-
*   tongued wizards withdrew,*
And the hearts of the meanest were humbled and began to
*   believe it was true*
That All is not Gold that Glitters, and Two and Two make
*   Four—*
And the Gods of the Copybook Headings limped up to
*   explain it once more.*

As it will be in the future, it was at the birth of Man
There are only four things certain since Social Progress
*   began.*
That the Dog returns to his Vomit and the Sow returns to
*   her Mire,*
And the burnt Fool's bandaged finger goes wabbling back to
*   the Fire;*

And that after this is accomplished, and the brave new
*   world begins*
When all men are paid for existing and no man must pay
*   for his sins,*
As surely as Water will wet us, as surely as Fire will burn,
The Gods of the Copybook Headings with terror and
*   slaughter return!*

CHAPTER 1

The Bear

"I have a duty to speak the truth as I see it and share not just my triumphs, not just the things that felt good, but the pain, the intense, often unmitigated pain. It is important to share how I know survival is survival and not just a walk through the rain."

~ Audre Lord

"What was that?" Janet hissed, shaking Lionel's shoulder. He grunted quietly, rubbed his stubbled face, and swung his legs off the rumpled fur-covered bed. Janet was sitting up in the dim light from the dying fire, her hand on her growing belly, white-blond hair tumbling over her shoulders. "Did you hear that?" she hissed again.

Lionel heard it that time. It was a low, snuffling sound, very close to the thick wooden door that was recessed into the slope of the mountain. Padding on cold bare feet Lionel crept quietly to the east-facing window of their dug-out cabin. He picked up the CZ Ranger .308 that he kept ready and silently unbarred the wooden shutters, gently setting the iron bar on the floor. He peered out the window into the misty night.

Through the dancing wraiths of fog, Lionel spied a large, darker shadow by the light of the gibbous moon. It was moving silently along by the fenced garden, heading towards the hives.

He hurried quickly across the cold floor to the door, unbarred and opened it.

Ignoring Janet's hissed, "be careful!" he stepped into the opening, levelled his rifle, peering through the scope. Not for the first time, he wished he had invested in a night-vision scope. Cold air and mist drifted through the door, raising goosebumps on his bare torso. He ignored it, located the dark shape, and squeezed the trigger.

Immediately after the deafening crack split the night, a loud resonating roar reverberated as the animal reared up onto its hind legs. Lionel squeezed the trigger again. The roar sounded again, and a huge dark form dashed for the encroaching trees.

Lionel slipped his bare feet into the boots by the door and grabbed his jacket off the hook. "Where's the flashlight?" he muttered, groping the closet shelf in the dim light. "Here it is." He dropped it in his pocket and went out. "Bar the door and wait for my knock, keep your gun beside you," he said and closed it.

Janet sat trembling for a few moments, heart pounding, ears straining in the night silences, then she leapt out of bed and hurried to bar the door. She stood looking out the window with the shutters ajar for several long minutes, her tall slim body vibrating with her terrified breaths and her dreadful imaginings. Night and creeping predators howled in her swirling mind.

There was nothing to see or hear outside now, except the twisting tendrils of mist and drifts of cloud over the moon and the roaring of her heartbeat in her ears. Silhouettes of darker trees against the dark night. Not even the grey owl down the mountain was hooting. The dash of the waterfall off to her left was drowned out by her panting breaths.

Janet found herself praying incoherently. Please God, keep Lionel safe. Please God, bring us back to civilization.

Please God, keep my baby safe. Please God oh please God oh please, let the world go back to normal.

How long was it now that she'd seen no one other than her husband Lionel? It felt like eons of loneliness. Somewhere out there everything she'd ever known was ending - at least that was what Lionel had said would happen. For two years he'd fought, tried to wake people up to their peril, made videos, and joined activist groups of medical experts. She'd watched him roused to horror and disgust with the masking and the lockdowns and the utterly irrational inconsistencies.

It had happened so quickly: Lionel had gone from an eminent immunologist with multiple peer-reviewed scientific papers and a world-class specialist consultation clinic to a mountain man now hiding in the highlands of northern British Columbia hunting a bear in the middle of the night. Their beautiful home was gone, her friends at Bible study – where were they now? Her parents – were they even alive? Everything she had ever known and loved was gone and now her daily reality was so – silent, solitary. The world had changed, and she wasn't ready for it. How was this even possible?

As Janet bent down to pick up the cold iron bar and close the shutters, she realized that tears were running down her cheeks. Ignoring that wet rain, she dropped the bar into its iron braces, shivered, and went back to the warmth of the bed.

Janet had almost dropped back into a restless sleep when Lionel's knock roused her. "I don't think I hit him," he responded to her anxious query. "I didn't see any blood. I'll check again when the sun rises. Huge prints, though. He's a big one."

He removed the clip from his rifle and put the CZ back on the wall rack. He tossed his jacket onto the rocking chair by the fireplace and crawled back into bed. Janet reached out and drew his cold feet to her warm legs and he was soon asleep. She listened to his comfortable breathing for a long time before she managed to fall asleep again.

The morning sun had burned away the mist by the time Janet got up. Lionel was already outside, chopping wood and feeding the chickens that were housed in the log coop next to the garden. Gulping against the familiar morning nausea, Janet nibbled on a homemade biscuit while she brewed coffee in her beloved French press.

Lionel came in shortly, bringing in wafts of freshly chopped spruce and a slight aroma of sweat. This rough living agreed with him. He bore little resemblance to the distinguished young man she'd married seven years ago. He was bigger now, muscular from the hard work he had to do to maintain their rustic way of life. His thick wavy brown hair was shaggy and he shaved weekly, not daily.

Lionel dropped a kiss on her forehead and briefly ran his hand over her belly. "Good morning," he said. Janet wondered if he was greeting her or the tiny child curled up inside her. He didn't talk much anymore. It was almost as if the battle he'd waged out in Calgary had stolen all his words away. He had spilled his words into his YouTube videos, he had poured his words into warning articles and podcasts. Now he had very few words left. So few words for her. She was so lonely sometimes. The green silences of the mountain seemed to soothe him, fulfill him and cleanse him. It was different for her.

She went to the big iron cook stove, put a chunk of wood inside, and stoked up the fire. The coffee was ready, so she poured a cup for Lionel and herself. "Did you see any sign of the bear?" She placed the French press on the table.

Lionel shook his head. "No blood at all. I didn't even wing it. I did see bear scarring on the aspens a ways down the mountain and a lot of prints around the chicken house and goat shed, though. He looks to have attempted entry. Good thing they're sturdy. I think I'll stick around for a few days. I was wanting to get an elk or deer this week to add to our supplies, but I think I'll wait a bit and see if he comes back around."

He dug into the eggs she placed in front of him. She sat down across from him, one leg bent under her, and nibbled a piece of toast.

Over the next couple of days, Lionel spent some time getting her to practice with her .270 Browning Winchester and the Mossberg pump-action 12 gauge. He wanted her to learn to shoot so she could protect herself. She preferred the smaller Ruger .22 rifle because it didn't kick as much.

"Don't you think our little butterfly can hear the gunshots?" she asked, laying her hand on her stomach when a particularly strong flutter happened somewhere inside her in response to a volley of shots. "I bet it's scaring her."

Lionel laughed. "Don't worry, little butterfly," he said, laying his hand gently on top of hers, "she - or he - will be shooting guns at two years old."

That night he curled up against her, his hand caressing the small mountain of her middle. "Do you know how rare babies are going to be soon?" he asked.

She sighed quietly and snuggled against him. "What did George have to say tonight?" She was referring to his bi-weekly ham radio call with his long-time friend George who was still in Calgary. Talking to George twice a week was the only way they kept in contact with what was happening outside.

"Well, like I said, babies are going to be rare soon. He's had two female patients who miscarried this week. He still won't admit it's the jab, though." Lionel rolled onto his back and stared up into the dark rafters above him, lit only by the flickering fire in the fireplace. "He was really upset about a baby girl that went into anaphylactic shock after nursing from her mom. She'd got the jab that morning. The baby died, but he claims it was just an allergic reaction unrelated to the mRNA injection. He was always skeptical about what Viv and I told him, he always thought we were alarmists."

Into the long silence after these words, he spoke again. "I'm heading out early in the morning. When you go out, keep your .270 loaded beside you and stay near the cabin. I haven't seen any sign of the bear since the other night, so you should be fine. Just be careful." He took her hand and raised it to his lips. "Good night, Janet." He brushed his hand over her belly. "Good night, Butterfly."

The birds were just starting to twitter their morning greetings when Lionel heaved his pack onto his back and headed out the door. Janet sleepily got out of bed and followed him. He bent slightly to drop a quick kiss on her lips. "Good luck," Janet murmured. He heard the bar drop as he started his trek up the mountain.

Exhilaration filled him. Even as a child and later as a med student he'd loved hiking through the mountains and going for hunting trips with his father and his older brother Michael. Getting out of town, away from the noise and annoyances of everyday life had restored and empowered him to go back, study hard, and reach the pinnacles of academic excellence none of his family had ever dreamed of. He'd completed his medical training in record time and received a grant from the Alberta government to study immunology at the University of Guelph with the renowned Dr. Byram Bridle.

Lionel moved up the mountain eastward. Using the fallen tree bridge he soon crossed the fast-flowing creek above the waterfall that provided power to his home. He paused in his climb to survey the scene before him. The morning sun was just rising beyond the mountain range behind Dark Mountain. Most of the winter snow had melted, except for areas which rarely saw the sun. The air had that translucent quality that only a cool April morning can have. He inhaled the scent of spruce and pine and water from the rain the evening before. He still marvelled at how beautiful this country was. Every time he paused to soak in the beauty, he would think, "This is God's country! This is the way He meant it to be."

He unslung the binoculars and scanned above him and further to the east. In the far distance, just beyond a ridge of mountains, a hovering helicopter caught his eye. He tracked it briefly, wondering what it was doing out in this wild country, then he scanned lower. Only a few soaring hawks or eagles. But he had confidence his prey was out there. This trail he was following was made by the elk and there was fresh scat here and there. If he didn't find them today, it would be tomorrow.

His mind wandered to Janet. Why wasn't she happy? Why couldn't she share his enjoyment of the simple life they lived? Why couldn't she see the marvels he saw? Sure, she had left behind her parents to whom she was very attached, but they had both taken the jab and chosen to believe the government narrative – in spite of her pleading with them not to take it.

Lionel sighed, taking note of a burrow that looked to be occupied. He would set a snare there and see if he could get a few rabbits.

Janet's parents were involved in pastoral and mission work. That was the reason they'd given for electing to be vaccinated.

"Many of our members are elderly," Daniel, Janet's dad had explained. "Some of them live in assisted living facilities. Only vaccinated people are allowed to visit." He had believed the claims that the jab was 'safe and effective' and would protect the elderly and immune-compromised.

Of course, not long after, all assisted living facilities had been closed to all visitors including family members. Almost immediately after, though fit and formerly healthy, Daniel had a heart attack. He was recovering after a double bypass when Lionel and Janet left Calgary for their mountain refuge. George kept Janet and Lionel updated occasionally about Janet's parents and had also conveyed the good news to them about the coming grandchild.

Lionel's meditations were interrupted by a flock of blue grouse fluttering up around him to land in the branches of the evergreens. He laughed. "Don't worry, guys! I don't have my .22 with me." Shaking off his somber meditations, he continued his hike up the narrow path, the beady eyes of the immobile birds watching him as he went by.

By early afternoon, he'd reached the upper slopes of the mountain. A scan with his binoculars located the herd on the flat meadow overlooked by a jutting promontory. It looked like at least 20 elk with a magnificent bull and several immature ones and more than 10 cows with their calves. "I just want one of you today," he grunted and removed his Ranger .308 from the holster on the side of his pack. He scoped the distance and decided he needed to get a shot from the clump of hemlock some 300 metres to his right on the face of the slope. He silently re-holstered his rifle and moved back under the cover of the trees.

It took about two hours of quiet, careful movement through the bush to reach his goal. He lost sight of the herd while working his way southward and downward. When he approached the hemlocks, he noiselessly placed his pack on the ground, took his rifle, and crept through the thinning area in the trees.

The herd was restless. Some of the cows that had been lying down were on their feet. The big bull had his head up, flaring his nostrils. Many of them were milling restlessly and cows were squealing for their calves. Lionel went down on his belly and carefully eased his way to a good vantage point. The bull barked and tossed his head. Lionel raised his upper torso up onto his elbows, took careful aim, and gently squeezed the trigger. His target was a healthy-looking bull that looked to be a couple of years old. He saw one elk rear up. Barking and bugling filled the afternoon air along with the squealing of cows and calves. The herd scattered and headed into the brush across the meadow.

Lionel whistled with satisfaction. His target was down. He went back to his pack, gathered it up, then approached the downed animal. It was a clean shot through the left shoulder. He roped up the legs and dragged it to the two birches he'd already marked out for the purpose. Soon, the hanging bar was rigged up, his game animal gutted and cleaned.

When he was done, the sun was dropping behind the mountains to the west. Lionel decided this was as good a spot as any to spend the night. He lit a fire, ate some of the food he'd packed, wrapped himself up in his waterproof bedroll and fell asleep quickly, lulled by the chirping crickets.

It was drizzling slightly as Lionel headed down the mountain the next morning with his tarp-wrapped game dragging behind him. It was slow going, taking care not to rip the tarp on roots or rough surfaces, but Lionel had done this many times before and, in lieu of the hunting sled he used in his youth, his tarp was the heaviest gauge he'd been able to buy. There was still snow in shaded areas and rain-wet grass that made his task much easier. By mid-afternoon, he was approaching home. He crossed the creek, allowing the tarp-wrapped elk to drag into the icy spring-melt water. He was resuming his approach to home when he heard the screams.

Fear exploded in his head. Lionel dropped the rope and, with frantic fingers, unbuckled the belt of his unwieldy pack and dashed towards the clearing. Breaking through the fringe of tamarack that ringed his clearing to the east, he saw a huge brown shape, reared up on its hind legs. Janet was on the top bar of the wooden fence by the henhouse, desperately trying to climb onto the roof all the while pointing a weapon at the roaring horror that was barely ten feet from her.

A shot rang out. It was the sharp crack of a .22.

"Nooooo, Janet! Nooooo!" His gasping howl tore out of him. Lionel's stomach contracted; she had not kept the more powerful rifle with her.

As he ran, he was dragging his rifle from its holster on the side of his jouncing pack and he was trying to shrug the straps off all at the same time. He stopped when the pack fell to the ground, his frenzied fingers fumbled at the leather ties on the back of the pack, searching for the loaded mag he'd placed in there that morning. All the while, he was howling at the top of his lungs, trying to attract the monster to him. The roaring continued unabated, along with the screaming and another crack from Janet's small rifle. He found the mag, snapped it into his .308.

The gigantic, humped animal was on all fours now, blood streaming from one side of its face. The small calibre bullet striking the side of its head had served only to enrage it more. It took only moments for the enormous shaggy monster to reach the frantic woman who was on the edge of the henhouse roof now, trying to use her ineffective weapon as a club to fend off the beast. The small rifle struck it on the skull at the same time as the six-inch claws on the enormous right paw of the upright grizzly made contact with Janet's vulnerable clothing and flesh.

The .22 bounced off its skull and flew away across the chicken run. With the impact of the gigantic, murderous paw, Janet's fingers slipped loose off the ridge of the henhouse roof and she crashed to the dirt. She was still trying to get away, twisting and screaming. The bear fell back onto all fours and swiped at her again, just as Lionel raised his rifle and took his first shot.

The powerful round slammed into the hindquarters of the shaggy creature. It reared up and away from Janet's crumpled form. Another shot struck it in the shoulder. It was on its hind legs now, towering over Lionel and swiping at him when

Lionel's third shot, at point-blank range, hit it in the centre of its wide-open roaring jaws.

Lionel didn't stop to see the monster fall, he vaulted over the fence into the chicken run where the terrified birds were still huddled, crouched as far away from the fray as they could.

Gasping Lionel fell to his knees beside his wife. She was lying in a growing pool of blood, half on her stomach, arms splayed, her face turned away from him. Her body was shuddering, and a low mewling sound was coming from her. There was a dreadful gash in her right shoulder and down her upper arm with the bone of the humerus visible through the ribbons of her flesh, the slash was so deep.

Waves of dread washed over Lionel as he gently turned her over, intending to gather her up in his arms. When he saw the damage on her lower body, a tortured groan broke from him.

"Janet, Janet, honey, stay with me. Janet, Janet, Janet, it'll be OK, you'll be OK."

He gathered her shaking body in his arms and carried her into the cabin and gently laid her on the bed. Her wide-open eyes were glassy, mewling cries continued to escape her slack mouth.

Lionel groped in the cupboard where he kept his medical supplies, not noticing the smears of blood he left on every surface. This was his wife, his companion in exile. This could not be happening. Oh God, this couldn't really be happening. She couldn't die, she was his Janet, he couldn't do this. He found his hands shaking, sweat and agony blinding his streaming eyes, bloodied medical supplies falling like carmine hail to the stone floor. On his knees now, scrabbling through the fallen equipment, he stopped.

Breathe. Slow down. Breathe. Pray. Get what you need. Now get up.

Lionel located the case of surgical tools and the other materials he needed. His breathing calmed, he reassured softly, "It'll be OK, Janet, stay with me, you'll be OK."

Using the sterile scissors, the trembling in his hands sternly controlled, he cut away her clothes to expose the ragged gashes that started on her left hip, across her abdomen and deep into her right thigh. Her body was already convulsing, trying to save her by rejecting the tiny human curled up in the nest of her womb.

Lionel took out his suture kit. He administered a shot of morphine and flushed the area with a bottle of saline, then began to stitch. Blood-soaked towels were soon heaped around his feet as he struggled to repair internal damage. Images of sepsis and abscesses he squelched and continued to pray. He rigged up a saline drip in a desperate endeavour to replace lost fluids. By now, she was unconscious, her face ghastly pale.

Lionel worked quickly, closing the worst of the gashes first in an attempt to staunch the bleeding. He had to stop at one point and gently wrap the tiny infant her body thrust out.

An eternity later, he finally ceased his work, covered the seeping wounds with gauze compresses, and gave her an injection of antibiotic.

He did his best to clean up the bed, gently easing the blood-soaked bedclothes out from under Janet's silent body and slipping clean sheets in their place. Lionel bathed as much blood as he could off his wife. Her glorious blond hair was tangled and full of blood and there was nothing he could do about that. He covered her with the warmest blankets and stoked up the fire.

Drawing a chair up beside her, he held the kitten-sized baby girl cradled in one hand. He had wrapped her in the partially finished baby blanket Janet was knitting with the fluffiest yarn. This tiny child did not have a chance once the bear ravaged her mother's body. She was so tiny, yet so perfectly formed. Her minuscule fingers and toes and her perfectly formed ears brought tears to his weary eyes. There had been so much potential for life here, and it was torn from her. He saw her die, her beating heart stop because her lungs weren't formed enough to breathe.

"Go to God, little Butterfly," he murmured, then he bowed his head and prayed for her mother.

Two hours later, when Janet stirred and moaned, he gave her another shot of morphine and one of antibiotics.

Sometime, deep into the black ocean of this night, when the fire had died down to purple embers and Lionel had fallen into an exhausted sleep, Janet woke up.

"Lionel, Lionel," her whisper was enough to rouse him.

He was immediately kneeling at her side. "Janet," he murmured back, "honey."

"She's gone, isn't she? Butterfly is gone." Her voice was almost inaudible. Somehow, in the midst of the horror of pain and anguish, the mother had felt her body thrust her child out. Now, she had roused to grieve, though life was fading from her.

Lionel stroked her pale matted hair. "Do you want to see her?" he whispered gently.

He took a moment to turn on the lamp beside the bed, picked up the tiny bundle he'd placed in the bassinet he'd built with so much anticipation and joy, and carried the child to her.

"Thank you," she said, cradling the tiny, swaddled body to her breast. She closed her eyes.

Lionel touched her forehead. It was cold, as though her body could not generate enough heat. He got out his medicine kit, prepared to inject her IV with more antibiotics.

"No more," she murmured, "let me go."

He put away the kit and sat beside her in his chair. An ember fell in the fireplace.

"Do you remember where we met?" his voice was soft and sad. "You were so beautiful, with your shining crown of hair. Remember all those Bible studies I attended, just to see you?"

Janet's face relaxed, a bit of a smile on her pallid lips.

"I chased you until you finally agreed to date me. When you agreed to marry me, I was so happy, I couldn't believe how lucky I was." His voice caught a little. He was remembering that first rush of love. "I still can't believe you gave everything up for me. You were so generous, so giving. I didn't deserve you."

Janet's breath was coming more shallowly now. Lionel reached out and gently removed the IV from the hand that was cupping the tiny body of her child.

"Oh, Janet, you didn't deserve any of this. I'm so sorry, I'm sorry for everything. You deserved so much and I didn't give it to you." He didn't notice the tears running into his beard and a sob tore out of his chest.

Janet's breast finally stopped moving. Lionel fell to his knees and let the anguish overwhelm him. When he raised his head, he saw the first light of the dawn coming through the window.

By noon, he had built a pyre in a clearing up the face of the mountain. The rain from the previous day had stopped, though the skies were louring and threatening rain later that evening. Lionel laid his wife and tiny daughter to rest on the heap of wood wrapped in the best linen he could find in his stores. He hunkered down next to the pyre, his hands buried in the shallow soil covering the rocks and bones of the Dark Mountain and he wept.

He wept for the lost promise of the life that was gone. He wept when his guilt at having not loved Janet well enough swept over him. He wept for the world that was willingly marching to destruction. He wept for his friend George who was going to die and didn't believe it yet. He wept and refused to think of Viv because that would be one more betrayal of the woman lying silent on the pyre.

When his tears were finally exhausted, he lit the fire and stood silently as it consumed his companion in exile. By the time the fire died down, a slow cold drizzle had begun. He would be alone now.

C H A P T E R   2

Mission

"Great nations do not succumb through lost wars, but rather through racial decay and the destruction of their internal order."
~ Adolf Hitler

"Why, O Lord, do You stand far away? Why do You hide Yourself in times of trouble?"
~ Psalm 10:1 ESV

"Going outside for a smoke, Grandfather," Norm called to the old man lying in the storeroom on a small cot wrapped in a warm blanket. The young man pulled on his bulky blue parka without bothering to zip it up and went out into the snow. He snapped the Christmas light switch off as he went out into the early morning radiance.

He had placed a cigarette in his mouth and flicked his lighter when through the gently swirling flakes of the mid-winter morning he spotted an extraordinary sight.

The flame of his lighter went out, he removed the unlit smoke from his mouth and stood still in disbelief. It looked like a bear walking on its hind legs on snowshoes pulling a sled! The apparition was walking steadily, in the peculiar wide-legged gait of the snowshoer, across highway 37 from the east. Snow was clinging to the heavy fur on its head and shoulders.

As the form approached, Norm saw it was a man. His shaggy hair and beard, rimed with snow and ice, were the same colour as the enormous bearskin coat. The man's head-covering was made of the upper skull of a bear, his mitts were made of bearskin, and his legs were wrapped with bearskin bound with leather straps. Even his snowshoes were the bear-paw type. The sled pulled by the man was hand-made with polished runners and an elk-hide covering.

As he approached, Norm was transfixed by the fathomless ice of the man's eyes, drawing him into some unknown depths of cold and loss. Rousing himself, he replaced the cigarette in his mouth and lit it, cupping his hand around the small flame.

"Hey, good morning," he said when the man halted. He drew deeply on his cigarette and let the smoke drift out his mouth and nostrils into the crisp winter air.

"Good morning." The man's voice was the low growl of someone who hasn't spoken in a while. The bearskin-clad man shrugged off the sled's harness that crossed his shoulders and chest. "You open yet?"

Norm nodded. "We open at 7 am, eh. We used to get truckers through here wanting an early start and some supplies."

"What do you mean, 'used to'?" The man removed his snowshoes and placed them on the sled.

"Not so many anymore," Norm answered. "I call head office, they say they're sending a shipment... when they answer, but nothing ever comes. Sorry, we're getting low on supplies."

"I see." The man stamped his boots free of snow on the mat before the door. He then shook some of the snow off his headgear and coat and entered the Super A.

Norm sucked in a few more quick drags on his cigarette, threw it in the snow and followed him in.

"Grandfather! You're up?"

The sick old man was standing at the cash desk. His deeply creased ancient face looked almost skull-like as he braced himself on the glass counter. He had removed the oxygen cannula, and his breath was shallow and strained.

"It is my time, my son. I must speak with Bear Heart before I go."

"Who, Grandfather?"

"Please tell Bear Heart to come to me. I have a message for him." He stumbled as he turned and Norm hurried to his side. He slung his arm around the old man's frail body and they made their slow way back to the storeroom.

Lionel, for it was Lionel, had taken a basket and was wending his way through the meagrely stocked aisles of the Super A. On the way in, he noted the scarcity of chocolate bars and chips that would usually be on display at the check-out desk, so any food he could find would be welcome. His bearskin mittens were in the cart, but he still wore his bearskin coat and bear skull headgear. He was loading up with what sparsely available canned fruits and vegetables he could find. He'd found a bonanza of freezer-burned fruits and vegetables in one of the freezers and was feeling pleased about that. There had been no garden last summer and vegetable and fruit stores had dwindled to non-existent. He had mounded the three loaves of bread left on the shelves, a large bag of Jasmine rice and the few oddly shaped types of pasta he found on top of everything into the cart when Norm came up behind him.

"Uh, excuse me, I think my grandfather wants to speak to you."

Lionel turned and looked at the thin young Indigenous man. "OK," he said. *I wonder what he wants?* His thoughts were fleeting; if it was conversation the grandfather wanted, Lionel had none for him.

"Come this way."

When they entered through the swinging doors into the dimness of the backroom, the old Native man was seated on a blanket laid out on the floor. Puffs of sweet-smelling smoke rose from a twisted braid of herbs in a bowl in front of him on the blanket. He was chanting softly, in his trembling old voice, as he beat gently and rhythmically on a drum, his eyes closed.

"You must come, Bear Heart," he said, placing the drum on the blanket, "and I will tell you the dream the Creator gave me for you."

Lionel sank down, cross-legged on the blanket. *For me? I haven't talked to God in a long time. I am estranged from Him. Why would He have a message for me?*

The ancient elder's weak old voice almost mesmeric, he began to speak.

"I am old, Bear Heart. I have lived a long time. I have lived to see the white man come and take away my children and my children's children to their schools. I have seen them come back, their souls wandering. They could not speak the language of the Tahltan people. They did not know how to live on the land, they no longer knew our ways. Our sisters, our daughters, our mothers, our wives disappeared, and nobody helped us look for them or stopped them from being stolen from us. Our children wander in dark paths and lose their way in alcohol and drugs because they can't find the spirit of our ancestors.

"Now, my people are dying. The Creator has sent Eagle Spirit to show me that once again the white man has come to destroy. This time they came with their needles and their promises of safety. I am dying, soon the Creator will gather me to my ancestors. Before I go, He has given me a dream. All my children will die soon, they too will be with our ancestors. The Indian women's wombs are emptying. The brothers and the fathers are dying. They are wanderers that have lost their way."

The elder continued, telling of the tears of Mother Earth. How she groaned for the distress of the people of the world. Of the wanderers who are spirits that can't go home, roaming the earth away from their bodies. He spoke of the Creator, who allowed Wendigo to enter the hearts of the dark men who plotted the destruction of the world.

The old man's words washed around Lionel carrying him into a world of loss and despair. Chasms of familiar sorrow sucked him into their depths and he swayed where he sat, lost in the slough of months, bereavement, and solitude.

The ancient Native reached up and removed an eagle feather from his headband and handed it to Lionel across the blanket with his trembling hand.

"Bear Heart will live because he is strong. Eagle Spirit from the Creator has shown me that Bear Heart would come from Dark Mountain. He showed you to me as the man with the heart full of courage that will save the children, save the butterfly."

Lionel had sat, silent and still, unable to tear himself voluntarily away from the stygian ache he had carried for so many months. With the mention of the butterfly, his head jerked. A sudden vision of Janet came to him, her hand on her belly as she spoke of their butterfly. He had carved, nearly a year ago, the words "Beloved wife Janet and her precious Butterfly" onto a slab of wood and placed it on the mountain where he had built their pyre.

The old man's voice was fading. He swayed where he sat. "Bear Heart, soon I will be gone. Soon the Tahltan people will be no more. You are a man of the land. You will carry on after we are gone. Save the butterfly. Save the stolen children, the lost children. Your heart is full of courage. Beware the black bird, it is looking for you. Go with the blessings of the Creator."

He rose slowly and wearily from his seated position. Norm, who was sitting silent by the door, jumped up and helped him to lay down on the cot. He picked up the blanket after Lionel stood up and draped it over the old man's thin body.

Lionel silently left the sombre storeroom and completed his shopping. The old man's words swirled through his head along with derisive laughter. *I am not courageous. I am not a hero. I couldn't save my wife or my child and he expects me to save – children? The butterfly? The Creator? God? I haven't spoken to God for so long that I can no longer feel His presence and God had to give this man a message for me? It can't be me he's talking about. He's a crazy old man.* Then, an unrelated question came to mind.

At the cash, his ice-coloured eyes met the dark brown ones of the young Native.

"When did they come?" he asked.

Norm immediately knew what he meant. "They came in vans, a doctor and nurses in uniforms. They told us we would be safe if we took the shot. They said Indians get sick easier than white people and everybody had to get a vaccine to be safe. It was maybe October. A couple people got sick, but when they came back a month later, everybody got the second vaccine anyways. They said everything would be fine." His voice rose a little. "It wasn't fine. My sister was pregnant with her first baby. The day after she took the shot, she lost her baby. My auntie got a really bad headache right after she got the second shot. She died that night. My grandmother's brother started talking strangely. Now he doesn't even know how to talk - or feed himself or go to the bathroom. That happened to some of the other Indians. A bunch of Indians in town have pain inside them the medicine man says is cancer. He's dead now, himself – they said it was his heart. Others got sick, went to sleep and never woke up. It took a while, some weeks, some months, but it was not safe."

"I'm sorry," Lionel said, his icy blue gaze filled with fathomless sorrow. *So much death. So much destruction. So much loss. Why God, why?*

"Yeah, but they're not sorry. Never see those medical vans anymore now we really need them. No doctors either, just a helicopter stops by every month. They ask if everything is OK and ask a bunch of questions, usually about some white man and woman, but they don't offer any help..." his voice trailed off. Working mechanically, he finished tallying up Lionel's purchases.

"How much do I owe you?" Lionel pulled a roll of bills from an inside pocket.

"Sorry, man, no more cash. You know what, it's OK, don't worry about it. I'll use my grandfather's credits - you know, Socdits. He's got lots."

Lionel gathered up the bags of groceries Norm packed for him. "Thanks," he said. So, the collapse of the fiat system had happened. No more cash. Probably Socdits was what the Chinese social credit system adopted in Canada was now being called. Why hadn't he heard about this from George? How many times he'd told his friend this was the end game and George never believed him. Odd about the helicopter, though. He went outside to his sled.

Norm followed him, thin body tense and anxious. Grandfather thought this man was important. Maybe he had some answers. "What will you do? Will everybody die? Will my people die?"

"I'm not sure, but it's not good, I'm afraid. I'm sorry, there's nothing I can do."

Lionel finished packing his groceries into his sled and covered and bound them securely in place. Norm stood watching him, lighting another cigarette, a desolate expression on his dark-skinned face. Bending, Lionel strapped on his snowshoes then shrugged the sled's harness back in place over his chest.

"Goodbye," he said with pity in his voice.

"Goodbye, Bear Heart."

Bereft, weighed down by anxiety and loss, Norm stood outside for a long time watching the man follow the snowy cleared path eastward. Soon he vanished behind the snow-covered pines around a curve in the path. This white man had no answers and Grandfather's illness had deluded him into thinking the Creator had a message for him.

The trek back to Dark Mountain and his silent, empty refuge seemed shorter than the road to Dease Lake. Lionel did the 20 km over three days, the same as the trip out had taken, but this time he was preoccupied. Over the first day of his trek home, his thoughts were incoherent and wrathful.

The same rage he had felt in the grocery store surged through him. The old Tahltan Native expected him to save the world, save the children. What children? Stolen? Lost? What did that mean? The world could not be saved. God knew he'd tried for so long to wake them up. Just months after they had announced the masking and the lockdowns, hadn't he done what he could to make people aware of what was going on? Could he have done any more? He lost everything in the outside world because he'd fought so hard. All he had left, now that the bear had robbed him of his companion, was the cabin he'd bought from a grieving engineer and the pelts of Janet's killer.

After the initial anger, Lionel felt waves of confusion and sorrow flood over him because he was reminded of Janet and his child. He felt again the dark despair of those months after her death. He stopped hunting and started living off his stores of food. By fall, a fox or a fisher marten had gotten most of his chickens because he kept forgetting to close them in. His goats had wandered off and been killed by some predator, the bees had swarmed to some unknown place, and he didn't have the energy to care.

All he had cared about was tanning and preparing the skin of the monster that had killed his wife. Months of scraping and manipulating, cutting and sewing in a petty revenge against the demons of loss and anguish. He stopped bathing and his hair and beard had grown long and matted. The dug-out cabin once kept so clean by Janet grew dirty and neglected with dead leaves and mud tracked throughout. He questioned his existence and raged at God, his Bible gathering dust on a shelf.

He knew that so much of it was guilt.

No, he hadn't loved Janet enough. From the moment he met Viviana, who was by then engaged to George, he was lost. She was the complete opposite of Janet. She was small and slender, with a smooth asymmetrical bob of black hair and black wings for eyebrows. But she was so intense, so alive! He'd fought the attraction. It was so irrational! His own wife, whom he had married just the summer before, was stunningly beautiful with a crown of glowing pale white-blond hair. Men envied him his wife, yet somehow Viv had captured him with her brilliance and her vivacity.

George had asked him to be his best man. How could he refuse? Of course, at this point he had not yet plumbed the depths of his attractions to Viv. George was his best man at his own wedding after all.

Later, George completed his internship at Vancouver General Hospital and relocated to Calgary with Viv. After Lionel completed his immunology specialization and opened his consulting practice, he had needed a partner for his office with advanced qualifications as an allergist. Viv had qualified in the treatment of allergies using conventional and alternative treatments; exactly what he needed at the clinic. Asking her to join him seemed a perfect move.

They were so well matched professionally! How many long hours they had spent together in heated discussions over this or that problematic case of Lupus, sarcoidosis, or asthma. Discussions over coffee, while jogging together down trails in parks, or leaning over microscopes in the laboratory. Long conversations, as the pandemic closed in, over how to fight back against the narrative. Lengthy debates over the Biblical implications of fighting governmental mandates.

He remembered the growing turbulence of his feelings for her. How he found himself treasuring the way her black brows would draw together when she was puzzled or annoyed. How her hair gleamed blue in certain lights. How her large dark eyes noticed everything. The strong grip of her small hand when she reached out to grasp his arm when she was excited about a discovery. He knew this preoccupation was wrong. He'd fought it and prayed about it. George had had no idea what he was feeling.

He thought about George. They'd been friends since high school when they were on the football team. They were both going into medicine and looking for a football scholarship. George got his scholarship at the University of British Columbia; he'd gotten his at the University of Calgary. Both had gone into medicine. His friend had supported his decision to leave Calgary when his medical license had been revoked, though he had never understood Lionel's urgent need to expose the lies that the government, the media and the medical system were telling about the China virus pandemic.

The winter sun had set behind him and slow white flakes were swirling when Lionel stopped his eastward progress and made camp. Night came early in December this far north. He figured it was around 5 p.m. when he stopped.

Lionel dug his nightly burrow into a deep snowbank and used the dry branches and twigs he'd collected through the day to make a fire in a clearing near his burrow.

His supper was beef stew, heated right in the can. He barely tasted it as he spooned it into his mouth, staring into the fire, night shadows deepening around him.

His wife was dead, his hopes and dreams of a family living with him in his refuge were dead. The world was dying.

The young Native's words had confirmed it for him. Just a few years after he had started his campaign against the lies and dishonesty it was all breaking down. He thought of his last conversation with George before he left for Dease Lake on his supply run. George was different that time. Very different.

It was nearly two weeks since they last talked. Lionel was getting worried. He sat down and tried to connect at 8 p.m. as they agreed that summer day before he left Calgary. That was when they both obtained their licenses and bought their ham radio systems.

George was missing more and more of the biweekly calls by then. Lionel knew there was something wrong. The George he knew from before would always laugh and tell jokes. Lately he was vague and distant and he never seemed to say anything real since Janet died. He didn't talk about his practice. He rarely said much about Viv or anything important.

It was almost 8:30. Lionel tapped the call button for the umpteenth time.

"This is Dark Mountain, come in Windy."

The radio crackled briefly. "Windy here. Hey."

"Hey, man! Good to hear your voice! Everything OK over there? Over."

Long pause with only crackling sounds of static. Maybe two minutes.

"Come in, Windy. What's up? Over."

"Yeah, hi. Lionel, man, you were right. Now it's all gone to shit..." His voice trailed off.

"Hey, George, you OK? What's going on? Over."

"You know all that stuff you and Viv studied and wrote about. All those videos and podcasts you did. You knew. You knew everything even back then. Viv never says 'I told you so', but she has every right! You see, they said I had to be an example. They said everything was going to be OK. So I took the vaccine. But they switched it because Viv didn't come. They told me 'control your wife'. But she didn't come." George's voice died out again.

Lionel clicked the mic, ready to respond, but George was still talking.

"It's all going to shit, Lionel. Kids are dying." His voice rose and he was talking faster now, his words difficult to decipher through the airwaves. "They gave it to kids... I gave it to kids... it's my fault... so many dying...myocarditis, pericarditis, seizures, blood clots, dead – just dead...oh God, it's horrible..."

"Roger that. George, are you saying they gave the injection to children? How young?" Lionel was agitated. What he was hearing was worse than he'd imagined.

Long pause.

"Oh man, it's so bad..." It almost sounded like George was crying. "They said it was safe for five-year-olds, they gave it to little kids... and they wouldn't even have died from the virus, but they gave it to little kids anyways. Right in the schools... in the SCHOOLS, man!"

Another long, crackling pause. Lionel waited to see if George would continue.

"Lionel, listen, I joined them because Dad was with them, he said Johnsons had always been in the club. I mean, they talked about God, so they must be good, right? It was fun... it's not fun anymore. Oh, you know, I should have listened to you. I should have listened to Viv, now it's too late... Oh, crap, man, this city is going to shit, everything is going to shit. People dead, that plane crash when the vaxxed pilot dropped dead. So many people died. They were picking up pieces of bodies for days, spread all over the streets of Red Deer. So many more people are going to die... and there's *so many* people getting sick: Bell's Palsy, Guillain-Barré Syndrome, strokes, heart attacks, rampant cancers, sudden deaths for no reason... it's so bad... I KNEW, and I didn't do anything because they told me not to say anything and to go along, they said we were the chosen people... now I'm going to be just like those poor people, soon..."

"Roger that, who is 'they' you keep talking about? Over."

George continued as though Lionel had not asked the question. "Listen, Lionel, there's something they didn't know would happen. They didn't know that even if they didn't get vaxxed they would get sterile. I just figured it out. The Dean's wife and a couple of the other wives, bad stuff happened. Miscarriages, sterility, bad stuff. You talked about shedding, you and Viv. You guys were right about everything. I told Viv to stay away after I found the evidence. She said she'd be OK because she's taking some supplements to fight the spike protein. But you were right. Oh, shit, you were right..."

"Roger that. Is Viv OK? Where is she?"

Long pause. Radio crackling noises in the dim room where Lionel sat, gripping the mic.

"Come in, Windy. Over."

"She's OK. She'll be OK. I'm sorry, it's over, everything is gone to shit, oh man, I have to go."

A click and silence. Lionel tried to raise George for the next half hour without success. He was still deeply troubled as he headed out on his supply run.

So now, hunched in the snow under the dancing northern lights, by the crackling fire in the silence of a winter forest, Lionel felt eyes on him. He shrugged off his glum memories and slowly reached for his Ranger .308. His hand stopped moving when he realized that his silent watcher was an Arctic Fox, its white coat blending seamlessly with the snow, only its black nose and reflective eyes giving away its position.

"You hungry?" Lionel spoke softly, quietly opening the bag of stale bread beside him and extracting a couple of slices.

He wiped them around inside the nearly empty can of beef stew, then tossed them to the fox. It sniffed them, then gulped them down. It then lay down, its head on its two stretched-out legs and, looking exactly like a dog, closed its eyes.

Lionel soon withdrew into his snow burrow after securing his food under the heavy elk hide on his sled. When he woke up the fox was gone.

By the time the late-rising winter sun crested the mountains to the east ahead of Lionel, he had already done at least two kilometres. As he walked, he scanned for deer or moose prints and scat. If the scat was fresh, he was prepared to follow them and take it down to store for food. He saw a few rabbit tracks but didn't want to shoot them. He preferred snaring small game.

He trudged eastward in his bear paw snowshoes. The sky was overcast, and it looked like snow would be falling again before the day's end. He moved as fast as he could, dragging his loaded sled.

Disquieting thoughts of the black bird the elderly Native had spoken of caused him to glance over his shoulder as he trudged through the snow. What black bird? Looking for a white man and woman? What was that about? He thrust aside the man's strange words.

His mind wandered again, though his thoughts were not as tumultuous as the day before.

He thought of Janet and her sweet selflessness. She had given up her dream of becoming a vet and had started working in a vet clinic as an assistant, saying she could go back to her studies later. She worked while he did his postgraduate medical specialization with Dr. Bridle in Guelph. She worked and supported him while he struggled to set up his clinic. She was always there, encouraging him, praying with him, gracing their home with her gentle presence.

They had such a lovely home in Calgary. Her parents helped them purchase it, though he'd been quick to pay them back once the clinic started to bring in money. Daniel and Arlene; he'd been lucky to have them as in-laws. Daniel was an architect and had made a lot of money in his youth. When he retired at 50 and went into pastoral work dedicating his life to God, Arlene had joined him in missionary efforts among the immigrant populations in Calgary.

Janet had grown up in comfort and grace. What had he given her for marrying him? Unbidden images of her ravaged body rose up in his mind and again the guilt overwhelmed him as he remembered his conflicted love for Janet as his attraction to Viv grew.

He and Viv were working so hard with the front-line doctors and the nurses. There were so many lies they discovered!

Why had the chief medical officers of Canada, the U.S. and so many other countries been so determined to talk about the cases of the infected and the deaths, without pointing out that the deaths were of the elderly who would have died anyway from the seasonal flu? Other predictable deaths were of the many people with co-morbidities which would have done them in soon anyways – usually obese, often diabetic with multiple other issues. Dear God, people didn't even want to listen when he pointed out that no more people had died during the year than usually do throughout a flu season! Even the morgues did not report excessive deaths. Why was there so much misinformation to feed fear to the people who passively absorbed and BELIEVED everything they were told? What did these corrupt individuals have to gain?

What would they gain by killing millions and then billions of people with the vaccine they were trying to force onto the world? He knew the chief medical authority in the States was getting richer and more influential through his efforts to instill fear then promote the vaccine. Didn't he own some of the patents for that vaccine? A vaccine that was patented before the virus even appeared.

Lionel's mind travelled back to an interview he had listened to some time ago. It was an interview with a Russian KGB defector called Yuri Alexandrovich Bezmenov. He had outlined a plan for the take-down of western civilization, describing the first phase as 'demoralization' which is, in fact, ideological subversion. Well, that started even before the 1970s with the attack on the family and on morality. What had Yuri said? Something about how people are programmed to think and react to Pavlovian stimuli in a certain fashion so that they could be convinced that black was white and white was black. This would lead to an inability to assess true information even if authentic proof was provided. Lionel laughed ironically in his mind: the plandemic sure was evidence that this stage had been successfully implemented with the massive psy-op he had fought so hard!

After the demoralization was completed, the second stage of destabilization would take place followed quickly by the third stage of crisis. Well, crisis had come and the take-down of western – even world civilization was well underway by the time Lionel and Janet had bowed out. What was the world like out there now? Had it reached the final stage of normalization? Were people now viewing totalitarian governments as acceptable and people dropping dead or dying as normal?

Snow swirled around him as he trudged, and a light wind arose and drove it into his face. Lionel stopped and had a drink of water from his pack, then continued his eastward march.

He thought of Event 201 in Geneva. It was a dress rehearsal for the pandemic funded by the same cabal that was behind the psy-op of fear being propagated through every media outlet.

He'd watched as hundreds.... and then thousands of reports came in about adverse events. He received emails from all over the world about people who were being suppressed from reporting the effects of the vax, people who were dying.

Lionel forced his mind away from the memories. The rage and impotence of those days were coming back, and he didn't want to think about that.

He thought again about Viv and Janet. He had never been physically unfaithful to his wife. He couldn't do that, and neither could Viv, of that, he was sure. It had always and only been unfaithfulness of the heart. He and Viv had only one conversation about their feelings for each other, just one. In that conversation, he had seen that she loved him as much as he loved her. He remembered how he had held her and kissed her, holding her small vital body tight in his arms. She had kissed him back and it was so intense. He thought of her mouth, the smooth rain of her black hair in his hands, her slender throat, the press of her body against his. He'd wanted her so much.

But they had both stopped. Almost at the same time. "No, this is wrong," he'd said, and she'd murmured, "I can't do this" almost simultaneously.

After the long minute, when they were both gathering their composure, pressed against lab benches on opposite sides of the lab, she spoke. "I'm sorry. Let's not do this again."

He agreed. He struggled with the knowledge that his feelings for her were wrong and prayed about it.

God took care of the matter.

Arriving at home, he found the letter from the Medical Council of Canada, telling him they may be withdrawing his medical license, based on advice from the CPSA. A few awkward days at work and it was almost a relief when he saw the summons to a meeting with the College of Physicians and Surgeons of Alberta in Edmonton.

A Dr. Shaw was present along with the provincial head of physicians and surgeons, Dr. Mendez. The chief medical officer of Alberta was also there.

Dr. Mendez plunged right in after the initial greetings.

"Thank you for attending, Lionel. I'd like to address some of your recent engagements as regards your YouTube video entitled…" Mendez consulted his notes, "Lies your doctor told you about the China virus vaccine."

Mendez then spoke for a lengthy three minutes about how it was unprofessional to go against the advice of the chief medical officer's directive and attack his colleagues. He then addressed Lionel's YouTube channel Awaken and remarked that there were still several videos on the channel that had not been taken down by YouTube, but that he would be writing an email, from his position of authority, asking that Lionel's destructive YouTube channel that was so full of misinformation be taken down completely.

"None of my videos violated informed consent nor propagated lies…" Lionel said, attempting to keep his annoyance hidden.

Shaw cut in. "Dr. Goudreault, your complete lack of professionalism and violation of our code of ethics will lose you your license to practice medicine in the province of Alberta…"

Lionel tried again, "I have not acted unprofessionally, nor have I used my videos to propagate lies, I merely brought my concerns about the…"

He was unable to finish. Shaw broke in again. "I repeat, you need to be following the directives of the WHO. Your videos are lying about the severity of the China virus, making false claims about..,"

"Excuse me," Lionel intervened, raising his voice as his annoyance grew. "I have used only verifiable statistics, many from government sources. It is you who are living in a dystopian world where lies are truth and truth must be concealed. Someday you will be held accountable for what you are doing..."

"Dr. Goudreault," this time it was the chief medical officer of Alberta, "this meeting was a courtesy to advise you of our deep concerns about your behaviour. We are not here to debate. I have asked Dr. Mendez to ensure mental health counselling is available to you as you seem to be under a lot of stress..."

"This is not a meeting, nor a debate, it is a panel of judges unwilling to listen to anything but their own narrative, irrespective of facts or proper scientific inquiry." Lionel's voice continued to be polite though louder, but it required a great deal of self-control. "I am only under stress due to your own unethical and dystopian behaviour..."

Dr. Mendez cut him off again, advising him that he was under investigation, and they would likely be advising the removal of his license to the Medical Council of Canada. He assured him that all mental health counselling facilities were available to him and that he should be taking some rest. Every other attempt Lionel made to speak was overridden by Shaw or the chief medical officer or Mendez himself.

"Thank you for coming to the meeting," Dr. Mendez finished, standing up and extending his hand to Lionel. "You can expect to receive a copy of my email to MCC as well as your email regarding our decision."

Lionel stood up. "Someday your dystopian universe will end and you will live to regret this," he said. He didn't shake anybody's hand, but strode, his body under strict control, out of the room, closing the door quietly behind him. He maintained his control, tightly gripping the steering wheel of his SUV, until he was south of Leduc. By then, the bile in his stomach had risen to his throat. He pulled over at a rest stop, walked into the trees and released his rage, his horror and his despair.

The emails from Dr. Mendez of the CPSA arrived in due course, as did the registered letter. He was told his medical license was suspended pending investigation and he would have to withdraw from the clinic, or they would shut it down.

By then Viv was also in trouble with the CPSA, because of her own activism. Tension at home with Janet was also skyrocketing and he knew he had to do something.

He'd heard second-hand about the ecological engineer Alan Tremaine's bug-out cabin from a long-time colleague who also had concerns about the so-called vaccine. It was almost like God had dropped this opportunity into his lap. With his funds from the sale of his house and his share of the clinic, he bought the cabin sight unseen and enough supplies for two people for at least two years. He also purchased a breeding pair of goats, a small flock of chickens, a large selection of hand tools and hardware and a sizable library of DIY books.

As he plodded, step-by-step, through the deep snow of northern British Columbia, he thought about the series of events that had led him here. He hadn't asked Janet's opinion or how she felt about it. He'd been so excited about the prospect of getting away before the collapse of western society. He was so sure it was coming. He didn't check with her, he just packed everything up and swept her away.

Janet was a people person. She loved animals and people. She was a missionary, a helper, so selfless and kind. She died and it was his fault.

By the third day of his trek, he knew what he had to do. He shared a quick breakfast with the fox that showed up at least once a day to eat whatever scraps he would give it. While trudging, step by step through the cold of the Canadian north, he knew he had to go.

Living like a hermit on the shoulder of Dark Mountain in northern BC was doing nobody any good. He had no wife to protect, no children to raise, so no reason to stay. Out there were people who were dying, people who were afraid and ignorant, people he had to help. His friend George seemed to be losing it and he had no idea what was happening with Viv.

No, he couldn't save the world. He felt again that twinge of annoyance when he remembered the words of the Native elder. He couldn't save the world and 'save the butterfly'? What did that mean? Save the children?

Well, he would start by going to Calgary to see what was happening there.

C H A P T E R   3

Rachel

I can be changed by what happens to me. But I refuse to be reduced by it.

~ Maya Angelou

Rachel dug industriously in the open can of baked beans; her spoon clutched in her small grubby hand. She was sitting cross-legged on the cluttered counter, empty cereal boxes and food wrappers in heaps. There was a persistent sour odour in the filthy kitchen that Rachel no longer noticed.

"Do you want some, Mommy?" she asked the murmuring woman standing vacantly by the window.

Rachel didn't expect an answer. Her mother hadn't spoken for at least three weeks since she'd had a weird shaking spell. She jumped off the counter and took the woman by the hand and led her to a stool by the dirty counter. She resumed her seat and, gently patting the nearly catatonic face, she spooned the cold beans into her mother's slack mouth. When the can was empty, Rachel jumped down again.

"C'mon Mommy, let's go to the bathroom."

After helping her on the toilet, she said, "K, Mom, I'm gonna fix your hair."

Rachel missed her mom's booming voice and the corn rows she had once made in her hair. She had tried to make some in her mom's, but now she couldn't even comb out the dense masses of her tight curls and resorted to pulling it back and putting combs in it. Rachel sometimes worked at combing out her own hair, but more often than not, she looked like a small explosion had taken place on her head.

Preparations for the day complete to her satisfaction, she said, "We're almost out of food, Mommy, so I have to go look for some."

Rachel sat down on the floor and put on her blue running shoes, then she picked up her pink jacket off the floor and put it on. She got the stool, climbed on it and unbolted the door. Rachel's 5-year-old legs were too short for her to reach the deadbolt which she tried to remember to lock every night. Just last week her mother had wandered out of the house while Rachel was sleeping.

She slipped out the door and secured it behind her with a broom stuck crosswise through the bars of the veranda. She couldn't lock it because her mom had put the key somewhere and it was lost.

Skipping down the stairs in the bright morning light, she saw her neighbour, Mr. Varga, lying in the long grass by his grey car. It was quite a few days that he'd been lying there and now crows were sitting on his head and pecking at his face. She knew Mrs. Varga was still in the house, but she had stopped speaking and even moving the day after Mr. Varga fell down and didn't get up again. Rachel had seen him fall and went and banged on their door to tell Mrs. Varga. Mrs. Varga started crying and trying to call people. She had even tried to drag Mr. Varga into the house herself, but he was too fat. That was around the same time her own mom started talking funny, so Rachel ran into her house and most of the time she tried not to notice Mr. Varga.

Soon after this, she went on her first food-hunting trip. All their food was gone, and Rachel was hungry and she wanted something to feed her mom. Now she was a pro at breaking windows and going into houses. She always knocked first, though. At Sunday School, they said it was bad to steal. She figured if there was nobody living in a house, maybe it was OK. She didn't go to the Vargas' house because Mrs. Varga was there and taking their food would be stealing. But, maybe since Mr. and Mrs. Varga weren't eating the food, it would be OK? She would have to think about that. For now, lots of the houses seemed to be empty, so she was finding enough food.

Usually, she tried not to notice the dead people, the people with weird things growing on their faces and the people like her mom. At first, she wondered if Jesus would want her to help those people and feed them like she did her mom, but she thought maybe Jesus would rather she just help her own mom. Lots of people had left town by now, or they were just dead in their houses anyway.

Rachel picked up the stick she always carried with her to fend off hungry dogs and trotted down the street singing 'Jesus loves the little children'. She liked that song because it said Jesus loved all the kids including the red and black ones. Her mom said her dad was an Indian, but she didn't remember him because he died in a car crash when she was little. She just knew her mom was black, so that meant Jesus must love her twice as much since she was both red and black. That made her giggle when she heard the song for the first time.

She dodged the two crashed cars at the corner. She saw that for now, the dogs weren't going to bother her because they were eating something on the ground. It looked like a person's arm, but Rachel didn't want to think about that.

At the corner of the street, she stopped and looked around thoughtfully. She still had to plan where to go to get some food. Her mom always said when she went out, "Watch for cars." That wasn't a big problem anymore since most of the cars she saw weren't going anywhere. A few were crashed with dead people inside or nobody was around to drive a lot of them. They were covered with dead leaves and dust or had broken windows and missing parts. She saw some other kids, sometimes, and there were a few adults around that looked normal still or just seemed to be sick or scared. Well, it was a few days since she saw anybody grown-up that looked normal.

Rachel put her hands on her skinny little hips and looked up and down the street. A lot of the snow had melted and there were puddles everywhere. She wished she had her rubber boots on, then she remembered that her mom had promised to buy her new ones because her pink ones were pinching her feet. She looked down at her velcro running shoes and decided to jump in some puddles anyway because her mom wouldn't even notice if she got them muddy. She already knew her mom probably wouldn't be buying her new boots now.

Bouncing through the lovely puddles on the street, she wove her way along the road seeking out the deepest puddles and singing her favourite Sunday School song at the top of her voice. Since her mom went funny, Rachel hadn't gone this far from home. Today, it was warmer, and the sun was shining. She decided without even thinking about it much, to go check out the grocery store down the road where her mom used to work. Maybe she could find a way in and get something nice to eat.

She paused at the pizza place, but she didn't smell any pizza. She wished there was somebody around to make some pepperoni pizza. Her mom would sometimes stop there and get one on her way home from work. Maybe there would be pizza in the grocery store she could put in the microwave at home. She resumed skipping cheerfully through the puddles, even though now she was muddy from her blue running shoes to her fuzzy black hair.

Rachel was almost to the grocery store when she heard what sounded like a little kid crying. She froze and looked around, trying to locate the source of the sobbing.

In a big parking lot across from the store where she was headed, she saw a beautiful big puddle. In the winter, before the plough people quit ploughing the roads, they had made a huge pile of snow there and it had melted and made a little ocean. She jumped joyfully into the puddle, then splashed her way to tall concrete barriers on the side of the parking lot. Instead of going between the barriers, she scrambled up onto one.

Standing on the one closest to a big blue sign, Rachel craned her neck and tried to locate the source of the crying sound. Turning in a circle, she saw a crashed car with a dead person inside. It had hit a big truck that was loaded with a bunch of dead pigs that smelled really bad. The truck driver was not visible. There were some big black birds sitting on top of the balcony of the restaurant and others pecking at somebody on the ground. The person on the ground didn't look dead, he was still moving.

She turned again and finally figured out that the crying kid was probably in the place where what her mom called 'trailer trash' lived.

By now Rachel was feeling cold because she was so wet. She hopped down and hurried through the tall dead grass to the first trailer and went around it. She saw a thin cat in a window and picked up a rock and threw it at the glass. It smashed and the cat disappeared. She walked up closer.

"Come out now, kitty!" she called. She waited and called a couple more times. After a few minutes, the thin cat appeared and jumped through the hole and slunk away quickly. Rachel tried to catch it, but it went too fast. Disappointed, she continued her search for the source of the sobbing. She heard it more loudly now.

Going around another trailer, she saw a small playground. The playground equipment was covered in dust and rotting leaves and the two swings creaked back and forth in the slight wind. Melting snow lay thickly under the trees on the north side of the area. In the middle of a spot with long brown grass from last year, a very small boy with blond hair was tugging on the arm of a motionless woman lying sprawled on her side.

"Mommy, Mommy, wake up!" he was crying between bouts of sobbing. The woman was unresponsive. It looked like the little boy had been crying for quite some time. He was very dirty, his batman t-shirt had mud on it, his blond hair was full of small twigs and seeds and his little jeans hung low because of a heavily loaded diaper. The grass beside the dead woman was flattened as though he'd slept there at least one night, and a couple of the big black birds were sitting on the top bar of the playground swing taking swoops at their future meal. As Rachel approached, she saw the tiny boy wave a stick at one that hopped onto the ground and tried to move closer.

She walked quietly forward, calling in a soft voice, "Hey, little boy, what's your name?"

The crying baby turned around quickly, stumbled, and fell. He abruptly stopped wailing. From his seated position on the ground, he rubbed one eye with his grubby fist, smearing the dirt on his face, and blinked teary blue eyes at Rachel. His little chest was still heaving with suppressed sobs.

"Hi, kid, I'm Rachel. What's your name?" she repeated, plopping down beside him on the cold grass.

He blinked his blue eyes again. "Mommy sleeping," he said, patting the stiff hand of the unmoving woman, "wake up Mommy."

"Your mommy isn't going to wake up. Come with me. What's your name?" Rachel jumped up and held out her hand.

The little boy pushed his way to his feet by raising his dirty diapered bottom in the air and then standing. He grasped Rachel's hand with his grubby paw and toddled along beside her.

"Me hungry, me want lunch," he confided.

Rachel eyed the tiny child trotting trustingly beside her. "You are stinky, too," she declared. "Your diaper is very yucky."

She happily ignored her own muddy condition. "You need a bath, you're all full of poo."

The little boy tugged at the waist of his jeans barely covering his diaper. "Hurt," he said in a distressed voice.

"Come on, we'll find some food. What is your name?"

"Me Matty. Find some food." he echoed.

"Matt? Your name is Matt?" Rachel continued holding his hand as they crossed the empty highway to the grocery store.

Matt stopped and pointed his tiny free hand at the KFC on the opposite corner. "Food? KFC?" he said hopefully.

"No, silly Matt, there's nobody to make the food at the KFC."

They stopped in front of Save-On-Foods. It looked like somebody had already had the idea to get food there. The door hung open and some of the windows were smashed. She checked Matt's feet. He was wearing rubber boots, so he was OK. "Come on," she said and led the way inside.

It looked like all the cash registers were emptied. Their drawers hung open and some were on the floor. Most of the shelves looked quite sparse, but there was some food.

Rachel glanced around quickly and spotted a shopping cart. "Come on," she said again and skipped happily to the cart. "Can you climb up?" she asked, "I'll push you."

She ended up having to shove him on the jeans covering his dirty diaper to help him clamber up. "Ew, you're super stinky," she commented as the little boy plopped down in the bottom of the shopping cart. Delightedly pushing the cart even though the handle was above her eye level, undeterred, she rolled it cheerfully along an aisle of the grocery store. "What do you want to eat today?" she asked as she skirted the motionless body of a middle-aged woman in a Save-On-Foods green uniform. A rat skittered away as she passed. She saw some of her favourite cereal, so she dropped it into the bottom of the cart beside the child. In the cookie aisle, she saw a lonely bag of Oreo cookies, but it was too high to reach.

"Wait here," she commanded and ran back to pick up a pail she had seen on the way in. Dragging it behind her, she came back to the shelf. Over ending the pail, she scrambled onto it. The Oreos were still too high. She managed to grasp the corner of the bag by climbing onto the shelf above the top of the pail. Pulling it towards her, she realized it was mostly eaten by mice. She hopped down.

"No Oreos today!" she announced and resumed pushing the cart.

Matt looked sleepily at her. "No Oreos today!" he echoed.

She found an aisle with quite a few cans of food still on the shelves. She dropped them happily into the cart. Peaches, fruit cocktail, pears, that was a real treat! She found some cans of soup and stew and they went into the cart too. Crackers, three boxes of crackers! As she moved along, she joyfully named each food item she found and Matt echoed the words in an increasingly sleepy voice. She didn't forget to check the freezers for pizza and found a couple. The picture on the box didn't look like they had any pepperoni, but she'd already found a package in the fridge.

By the time they had half of the cart crammed with food that was not filled with tired baby, they reached the diaper aisle. She looked critically at the now sleeping child.

"You have to learn to go potty," she declared, "there's no room for diapers and I'm not your mommy. Diapers are icky."

The sleeping Matt didn't respond, but the decision was made.

The next aisle was clothing and some shoes. Oh, joy! She found a pair of red rubber boots that were only a little bit too big. She sat down on the floor and peeled open the Velcro of her running shoes. Her dirty socks were drenched so she looked hopefully around. Socks! Lots of socks were hanging on metal hangers! Off came her socks and some pretty printed ones went on, then her beautiful new rubber boots.

Rachel eyed the sleeping Matt thoughtfully. His jeans were smeared with the poop and pee that had leaked out of his loaded diaper. Poking through the sparse shelves of kids' clothes, she found some pants that looked like they'd fit him. She found another batman t-shirt that looked almost exactly like the one he was wearing.

She climbed up on the side of the shopping cart to hold the clothes against his peacefully sleeping body. Good, the pants would probably fit, but the t-shirt was too small. She opened a couple more t-shirt packages and found a minion t-shirt that was bigger. He would need a jacket too. After pulling down most of the boys' clothes on the hangers and climbing onto the cart at least a dozen times to check sizes, the only thing she found was a dinosaur raincoat. That would have to do.

Rachel poked around a couple more shelves. Cool! A green t-shirt with flowers and butterflies on it for her! She promptly pulled off her muddy pink jacket and blue t-shirt and donned the beautiful green one.

Oh! Boys' and girls' underwear! Matt would need some because she was going to potty train him!

Matt slept all the way back to her house. He didn't feel the pile of food in the cart with him collapse onto his sleeping form. He didn't see the dead people and the scared people. He didn't see the big black birds and the crows eating the eyes of the corpses. She pushed the cart briskly past all that to the front of her house. She was panting heavily by the time she arrived, it was a hard job getting up the slope in the road to her house.

Parking the cart in the grass, so it wouldn't roll away, she climbed up its side to pat Matt's face. "Hey, Matt, wake up!"

The little boy's face turned sideways, and his dirty fists rubbed his eyes. "Mommy?"

"No, it's Rachel. Wake up, we have to bring our food inside."

His face crumpled a little, but Rachel pulled him to his feet. She clambered out and helped him over the side, scrunching up her face. "Ew, after we get the food inside, you need to take a bath, you're super super super stinky!"

"Super super super stinky," Matt repeated, forgetting to cry.

After climbing back into the shopping cart, Rachel started to throw the food onto the long, neglected grass of the lawn. Matt giggled happily, running back and forth trying to catch the smaller items. She didn't throw the cans at him, of course, because they were heavy, she just dumped them on the grass right beside the cart.

At one point, Matt stopped and point a tiny finger at the fat man lying prone in the long grass in the next yard.

"'Achel?" he queried, "man?"

"It's OK, don't look, he's dead. C'mon and help me."

They worked together to bring the food to the veranda. Rachel removed the broom from the bars. Her mom was still sitting vacantly on the stool where Rachel had left her.

Matt didn't seem to notice her as Rachel handed him a handful of crackers once all the food was in the house. He was munching them contentedly, sitting on the floor surrounded by cans and boxes of food. Rachel sat down beside him and opened the box of cereal and ate it dry. She had checked for milk at the grocery store, but it was all really smelly, some even had split open and spilled in the fridge, so she didn't think she wanted it.

When they finished eating, Rachel took off her boots and Matt's boots. She hauled Matt to the bathroom and ran the bath. He stood beside her and tried to put his hands in the water.

"Do you want bubbles?" she asked. She located the bottle of bubble bath and dumped in more than her mom usually did. Lots of bubbles was better than just a little, so lots of bubbles it was! When bubbles started floating around the bathroom, Matt started laughing and chasing them. Rachel caught him and pulled off his t-shirt.

"Bath time!" she said, just like her mom used to say to her.

He joyfully pulled down his pants and stood with his red irritated little bum covered with poo. "Yucky," he said helpfully.

Rachel looked at the clean water and bubbles and the poo caked on his bum. She found a towel and rubbed off as much as she could. Matt whimpered a little but didn't resist. She pushed the whole mess into the corner and tried to lift him into the bathtub. He fell into the cloud of bubbles and a huge wave of water drenched her. She shrugged and pulled off her own clothes and climbed into the tub with the little boy. He was sitting and slapping at bubbles and laughing. Plopping into the tub hadn't fazed him even a little bit.

The two children played in the tub until the warm water had cooled and the bubbles were gone. Neither thought about washing themselves, but when they climbed out, most of the mud and poo had come off. There was no adult to bother them about the dandelion fluff in Matt's hair or the lint and other oddments in Rachel's.

"Food?" Matt said hopefully. He was preparing to run wearing only the towel Rachel had draped around him to the kitchen to the stash of food.

"Wait, Matt." Rachel wrapped herself in a towel and ran to the kitchen and found the clothes she had collected for him. She brought him to her bedroom and looked for some clean clothes for herself. She helped him into a pair of the new underwear she had found. He scrambled into them, one leg at a time, holding onto her shoulder.

Soon they were both dressed. In the kitchen, she opened a can of chicken noodle soup. She and Matt ate, then she fed some to her mom. When she finished feeding the last of the soup to her mom, she noticed Matt's pants were all wet.

"Matt! Did you pee your pants? You're supposed to pee in the potty!"

The baby was starting to cry, so she took his hand and led him back to the bathroom. She pulled down her own pants and hauled herself onto the toilet. He stopped crying to watch her curiously. She peed loudly and showed him the pee in the toilet.

"See? You try it now!"

Rachel flushed the toilet, then she helped him take off his wet pants and heaved him onto the toilet. He teetered nervously, gripping the seat with his hands. A look of concentration was on his face. There was no sound of pee, but he slipped off after several seconds and looked hopefully into the toilet.

"Pee?" he asked, his face half in the toilet. Rachel looked in, too.

"I don't think you peed," she said judiciously after a moment.

Matt flushed the toilet proudly anyways.

"Oh, no, I don't have any more pants for you! I guess you'll just have to wear some underwear for now." Rachel led the little boy wearing only a minion t-shirt back to the kitchen where the trio-pack of underwear was left earlier.

After putting on the fresh pair of underwear, Matt followed Rachel into the basement where they played with some of her toys. He peed in his underwear again, and she showed him again how to pee in the toilet.

By the next morning, Rachel decided she had to learn how to use the washer. Especially since her mom had peed her pants because Rachel had forgotten to take her to the toilet the night before.

She got Matt to help her gather up the dirty clothes lying around the floor. Nobody noticed the wrappers and other stray items that got into the washer when Rachel clambered up and dumped them in. She got the bottle of detergent because she knew some of that had to go in the washer. It was too heavy to lift, so she took the lid off the bottle and tipped it and put some in the lid. She did that four times, emptying the lid into the washer each time. She looked at the array of bottles on the shelf in the laundry room and couldn't decide which other one she needed to use, so she opted to put a lid of each of them into the washer. They all smelled better than the dirty clothes, so she figured it would be all right.

Climbing onto the washer from the upended mop bucket, she poked experimentally at the buttons on the washer. Nothing happened when she poked the first two, but when she pushed the third one, a bunch of lights came on, then again nothing happened.

"Dumb washer!" she snapped and angrily pushed a button that hadn't worked before. It worked!

Matt was standing at the door of the laundry room with cracker crumbs all over his minion t-shirt. He was wearing a pair of her underwear.

"Dumb washer!" he echoed seriously.

Rachel hopped down onto the mop pail then to the floor. The washer made watery sounds, satisfying Rachel.

She took Matt to the bathroom with her mom. Her mom sat down and peed with Rachel's help, then - oh victory! - Matt sat down and peed in the toilet for the first time!

"You peed, Matt! Good boy!" Rachel clapped happily. The semi-catatonic woman behind her clapped also.

"Good boy, Matt!" the little boy echoed with a smile on his face. They stood and admired the faintly yellow water then Matt flushed the toilet.

"So, when you need to go pee, just tell me, OK?"

Rachel took her mom by the hand and led her into the kitchen. They all ate fruit cocktail for lunch out of the can.

C H A P T E R   4

Abi

Children have a lesson adults should learn, to not be ashamed of failing, but to get up and try again. Most of us adults are so afraid, so cautious, so 'safe,' and therefore so shrinking and rigid and afraid that it is why so many humans fail. Most middle-aged adults have resigned themselves to failure.

~ Malcolm X

Rachel danced in a circle holding Matt's little hands and shouting with glee. Matt was toddling on his little legs and grinning proudly.

"You did it, Matt, you did it! One whole day and night without peeing or pooing in your pants! Good job!"

It was another sunny day after a week of wet flurries and rain and they were in the tall grass at the back of the house. Almost all the snow was gone and the days were getting warmer all the time. It had taken less than two weeks with fewer and fewer mistakes on Matt's part for this celebratory day to arrive.

"Do you want to ride in the wagon? We need to find more food. You have to walk back though if we find a lot."

"Matt walk back, Matt is big boy now." The baby smiled happily at her.

The shopping cart was gone from in front of the house. Rachel was pretty sure it was those kids in the apartment building across the road that had taken it. They were bigger than her and sometimes would throw stuff at her and call her names. There were five of them, two girls and three boys. Rachel had also seen an old grumpy man that wasn't dead yet and a few other adults that looked normal except they were wearing masks and plastic things over their faces and looked really scared. Maybe they would die soon like everybody else. The kids didn't seem like they were going to die.

Rachel knew there was no food left in any of the houses on her street. Last week she checked the houses across the road, and somebody had broken into all of them. She would have to go further today. Maybe it was time to check some different places.

Rachel helped Matt scramble into the little plastic wagon she found a couple of streets over in the ditch. She picked up the rope and started pulling. One of the wheels was wonky, so it wasn't easy and jolted Matt around some, but he didn't seem to mind.

At the first street corner, Rachel stopped and looked thoughtfully both ways. There were lots of big black birds sitting on verandas and roofs. They were probably looking for more people to die, she thought.

She was terribly distressed a few days ago when she was foraging near the public library she used to go to and saw Mrs. Lindstrom the librarian. She was sitting down and crying on the side of the road, her normally beautifully arranged silver hair dirty and messy.

"Help me," Mrs. Lindstrom sobbed. She sounded like she had something in her mouth and her words were all mushy.

Rachel had approached cautiously and saw that Mrs. Lindstrom's whole side of her face looked like something had pulled it down. She couldn't seem to get up because one leg wasn't working.

"Mrs. Lindstrom?" Rachel hunkered down beside the woman. "Are you going to die?"

The woman extended one arm, the other was at an awkward angle and didn't seem to be working. "Help me," she slurred again.

Rachel got up and looked around. There didn't seem to be anything she could use to help Mrs. Lindstrom up. The big rock by the gas station was much too big. There were no pails or anything she could use to help her get up.

"Do you want some food? I can get you some food."

"Call mother ...help, please, help me."

"My mommy can't help you," Rachel was distressed. "I can get some food for you."

The woman resumed weeping, so Rachel ran to the gas station. The door was smashed, and all the shelves were almost empty. She found a bag of peanuts under one shelf and a bottle of water on the floor.

When she ran back to Mrs. Lindstrom, she was lying down on her side on the sidewalk, still crying. Rachel hunkered down again and tried to feed the peanuts to her. The woman flapped her hand and turned her face away. Rachel opened the bottle of water and put it to Mrs. Lindstrom's lips. Some of the water leaked out of the fallen side of the woman's mouth. Rachel was pretty sure she got some into her because she thought she saw her swallow.

"Wait here," Rachel said, ignoring the fact the woman certainly couldn't go anywhere. She dashed the three blocks to her house as fast as her short legs could take her. While she was there, she checked inside to see if Matt was still sleeping on the sofa and her mom was still laying on her bed where she'd left her. When she got back with the little wagon thumping behind her, Mrs. Lindstrom was shaking violently, white foam coming out of her mouth.

Rachel tried to give her more water, but Mrs. Lindstrom kept on shaking for a while, then she stopped. When Rachel saw she was dead, she pulled her wagon back home, crying a little. Mrs. Lindstrom always read the little kids stories during Story Hour on Saturdays and gave them cookies. She'd been going to Story Hour for as long as she could remember. Now Mrs. Lindstrom was dead and there would be no more Story Hour.

Now, Rachel stood at the corner of the street with baby Matt in the wagon and hoped she wouldn't see anybody she knew again. She didn't like seeing people she loved die. She looked thoughtfully down the road towards where Matt used to live. She knew there were restaurants and at least one more grocery store in that area. Maybe she could find some food at one of those places. She headed briskly down the hill in that direction, Matt bumping and thumping in the little wagon behind her.

At the corner of the highway, she stopped and looked around.

"Food?" Matt pointed hopefully at the A&W. She eyed it thoughtfully, but it looked pretty smashed up. It seemed like mostly everything in it was gone.

"I think other people got there before us," she said. She pulled the wagon towards the convenience store next to the gas station. All the windows were broken, but the door was still closed. Looking in a hole in the window, the children could see it was a mess in there. The flags and maps and books were ripped up and spread around along with other things people didn't need any more like keychains and little statues. All the rows of chocolate bars were empty, the boxes strewn over the floor. The chips and snacks were mostly gone, but Rachel spotted some cans and bottles on the shelves.

She looked at the door, but it seemed to be locked. When she tried the handle, it wouldn't open. She looked critically at the broken holes in the windows and found one window that was broken right to the bottom. Muddy footprints showed that the other kids - it was kids because the prints were smaller than an adult's - used this hole to get in.

"Just a sec," she said to Matt. Her legs were longer, so she could climb in carefully and not get cut on the glass. She climbed on the window ledge and cautiously stepped through the big hole without touching the jagged sides. Jumping off the inside ledge, she ran over and picked up an armful of flags and a red and white towel with a maple leaf on it. Spreading them on the inside of the window, she reached out and hauled Matt through the hole. He came through so fast, they both landed on the floor inside, Matt on top of her.

Laughing, they scrambled to their feet. They spent the next 15 minutes picking up cans and different foods and dropping them out the hole in the window, planning to collect them and put them in the wagon outside.

To Rachel's dismay, when she got to the window with an armload of dried noodles, all the food on the ground was gone. Two big kids were standing in front of the store across the road and laughing. They had all their food, and they even had put it in their wagon!

Matt came up beside her just then with his offering of a bag of Cheezies that had only one corner nibbled by mice. He stopped and looked out over the edge of the window.

"Food!" he gasped, pointing at the kids.

Rachel dropped the noodles on the floor and scrambled over the ledge catching her leggings a little on a piece of glass.

"That's our food!" she shouted. She rushed across the road at them just as a black pick-up truck came barreling down the highway, knocking an unkempt, vacant-eyed woman to the ground and running over her. Rachel made it safely to the side of the highway undeterred by her brush with death and dashed at the kids. The truck continued down the highway at high speed, clouds of diesel exhaust in its wake.

When Rachel tried to grab the rope on the wagon, the boy who looked to be at least 9 years old laughed and knocked her down. She jumped up and tried again. By then, the girl was running down the road dragging the wagon. The boy stayed and tried to push her again.

"Little black baby, you can't take that food. It's ours!" he jeered. "We found that food first!"

Tears of anger in her eyes, Rachel scrambled to pick up the box of cake mix and the can of tomato soup that had jounced out of the wagon because of the wonky wheel. She saw there was a trail of food, but the big boy saw it too and ran and started collecting it.

Rachel stood, holding the cake mix and soup. Her face was flushed with anger. "You're bad kids!" she shouted. "Jesus will put you in hell!"

Matt, inside the convenience store, shouted too. "Jesus put you hell!"

Rachel, back at the window, clambered onto the ledge and went inside more carefully than she had gone out. Noticing the knee of her leggings was ripped from falling down and she was bleeding at another rip from the broken glass, she ran to the aisle with first aid supplies and happily put a bunch of Band-Aids on her wounds to cover the bloody bits.

Matt watched her, then held out a finger that had a tiny scratch on it from a minor injury a couple of days before. "Me boo-boo!" he announced, so Rachel wrapped a big Band-Aid on his teeny finger, wrapping it around twice. Matt held it up and admired it proudly.

"Help me find a box or a basket," she commanded. "There's more food here, so we'll take it.

"Pee time," Matt said plaintively, finger forgotten. Rachel walked around until she found the toilet. It was really dirty with other people's pee and poo.

Matt wrinkled his nose. He had already dropped his pants but was disinclined to climb on the toilet. "Stinky," he said distastefully. "Yucky."

"You're right! C'mon." Rachel helped him pull up his pants and led him to the back door that she had spotted when she was looking for the toilet. She'd seen that it was a push bar door and would probably open. Looking around, she found a crate and dragged it over so the door wouldn't shut and lock when they went out. She remembered that doors like this locked because she got locked out once when she went to the back of the store where her mom used to work.

She pushed hard on the door bar with Matt grunting to help open the door. They didn't manage to open it enough to get the crate in the opening, so she used one of her boots instead. When they went into the back alley that smelled horribly of rotting garbage, a bunch of cats scattered, yowling.

"Kitties!" Matt shouted happily.

"I don't think they're nice kitties," Rachel said, then she showed Matt how to pee against the wall.

He was delighted with his new skill. "You pee!" he commanded.

"Silly boy, girls can't do that! C'mon, let's go get the food!"

Together they pulled hard on the door. Rachel's boot fell out. She picked it up, they squeezed through the door and she put the boot on over her slimy sock.

Matt tried to pick up the crate. "Box!" he announced, heaving at it.

"Good idea! You take one side and I'll take the other." Stumbling, they hoisted up the crate and staggered together to the front of the convenience store. On the way, they found a green rolly crate that had a handle. Rachel dropped her side of the heavy crate they were carrying.

"Look, this is perfect!" It was on its side; she righted it and joyfully pulled it to the fallen goods.

Matt toddled after her echoing, "Dis is perfect!"

They dumped everything into it that they could find. There wasn't much because the bad kids had taken most of the remaining food that was still good. Rats and mice had made headway in a lot of the food. Raccoons had not limited their foraging to the garbage in the back of the convenience store. They had found their way in through the broken windows and helped themselves as well.

The rolly basket was only half full. Rachel pulled it to the broken window and looked carefully up and down the road for the big kids. There was no sign of them, so she and Matt heaved the basket up to the window ledge. It fell on its side outside, and they scrambled after it.

They were soon walking up the street, pulling the green rolly basket behind them. Rachel kept checking around to make sure those kids weren't anywhere. They ignored the unfortunate woman that had been run over by the truck. She was still moving, but the big black birds and the crows were already showing an interest in her.

"We need more food, Matt. Where should we go?" Rachel's question was rhetorical, she stopped and looked around. She noticed the dragon restaurant looked undamaged. None of the windows were broken, the blinds in the windows were all closed as well as the door.

They crossed the road carefully after Rachel looked to make sure there were no black trucks or any kind of car coming.

At the restaurant, Rachel stretched up onto her tippy toes to look through the bottom pane of the window in the door. It was one of those windows with a design that makes it hard to see inside, so she had to move her face around a bit to see anything in the dimness inside the restaurant.

She stepped back with a gasp. "Oh!" she exclaimed, "somebody is there with a gun!"

"A gun," Matt echoed uncomprehendingly.

Rachel thought for a bit. "I don't think they moved." She stepped back to the window again and peeked carefully inside. An Asian woman was seated on a chair at a round table right in front of the door. A dangerous-looking gun rested on the table with the barrel pointing straight at her. Rachel squinted carefully at the woman. No, she wasn't moving and her eyes seemed to be shut. She knocked experimentally on the window and the woman still didn't move.

"I think the person is dead," she said matter-of-factly. She didn't see any rocks to throw to break the window, but there was one big can of stew in the bottom of the rolly crate the big kids hadn't gotten. She decided not to break the window in the door because it was really pretty and the dead Asian lady with the gun was right in front of it.

She heaved the can of stew at the window next to the door. It bounced off and almost hit Matt. "Be careful!" she cried and pushed him gently in front of the building next door with the big blue and red balloon on the front of it. He squatted down and watched what she was doing with interest.

It took four throws before the window cracked. Two more, and it shattered. Now she had to figure out how to get inside because the window was quite high up. These were problems she was used to dealing with since she had done it so many times before.

She carefully placed the food in the green rolly basket on the sidewalk, all except for the big can which was looking quite dented now. Balancing carefully on the up-ended rolly basket and avoiding the wheels, she used the can to finish smashing the bottom of the window. She took off her discoloured pink t-shirt (a few of her washing jobs had changed the colour of all their clothes) and laid it on the edge.

Just as Rachel was about to clamber through the window dressed only in her ripped leggings and bandaids, she heard a small cry from inside the restaurant. She paused and looked around the dimly lit room. She didn't see anything other than a bunch of wooden tables and chairs with red seats. Undeterred, she climbed through the broken part of the window.

Jumping down to the floor, she looked around to make sure there were no people with guns present other than the dead lady at the door. Grunting, she pushed the round table that had the gun on it to one side and opened the deadbolt on the door by climbing on one of the wooden chairs with the red seats.

"Come in, Matt," she called. While he toddled into the restaurant and stared around with wide-eyed interest, she took her t-shirt from the window ledge and replaced the noodles and other foods in the rolly basket and brought it inside. She also relocked the door so nobody else would come in that way.

Rachel shook out her t-shirt to make sure there was no glass in it and put it back on.

"Help me look for food," she instructed.

They walked hand-in-hand through the restaurant looking around them in the dimness. It wasn't so dark at the back because there was a series of lit fridges and freezers with glass doors.

Oh, joy! The fridges had a lot of food. She dropped Matt's hand and used two hands to heave open the door of the first fridge. There were some blocks of cheese and bags of grated cheese. She thought she could use that cheese for food so she took the nearest block of orange cheese and put it in her basket. It was quite heavy, so she was using two hands to carefully place it there when she heard Matt talking, and he clearly was not talking to her.

"Hi," Matt was saying.

Rachel left the fridge and allowed the door to swing shut and went to Matt's side. He was squatting on his heels next to another fridge.

"Hi, me Matt," he repeated encouragingly.

"Oh, I know you!" Rachel exclaimed, "you go to my Sunday School!"

She squatted down on her heels beside Matt. "What's your name?" She was talking to a small Asian girl hiding there. She looked quite distressed, though she wasn't crying.

"Who are you?" the little girl whispered timidly.

"I'm Rachel and this is Matt," Rachel gestured at the little boy, then sprang to her feet. "Is there anybody else here with you?"

"That's my mom," the little girl was getting carefully to her feet, tears spirting suddenly from her eyes as she pointed at the immobile woman in front of the door. "There's something wrong with her. I want her to wake up, but she won't. My Ba - grandmother - doesn't even know she's there."

"Is your grandma ok? She's not dead?" Rachel asked encouragingly. "What's your name?"

"I'm Abi. My Ba is sleeping."

"Abi, me and Matt are hungry, do you have any food?"

Abi rubbed away tears with the sleeve of her sweater and went to the fridge nearest the big stove and opened it. There was a whole bunch of containers full of cooked food! Matt and Rachel stood by in wide-eyed wonder looking at containers of red chicken balls and chopped meats in vegetables and noodles. There were pans with food and bags of food.

"Nobody comes to the restaurant anymore," Abi explained, "but Ba keeps cooking. We have lots of food."

"Is there anybody here with you and Ba?" Rachel queried in astonishment. She hadn't seen hardly any living adults since Mrs. Lindstrom last week and she died, too.

Again, Abi's little Asian face crumpled in distress. "My Ong - grandfather - and my dad went to get supplies a long time ago because the truck didn't come. They didn't come back. Ba tried to call the company to see if they saw my dad and my Ong, but they didn't answer."

"They won't come back," Rachel said matter-of-factly.

Just then an erect older lady walked into the kitchen. "Good, you have flends," she said briskly. "Maybe we eat now."

"Oh, yes!" Rachel and Matt exclaimed simultaneously.

"Abi, you get your mother now," the old lady instructed, pulling out an assortment of dishes and containers.

Abi looked at her grandmother in distress, but she didn't say anything. The old lady didn't seem to notice her failure to respond and soon had some wonderful smells coming from the stove.

Suddenly remembering her own mother, Rachel turned to Matt. "You stay here with Abi and her Ba. I'm going to get Mommy."

"OK," Matt said agreeably. He'd pulled out some pots from a cupboard close to the floor and was happily thumping on them with a spoon. He didn't even look around when she unlocked the door and ran out.

It was a long time before she came back. Ba had set out plates and bowls of steaming dishes and Abi, Matt and Ba had eaten after waiting for a while for Rachel. The food was cold when Rachel came back with tears standing in her eyes.

"I can't find my mommy," she said. "I looked everywhere I could think of, but she's gone."

"Don't cwy, 'Achel," Matt said in distress, taking her hand. "Come eat food."

Rachel sat down at the table, but she didn't look inclined to eat. Ba removed the food and brought it back to the stove.

"I forgot to block the door," she said in distress, sobbing a little. "I don't know where she went."

"Mommy gone," the little boy's blue eyes were filled with tears.

Rachel's tears spilled over. "Abi, do you think Jesus will be upset with me because I lost my mom?"

Abi looked over the counter at the dead woman slumped over by the door. "My mom is gone too, she isn't going to wake up. I know that now." She sobbed, "Jesus loves kids. I know my mom's with Jesus, but I want my mom."

Rachel, through her tears, noticed that Matt's chubby baby face was all crumpled up and he was sobbing and Abi had subsided to the floor with her knees up and her face leaning on her knees and was sobbing too. Gulping down her own tears, she pulled up the hem of her discoloured t-shirt and wiped her eyes and runny nose.

"I guess all our moms are with Jesus now. He can take care of them for us."

Ba placed the heated-up food in front of Rachel. "You eat now."

Rachel obeyed.

Without even discussing it, Rachel and Matt took up residence at the restaurant with Ba and Abi. Rachel made a couple of trips to her house to get some clothes. She also found more clothes for them at the Red Apple store down the road. Abi, in a very superior fashion, had informed Rachel that she could read and that was the name of the store.

Abi and Rachel, working together, moved Abi's mom to the floor. Abi wanted to put her in her bed, but she was too heavy, so they compromised by putting her head on a pillow and covering her with a blanket to make it look like she was sleeping. Abi wept through the whole process until they put a screen they brought from their living room above the restaurant around the woman's silent form.

The next thing they had to do was block the broken window. They tried putting empty boxes on a table, but Rachel ruled that people could knock that down too easily. They thought of taping cardboard to the frame inside with lots of tape, but that was ruled out.

Abi, amid sobs, described how her mom had posted herself in front of the door with her dad's gun after some people came and rattled the door, then tried to break the lock.

It was Matt who inadvertently found the solution to the problem. He was trying to retrieve a ball Abi had found for him to play with. It rolled behind one of the fridges that was empty. He pushed the fridge to get behind it and it rolled!

Abi and Rachel worked together to push the fridge in front of the broken window. It completely blocked the hole. Abi then showed Rachel how the wheels locked.

During this time, Ba was feeding them lots of food. She always put out enough for at least five adults. Since the ones who were eating were three small children and an old lady, there was always too much food. She consistently told Abi to get her mother and sometimes included comments about her husband and her son-in-law. She'd make statements like, "men hungly when they work hard. Maybe they come soon."

Gradually, without noticing it, they stopped going into the front of the restaurant. The smell there was getting really bad, but nobody mentioned it, they just stopped playing there or eating there.

It was a little over two weeks after Rachel and Matt joined Abi and Ba that the old lady started dropping things. Rachel realized within a few days that something was wrong when Ba dropped the wok with the breakfast in it. She jumped up and helped Ba clean up the mess.

"Ba, are you ok?" she asked, but she knew she wasn't.

"Solly, solly," Ba said, but she was having problems holding the broom and dustpan. "I think I need lest," she said and went to her bedroom.

Abi was upstairs playing with Matt, so she didn't see what happened.

When she came down, Rachel had a container of noodles and chicken in the big microwave and was trying to remember what Ba did to make it work.

"Where's my Ba?" Abi asked.

"She's resting," answered Rachel. "Do you know how to make this work?" She was pushing buttons experimentally.

Abi went over and in a superior fashion clicked the door shut and pushed the right buttons. The big microwave soon dinged, and the children had their breakfast.

Abi's Ba never came out of her bedroom again. By the next day, she could not keep her balance to stand up and was complaining of a severe headache. She began vomiting the following night. The little girls tried to clean her up - or Rachel did. Abi was too busy crying, so wasn't much help. Ba died that night.

A week later, carrying as much food as they could in the rolly basket, they moved back to Rachel's empty house because the smell in the restaurant was getting so bad. Rachel didn't even notice that Mr. Varga was gone from the yard next door.

C H A P T E R   5

Viv

Propaganda is the executive arm of the invisible government.

~ Edward Bernays

In searching for a new enemy to unite us, we came up with the idea that pollution, the threat of global warming, water shortages, famine and the like would fit the bill. In their totality and in their interactions these phenomena do constitute a common threat which demands the solidarity of all peoples. But in designating them as the enemy, we fall into the trap about which we have already warned, namely mistaking symptoms for causes. All these dangers are caused by human intervention and it is only through changed attitudes and behaviour that they can be overcome. The real enemy, then, is humanity itself.

~ The First Global Revolution: A Report by the Council of the Club of Rome 1991

"I'm going to sit you up, now," Viv said gently.

The man lying prone on the bed muttered something indistinctly but attempted to sit himself up. Viv slipped her strong arms under his armpits and helped him, then piled some pillows behind his back.

She carefully measured liquid liposomal glutathione into his honey sweetened Chaga tea and held it to his lips. She managed to get most of it down in increments, alternately massaging his twitching legs and feet. George had lost his ability to walk more than two weeks ago, shortly after his heart attack.

The collapse of the fiat system could have triggered his illness, Viv thought. Savings and investments and pensions just vanished overnight. It was a worldwide event prefaced by politicians around the world on all the news channels in unctuous voices giving the same message: "Don't worry, this is just temporary as we switch over to our Central Bank Digital Currency. You won't lose anything coming to you. The system is in place to restore solvency. If you require emergency funds, please go to your local Service Canada, show your digital ID and we will apply appropriate social credits to your account."

Day after insolvent day passed after this announcement. The words were repeated verbatim by talking heads with reassuring smiles on every news channel in the First World countries: "Don't worry, this is just temporary as we switch over to Central Bank Digital Currency. Show your digital ID and appropriate social credits will be applied to your account."

With the overwhelming loss of their savings and, ultimately, their property, millions of people saw their only recourse was suicide. Entire religious cults chose mass annihilation, believing this was end times and the second coming was imminent. The economy ground to a halt. Smarmy world leaders continued to counsel calm, patience, trust.

Viv and George made the trek to Service Canada and lined up for hours with frantic people: sobbing, pleading mothers, desperate fathers, angry individuals who didn't want to submit to the digital ID and social credit system.

At the Service Canada office, Viv was awarded no social credits; she had no digital ID and had not been vaxxed. George was awarded with the base number of social credits coming to a single man with no dependents.

"How will I pay my mortgage? How will I pay rent on my office? I'm a doctor, I have supplies and staff I need to pay! This is not right! I am a member of the club; this should not be happening!"

"Be patient, sir, everything will turn out fine!" Cold-eyed fat man smiling with too many teeth failed to calm George.

Demands to speak to a manager elicited loss of toothy smile from the fat man. "You will get your due. Calm down!"

George did not calm down.

George and Viv were escorted off the premises with George ranting all the way. All the Service Canada locations were guarded by UN military by then.

George made some frantic calls to influential people. To each one, he raged, "I am a Fellow of the Bow River Lodge! That should count for something!"

He received placating responses from those who responded to his calls. He was not placated. It was only after he received a call from the Grand Master that he ceased his calls and his frantic pacing and seething. He shut himself in his office at home for the rest of the day and refused to speak to Viv. He had a heart attack that night. At just 32 years of age, with no history of heart disease, George required an emergency angioplasty.

George's health remained poor after his surgery. His sleep became restless and he would wake multiple times through the night. It seemed it was nightmares that troubled him. He would sometimes sit up abruptly in the dark and begin to sob. Viv would wake up and hold him in her arms.

"What did you dream about?" She asked.

"I dreamed... you were dead. I was on a flat red plain and there were corpses everywhere and I wanted to find your body... and I was so sad."

"It's OK, it's OK, I'm here." Viv held him as he wept.

He returned too soon to the office to treat patients because of the increasing need for doctors.

His emotions were on a roller coaster. Some days he would come home from the office or hospital weeping, other times his anger and rage would consume him, and he would pace through the house and refuse to speak to her. His sleep was choppy, with recurring dreams of red plains, demons and loss.

Their finances were in shambles as well. The digital currency problem was escalating. Just like the Canadian government's ArriveCan app had been a disaster during the protests at the height of the lockdowns, the digital currency roll-out was an absolute catastrophe. The ArriveCan app which was supposed to track the vaccine status of people coming in and out of the country had cost $60 million and provided an unreliable service with appalling bookkeeping practices. The roll-out of the digital currency was an even more unmitigated failure costing more than $100 million uniquely to build a security system to prevent hackers from helping themselves to unlimited funds. There were rumours that even these security systems did not prevent theft. That was just the beginning of the ineffectiveness of the system.

"You were right! You and Lionel were right!" George dragged his weary feet into the house from the cold dark one winter night. "That vax - it's killing people, people are dying, just like you said! Oh God! It's so horrible! You have no idea what it's like." He slammed the door on the icy wind and kicked off his boots. His wont was to neatly place them in the closet and hang up his coat. George was usually neat to a fault, finding Viv's impetuous messiness somewhat annoying. Tonight, the boots tumbled on their sides on the mat and were ignored and the coat he shrugged off did not get hung up tidily on a hanger but was dropped on the floor of the closet. He stalked off into the spacious living room in his sock feet. "I need a drink."

"I'm so sorry, George." Viv followed him and urged him into his favourite recliner. "Put your feet up. I'll fix you a drink."

"You can say 'I told you so'. You don't have to be so nice about it." George's blond hair was standing on end, his eyes haggard. He took the glass of Scotch she handed him and gulped it down in one swallow then extended the glass for more.

Viv fixed him a refill and sat down on the sofa. "Do you want to talk about it?" She picked up her own glass of white wine and curled her legs under her.

George took a sip of his second drink. He looked at her for a long time, sighed and ran the fingers of his free hand through his already wild hair. "It's pointless." Another long pause. "Shedding is real," he said at last. "I think I'm a danger to you."

Viv hastened to reassure him that she was taking measures to fight the viral shedding with pine needle tea and supplements. "I'm not worried. God will take care of us."

George shot up abruptly, kicking the foot of the recliner back into place. "God!" The word exploded from his mouth derisively. "I don't think God is anywhere to be found. Humans are such damn useless wicked selfish destructive things; I think He's probably given up on us and taken a nice long holiday before coming back to blow everything up! It's just a matter of time!" He tossed back his second drink, strode to the side table where they had a few bottles of their favourite drinks and poured himself another generous glass.

"I have to call Lionel," he said as he vanished through the archway into the back room where he kept the short-wave radio.

A couple of weeks after this exchange, Viv noticed that George had hand tremors. At night, his legs sometimes shook slightly as well. Early onset Parkinson's seemed a possible cause. It wasn't long before she doubted that diagnosis and suspected Bell's Palsy. George's handsome face drooped noticeably, and his speech was slurred. Now, just a few months later, it was evident that he was experiencing more heart damage. His office was closed because of lack of funding, which was a good thing since his condition was deteriorating significantly. He had given up his hospital rotation as well for the same reason.

One night, Viv brought him to the hospital in an Uber since she'd been unable to get a response to her 911 call and their personal supply of gas for their vehicles was now exhausted. At the hospital, they were severely overwhelmed and understaffed, so she had ended up bringing him home again after waiting for more than three hours and watching George's lips turn blue. She managed to extract some nitroglycerin from the one nurse she spoke to.

"Why are so many people here?" Viv had asked the harried nurse who checked George in.

"It's the China virus, whadda ya think? And why isn't that man with you wearing a mask? Are you vaxxed?" Clearly the nurse didn't want to have this conversation and all courtesy was gone.

"My husband is not wearing a mask because he's struggling to breathe since he just had a heart attack and needs help and the acetylsalicylic acid I've been giving him is not easing his chest pain. Now, are you going to help me?" Viv snapped back. Then, her annoyance at the dishonest narrative caused her to continue: "Furthermore, there are at least three people in this room that seem to have severe neural damage, possibly Bell's Palsy, two seem to have liver damage judging from their yellowish hue, there are maybe five people with skin petechiae from subcutaneous blood clotting, several with abnormal growths, and I'll bet there's at least four more in this room alone that have heart damage, possible cardiac infarction

- like my husband." Viv nodded her head towards the waiting area. "They're all urgent cases and DEFINITELY NOT China virus."

"What are you? A doctor?" The nurse's tone was quite rude this time.

"Yes, I am. Look, just give me some nitroglycerin tablets and I'll get out of your hair." Viv had noted that George was slumped over, and she was quite worried.

The nurse gave her a wild glance, scanned the packed waiting room, jumped up and left. Within moments she was back.

"Here, take these," she hissed, "the pharmacy staff all called in sick, so nobody's monitoring this." She furtively slid a small bubble pack of nitro tablets across to Viv.

Viv administered one to George immediately, since she was extremely concerned about his condition. The rictus of pain on his face improved noticeably within moments, so she deemed it best to leave the hospital to their own devices.

"Viv, Viv," the man slumped against the pillows muttered, reaching for her. Viv irritably switched off the TV she had installed in front of him. It was another vaccine pitch by yet another celebrity. It was getting worse, these vaccine pitches, ever since the president of the United States had started sending people door to door to administer the jab. The Canadian Prime Minister had threatened to follow suit, though it was still not evident if he had followed through. She knew some provincial premiers had done telephone campaigns to try to get people to take the jab. Now, of course, it was the bivalent China virus vaccine that was all the rage. It was all so insane.

Realizing George probably had to urinate, she pulled down the blanket and installed the urine receptacle. George slurred his thanks and a trickle of urine went into the blue plastic container. It was early days, but the glutathione and the tea did not seem to be doing much to alleviate George's symptoms. Even his balance and muscular coordination had been affected by now. She wished she'd been able to secure natural remedies sooner, but all the health stores were closed now. Too bad she hadn't thought of Amazon as a source for her health remedies sooner. She used George's Socdits, which was what the digital social credit system was dubbed, to do the purchasing. She wasn't sure she would be able to secure any more supplements through Amazon or any online source, though. It was at least a week since any mail was put into their mailbox at the post office and the last time she walked the four blocks to check it, the door was locked.

Not for the first time, she felt a wave of gratitude to Aunt Joan. It was her great aunt who introduced her to nutrition and health remedies that helped your body heal itself. In med school, Viv learned nothing about these things. She later discovered the Flexnor Report that explained how, as far back as the early 1900s, John D. Rockefeller had successfully discredited and ended all teachings about natural remedies in favour of big pharma indoctrination of doctors in medical schools all over the world. He'd done this by funding med schools to take control of their curricula. Discovery of the ability to formulate pharmaceutical drugs from petroleum products was making him rich and the Rockefellers wanted to ensure the steady flow of money. Subverting medical education was the route they had chosen.

Viv switched the TV back on for George, feeling she couldn't stay in that room that smelled of medicine, urine and despair. George appeared to have fallen into a restless sleep now, anyways. She went up the graciously curving marble stairs to her home office on the second floor. Thankfully, the internet was still working. She sat down on her comfortable sofa with her open laptop resting on her crossed legs and put on her half-lens reading glasses. She logged in to a secure site she used to communicate with a freedom fighter group in Canada and entered the middle of a conversation about a Dr. Valant who had written to all the members of his church throughout North America telling them to get the injection. He had included all sorts of scriptures from the Bible telling them to comply and saying that all those who raise alarm about the vaccines are conspiracy theorists and disobedient to God.

Annette, the woman who was a member of a congregation that had received the letter, was shocked. She wrote a letter to Dr. Valant who responded with a condescending brush-off.

"Now, all the elderly in long-term care homes associated with my church group have been injected and many have died," Annette was saying. "A few of them got the virus even after the shot or the boosters, but many became quite ill and it was attributed to a break-through infection or some other cause. But so many died..."

"So, nobody admitted it was because of the vaccine?" Richard, who was another member of the group, queried. "My church has been experiencing some persecution – you know, that new world religion they're trying to bring in – I can't help but wonder if people like this are plants from that lot. I know we're getting people coming in and speaking against the gospel and trying to change the message. We're living in weird times when they push vaccines even from the pulpit and try to change God's word."

Viv typed quickly, "I agree with you." She added, "Did healthy kids also take the shot?"

"Yeah, many have. Now they're going after those who haven't. It's also been included in childhood vaccine schedules without any fanfare so parents don't even know about it. Pretty shocking. Parents don't check. Doctors tell them babies and kids need their vaccines. We've been jabbing helpless babies and children for decades and nobody questions it anymore or realizes that over the last 60 years or so, kids went from getting five vaccine doses to more than 73 doses of at least 16 vaccines! Now they've slipped the China virus poison into the schedule on the advice of the so-called leading health agencies in the US! Of course, all jurisdictions in Canada followed suit like a bunch of brain-dead sheep!"

"Deaths or adverse events among vaccinated? Adults and/or kids?" Viv typed.

"Many, but they keep using the words 'safe and effective' and 'rare', just like the media. People who get sick are too afraid to suggest it's injection-related for fear they'll be shamed or lose social credits. Those who die, the medical professionals just attribute the death to something else like complications from a prior China virus infection or climate change – can you imagine?" Annette answered.

"When did doctors become concealers, not healers?" Viv typed rhetorically. "Can I send you an information article to share with people at your church?"

"You can, but most of them are unwilling to conceive of or consider any reason why the vaccine is dangerous and unnecessary. It's like their brains no longer work. Send it anyway, I'll try to get a few people to read it. If I help anybody, it's one more person who is awakened."

"Send it to me too," Richard said.

The discussion went on to the topic of food shortages. This was a theme they revisited often. Ontario and many of the eastern provinces as well as most of the States were experiencing severe problems with food acquisition. Since many of the farmers in the Netherlands and other places in Europe and even further east were divested of their farms by their totalitarian governments, the virtue-signalling Canadian and American governments sent large amounts of food to the EU to make up for their shortages, to the detriment of their own people. The United States and Canada had a lot of their farmland bought up by the software developer that was pushing the vax. He installed solar panels on some of it and grew genetically modified crops on some that proved toxic to human consumption. He also established a cricket factory on some of that land with the object of creating a cheap source of protein to replace beef and poultry. Viv reflected that conservative Alberta had escaped some of the shortages as there was still locally grown food available. The eastern provinces and many of the States had followed the trend of disallowing individuals to grow their own food.

Viv logged out of Telegram and went to her Proton email. She noticed with wry amusement that it was April 1st. Reflecting that the world was full of fools, she scrolled through her contacts and found Richard and Annette's emails. She had to open and download the encrypted file she wanted to send to them. Before sending it, she took the time to reread it and check her links.

The article began with the Kissinger Report or the National Security Study Memorandum (NSSM) 200 which, as early as 1975, called for population control through sterilization and abortion in developing countries. Viv's article then clearly outlined the collusion between the World Health Organization and GAVI, the Global Alliance for Vaccines and Immunization. The WHO was headed by a man who was not even a doctor and was previously a member of a terrorist organization. This corrupt WHO leader repeatedly lied about the severity and even the source of the viral infection that was said to be as lethal as the Spanish flu of 1918. When they went into China, they had falsely reported that the virus originated, not from a lab (which was indeed what had happened), but from bats in a so-called 'wet market'.

Viv snapped her laptop into tablet mode and began to pace around the room, scrolling through her work and clicking on links to check that they hadn't been broken.

At one point she found herself standing motionless in front of the wall featuring photos of her wedding. Happy people, such a handsome groom. Her finger trailed over George's face. She had loved him – hadn't she? Of course, she loved him. Slowly her finger wandered to the taller man next to him, wavy brown hair spilling over his forehead, smiling clear blue eyes. Ugh! No! She wouldn't do this! She spun around, placed her laptop on the chair next to her. Time for lunch.

She helped George eat their frugal lunch of rice and tuna, then read to him for a while. 'The Answer' by Icke usually put George to sleep very effectively.

Back at her desk, she continued her review. Her white paper went on to show how the WHO had been taken over by GAVI. This malevolent foundation had been founded by a corrupt software developer with a bizarre obsession for depopulating the world. Vaccines were his vehicle for carrying out this goal through predictive programming with movies and documentaries about pandemics and disasters preparing the world psychologically for full compliance with governmental mandates. And they did comply; by the tens of thousands and then by the millions. They lined up and took the vax because of the promise of safety and the threat of sanctions should they not comply.

Viv paused in her review of the document. Should she add more information about this evil software developer? Her fingers hovered over the keys, then she decided against it. There was so much in this article already that was almost impossible to believe. She continued her review and verification of the information links.

This Global Alliance for Vaccines and Immunization (GAVI) had achieved the impossible. It had full immunity and no accountability for any of its actions and had helped Big Pharma achieve the same. As a result, nobody ever was held accountable for the mass murder and millions of injuries caused by the injections. In the process, they had increased their obscene wealth.

Viv sighed, stood up and stretched. The paper was eight pages long, with diagrams and references. Maybe it was too long. Maybe nobody would read it. There was so much that could be added. She could have added how the definition provided by the WHO on herd immunity - and even the concept of immunity - was changed to enforce the use of vaccines as the only way to fight disease. She could have included the medical dishonesty about the use of the PCR as a diagnostic tool. The richest and most powerful families were in deep collusion for a Great Reset wherein the World Bank, which they owned, wanted to transfer control of all the world's wealth into their own hands. There was so much missing from her article, but so much that was condemning.

She finished checking all the links in her document and updated a couple of them. She attached the document to her email and sent it off to Annette and Richard.

It was time to think about their next meal. Finding food was getting more difficult. She could no longer go to grocery stores since they were insisting that she provide a scan of her digital ID if she wished to shop there. Of course, there was not much in the way of food in the stores since the trucks carrying food to the cities were getting rarer all the time and locally grown food was being hoarded by most people. She also had no Socdits and few places accepted any alternatives anymore. Churches and foodbanks still gave out food until recently without insisting on proof of vaccination, but their supplies were getting scarcer. She was needing to get more creative with meal planning, though she had quietly stocked up as much as she could last year before things got so crazy.

After dinner, she gave George another dose of the supplements she hoped would help with his vaccine injury: Chaga tea and glutathione and N.A.C. (N-acetyl cysteine) capsule which was supposed to help with nerve function. His breathing seemed less strained, and she wasn't sure, but it seemed like his lips weren't so blue. She sat beside him for a while since he seemed to want her to stay, grasping her hand in gratitude. She reached out and smoothed his dry straw-like hair with her free hand.

It was that thick beautiful blond hair and his dark blue eyes with laugh lines around them that had attracted girls in droves to him. His fit athletic body was appealing to the female populace at the University of British Columbia, but the real drawing card was his personality. He was the guy who was always kind, friendly and laughing. He'd never been the jock that pushed other guys around and racked up notches in his belt by the number of girls he slept with. He was gallant and respectful to women and inclusive and congenial to the guys.

Despite the hordes of women around him all the time, he had chosen her, and she could never figure out why. She never hovered or gave him special glances or saved seats in lecture auditoriums for him.

It was the first day of the Stem Cells course. She took a seat at the front of the lecture hall as was her wont, put on her reading glasses and opened her laptop. The devastatingly handsome George Johnson settled into the seat next to her.

"Hi, I'm George," he said, extending his hand to shake.

"Viv," she shook his hand. "I know who you are."

"Really?" he looked inordinately pleased. "How come?"

Viv popped open her file for the course notes and typed the date. "Aren't you on all the sports teams and fraternities on campus?" she queried, turning to look at him over her glasses.

He gave a little laugh. "Not quite, but close. You want to go for coffee after class?"

Viv looked at him, her black eyebrows shooting up, ignoring the fact that the professor had started writing notes on the board with the reading list. "You're inviting *me* for coffee?"

She snapped her gaze back to the lectern and rapidly typed the reading list into her notes. "Aren't you going to record the reading list?"

"Nope, it's all up here," he tapped his temple with an index finger. "And, yes, I would like to have coffee with you."

She soon learned that he had an eidetic memory and that he was extremely persistent. Though she continued to maintain her strong focus on academics, she quickly found herself recognized as the studious girlfriend of the popular George. He kept popping up wherever she was – in the library, study hall, cafeteria or even on the campus lawn under her favourite shady tree. He regularly invited her to his football games and, a mere two months after their first conversation, she found herself at her first varsity football game!

When she took her seat at the reserved spot in the stands, George jogged over to her and joyfully handed her a smaller version of his football jersey. It almost felt like a marriage proposal, it was done so ceremoniously and publicly. She laughed merrily, hammed gracious acceptance for the on-lookers and gave him his first kiss on the nose. From that day forth, it was official: he was her boyfriend. George Johnson, the popular jock from Edmonton, was the boyfriend of the studious Viv Watson from Kitimat.

Sitting beside her sleeping husband, Viv reached out and gently traced a line down his forehead, over his straight nose and finely molded lips. She remembered him doing this to her so many times as they lay cuddled together in their marriage bed. Then he would kiss her and kiss her and tell her how beautiful she was.

They loved each other so much during those early years. The only blip in their happiness was her puzzled attraction to George's best friend. That was forgotten quickly when they returned to British Columbia after their wedding to complete their studies and specializations. She saw Lionel a few times after that, but George and her work consumed her. She was so happy. *They* were so happy. She and George joined a local church in Vancouver, mutually agreeing that they did not want to be part of a large charismatic congregation, both preferring a smaller evangelical assembly. They attended a small group Bible study together when their busy schedules allowed. They both loved theatre and saw a few plays at the Queen Elizabeth and the Vancouver Playhouse. They jogged together when they could. Halcyon years...

Viv sighed deeply and, seeing that George was sleeping now, she gently disengaged her hand from his and left the room, leaving the door ajar. He no longer slept in the upstairs master bedroom with her since his first heart attack. She'd set up her former home office on the main floor as a bedroom since going up the stairs winded George so badly. George, who just two years ago ran 10 kilometres a day and barely broke a sweat.

Back in her office, she logged back into her email. An email from Unsleep, a member of a resistance group, was waiting in her inbox. Viv knew Unsleep was somewhere in Alberta, but that was all she knew about him. Viv's handle was DrLiv, which wasn't especially clever, she thought.

DrLiv (the email read), *look out your window to see an excrescence that is now ubiquitous throughout the city. Beware of 5G. It has been activated and the jabbed are in danger.*

What did Unsleep mean? She'd noticed the 5G towers were everywhere now. And very ugly to boot. She also knew that there were serious dangers related to short, high-frequency wavelength electromagnetic emissions. How did that affect the jabbed? Darn, why did Unsleep have to be so cryptic! Since beginning her correspondence with Unsleep, Viv developed a mental picture of Unsleep. She thought he was probably some wild-eyed prophet – once known as a 'conspiracy theorist' - who lived in a basement and trolled the internet for the latest atrocities committed by the cabal currently ruling the world. He probably didn't shower very often and shaving and hair-cutting rarely occurred. She often imagined meeting him since that wasn't outside the realm of the possible as they were both in Alberta and both fought against the government. She imagined he was likely socially awkward and barely articulate.

This business about 5G, though. Surely it was just alarmism?

Viv opened her Tor browser and searched for information on 5G and the vaccine. The more she read, the more her skin prickled with distress. She was a doctor, not a physicist, so she had to look up some of the references and terminology, but it was very possible that the vaccine, which contained graphene oxide was a conductor in the vaxxed people's brains to control their brain patterns! She had frequently wondered why such a high percentage of the contents of the vaccine serum was graphene oxide.

Pushing back abruptly from her desk, Viv rose quickly and hurried downstairs. In the kitchen, she brewed her third cup of pine needle tea for the day. The suramin and shikimic acid in the tea was what was saving her from the adverse effects of spike protein shedding and Viv took this tea faithfully. She was also taking twice-daily doses of the N.A.C., a powerful antioxidant she was giving George. Her tea was easily made from a readily available source of white pine needles in the local park.

Carrying her cup of steaming tea, Viv went to the large front windows in the living room. In the glow of the streetlights, she saw the excrescence mentioned by Unsleep. It was crouching like some foul unholy presence just one block away beyond the luxury homes across the road from her. Why on earth did they have to be so ugly? Viv knew they were going up everywhere – often overnight - and she'd decried how ghastly they were! This one, though! She hadn't even seen them put it up, but it was there! How was that even possible?

"Crap!" Viv exclaimed under her breath, immediately after putting the boiling hot tea unthinkingly to her lips. She quickly set the tea down on the glass top of the coffee table and hurried back to the kitchen for an ice cube. She slipped on a light jacket, picked up her tea again and carried it out to the private back patio. After sucking the ice briefly to cool her lips, she dropped it into the tea.

Viv calmed herself, sipping the cooling tea, listening to the crickets, and watching the bats swoop. Early April and the bats were already busy ridding the city of pests. Though the human world was falling apart, these small creatures of the night seemed completely indifferent. Viv was always happy to see bats, she knew that bat populations were on the decline since millions were killed every year by the ubiquitous wind turbines that were supposed to be saving the world from global warming.

For the first time in a long time, she allowed herself to think about Lionel Goudreault, somewhere in the northern highlands of British Columbia. She had grieved for him last year when he lost his wife but had no idea how she could help except by sending along her condolences with George. She'd never been close with Janet, not really. Janet was an extrovert, belonging to many Christian social and missionary groups. She'd been raised in material comfort in a prominent Calgary family.

Viv was the exact opposite. She lost her mother at 12 when she died of cancer, and her father was a humble natural gas worker. Viv tried to take the place of a mother to her younger brother William. The only reason she'd made it to med school was because of her great aunt Joan who was a naturopath and nutritionist and had left her an inheritance that had helped her through her first four years of med school, along with the various scholarships she won.

Viv slapped at a mosquito marvelling that they were already about this early in the season. She wished she could see stars in Calgary, but there was so much light pollution she rarely saw any.

What had happened to her family? When she had started the battle against the lies about the virus, her father tried to encourage her to walk away and just focus on her career. When the vaccine rolled out, her brother was one of the first to get the shot as soon as it was made available to his age group. His wife and two kids also took the shot as did her father.

Viv sighed and rubbed her eyes. Why oh why had she neglected to keep her brother, Will and her father informed while she was researching and warning about this so-called pandemic? She would never forget that terse conversation she had with Will nearly a year ago.

"Hi Will, I heard Dad is retiring. Are you and Elsie planning a party for him?"

Long pause. "Yes."

"That's great! George and I will need advance warning so we can arrange the time to come."

"No need."

Confusion. "Why? We want to be there for Dad!"

"Did you get your vax?"

Oh no! Not this! Not my family! At this time, George was still supporting Viv's battle against the narrative and had firmly rejected all pressure to be vaxxed. Viv sighed mentally and hastened to reassure William.

"No, but don't worry Will, George and I are well. We're taking all the supplements required to build our immune systems."

"You don't care about Dad or me or Elsie or the boys. You only care about yourself. It's your social responsibility to take the vaccine and you know it." The emotionless monotone voice continued, driving spikes of pain into Viv's heart. "Only double-vaxxed socially responsible people are welcome at the party."

"But, that's not true!" Blood rushed to her face, and she picked up her phone and started pacing around her office speaking vehemently into the phone's microphone. "Have you been following my research online? I sent you some links months ago and asked you to subscribe to my podcast. William, this is serious!"

"Your research!" Will scoffed. "You and a bunch of loonies get together and decide all the health authorities are lying and the science about the China virus is a lie. You'd think, after spending – what – a hundred grand on getting an education in medicine that you'd know better!"

Stunned and disbelieving, she tried to send some articles she'd written and research she'd done to her brother and father and they told her not to send any more of her conspiracy theories. Her dad had even said that he was sure Aunt Joan would be deeply disappointed in her.

Then what had happened? Maybe six months before his heart attack, George changed. From listening to her counsel and the results of her research into the vaccine and its detriments and the suspicious contents, he had started to talk as though the China virus vaccine was a good thing. From there, he commenced a round of coaxing, cajoling and even harassing in an attempt to convince her to take the vax. Why did he do that?

She took another gulp of her now cool tea, listening to the night sounds. It was remarkable how silent this once busy city had become. She could hear quiet twitters in the nearby alder tree where a pair of Bohemian Waxwings were setting up their nest.

The day George took the vax was so strange.

Viv had been sitting in her office putting together her next podcast. That was back when her office was on the main floor off the foyer. She heard the tones of the door lock code then the whining of the opening lock. It was early afternoon, much too early for George to be home.

"Get your jacket on, we're going out!" George's voice was sharp and urgent as he strode to her open office door.

Viv got up willingly. "What's up? Where are we going?" He had already opened the closet door when she got there. She bent to take her boots off the shelf preparing to don them.

"Never mind that, let's go!"

Something in his voice made her pause. She straightened, boots in hand, to look into his face.

"George? What's going on? Where are we going?" She didn't move, still holding her boots in her hands she turned to find him extending her jacket and wallet and trying to cram them into her arms.

"Hurry up!" he snapped.

"I am not going anywhere until you tell me what's going on!"

"We have an appointment at the health centre. It's time to give up your conspiracy theories, Viv. Come on!"

Viv tossed her boots, wallet and jacket onto the floor of the closet. "Stop that, George! You know very well the dangers of the vaccine..."

George's face reddened. "Why does everything have to be YOUR way? Why do I have to always do what YOU want?" His voice rose and he was shouting now. He had never shouted at her before.

Viv's blood did a slow burn. She put her hands on her hips. "That is not true and you know it!" *What is wrong with him? I've told him about my research into the dangers of the vax! What has changed? Why is this so important to him?*

His anger vanished as suddenly as it had appeared. He grasped her hands. "Please, Viv, please, it's just a little jab and it's over! Come on, I promise nothing bad will happen. *They* promised nothing bad would happen. Please, come on, I know some people had a slight reaction to the vaccine, but *we* won't. They promised!"

She stared at him incredulously. There were even tears in his eyes. *What is he talking about? Why does this mean so much to him?* "WHO promised? Who has the POWER to promise such a thing? Of course there's a risk! There's a HUGE risk but it's being covered up! George, people are dying! People are having all sorts of dreadful reactions! The long-term effects are unknown!"

For the following ten minutes his pleadings and urgings flipped back to anger and again to tears. Viv was unable to get George to admit who was pressuring him to get vaxxed or why he was so sure it would not harm them.

But, she didn't go with him. When he returned home, he did not speak to her for two days. And, the vax did harm him. And now he was dying.

Viv picked up her teacup and, re-entering the house, she froze. There was a man standing in front of the big window, only his silhouette visible against the outside light. Something about the set of his shoulders calmed her alarm.

"George!" she cried, "you're up!"

The immobile man at the window did not respond, he stood steadily gazing out the window. Following his gaze, she noted the 5G tower again and wondered about it.

"George," she repeated more gently after taking his arm, "are you feeling better?"

After a long moment, he turned his head towards her and his knees buckled. She caught him before he hit his head on the coffee table. "Let's get you back to bed," she said quietly.

"Viv," George said, "Viv, what's wrong with my mind?"

"What do you mean?" Viv asked, then, "I can understand you! You must be getting better!"

"I don't know. I hear voices in my head and my mind is...wrong."

"Come on, you need to get back to bed. We'll talk about this tomorrow." Viv pulled George's shrunken arm over her shoulder and helped him to the bed in the converted office. He was definitely better though. The nerve twitches and weakness seemed to be receding somewhat, and he could talk quite clearly.

Viv sat down on the chair next to the bed. "Do you need anything, George? Do you think you can sleep?"

He ran his hands through his hair. "Viv, what's wrong in my head? Why can't I remember anything? Why do I hear voices in my head? What is wrong with me?"

"Shhh, shhh," Viv said soothingly. "I'll make you some tea."

When she got back with the Chaga tea he was sitting again, his feet on the floor. His head was gripped in his hands, and he was rubbing his temples and swaying and whispering something indistinctly. The loss of his powerful memory seemed to be disturbing him deeply, but it was more than that.

Approaching with the tea, Viv caught the words, "Get out, get out of my head." Putting the mug on the side table, Viv helped George slide his legs back under the covers. She sat down beside him on the bed, making the shushing sounds again, and gently urged him to drink the tea.

"It's OK," she murmured as he finished and sat beside him until he settled and slept. "Goodnight." She drew the blankets up and switched off the bedside light.

Her own sleep, in the comfortable king-size bed piled high with fluffy pillows, was restless. By five she was awake and unable to sleep anymore. She decided to go for a jog, something she hadn't done since George had his second heart attack.

Viv donned her favourite running shoes and sweats and headed out the door, carefully locking it behind her. She first checked on George and he was still sleeping.

Running down Riverdale towards the park, she couldn't believe how much fitness she'd lost in just two weeks. When she ran, her mind wandered inadvertently to Lionel. They used to go for a run together at lunchtime every day.

Lionel. It was painful thinking about him.

It was her research, months later, that had shown her the utter corruption in the medical community and led her to have a better understanding of how Lionel was thrown out of the medical profession so quickly and with such finality. Other doctors who were fighting the misinformation about the virus and associated lies didn't get such abrupt ejection. Her own ejection was not so sudden. She'd received several warning letters from the Medical Council of Canada before her license was revoked. Lionel had only one meeting before he was ejected with finality.

She ran steadily, her breath puffing white in the cool morning air. Her path took her through a playground occupied only by birds and busy squirrels. By the south end of the park, her steps slowed to a lope and then stopped. What was she seeing here? How strange!

Next to a 5G tower between the two roundabouts, there were several military jeeps and a large black van. Some dozen civilians had either been drawn to the 5G tower or were herded there by the soldiers. A few were holding their heads as though in pain or covering their ears trying to block sound only they heard. Others silently looked empty-eyed at the tower even while the troops were converging on them. Several more were already sitting, unresisting, in the back of the van.

Scalp pricking with urgent warning, Viv ducked behind a nearby tree. A soldier was roughly gripping the arm of a balding older man.

"Wh-why do I have to go with you?" the man protested feebly.

"It's for your safety," was the response which elicited a harsh guffaw from a second uniformed man standing by the open door of the van. He then pushed the tottering protester into the van with the butt of his rifle.

Viv fled, stumbling and gasping and distraught. *For their own safety? How was herding these helpless people like cattle into a van 'for their own safety'? Hitting them with the butts of guns was 'for their own safety'? Piling them like human refuse was 'for their own safety'?*

When she got home, panting and dripping with sweat, her reeling mind was made up. She had to contact Lionel and get him to come home.

C H A P T E R   6

Leaving Dark Mountain

For I am convinced that neither death, nor life, nor angels, nor principalities, nor things present, nor things to come, nor powers, nor height, nor depth, nor any other created thing, will be able to separate us from the love of God, which is in Christ Jesus our Lord.

~ Romans 8:38-39 NASB

If you wish the sympathy of the broad masses, you must tell them the crudest and most stupid things.

~ Adolf Hitler

Facts do not cease to exist because they are ignored.

~ Aldous Huxley

It was raining at last. Lionel's friend the Arctic fox made a visit on the first of April, so he gave him a piece of an elk leg he'd taken out of the freezer the day before. The fox was coming less frequently of late. Some of his dense white winter coat was darkening to its summer grey colour.

Three weeks ago, he had made the decision to leave. Snow had kept falling in heavy wet flakes during those weeks, covering the conifers in a thick silent blanket. The drifts were already deep enough to bury him and he had tried to remember if last March there was so much snow, but he couldn't.

Now, he wanted to go. Well, he wasn't sure if he could leave yet, to be honest, since his jeep still wouldn't start. He knew he'd need transportation since walking to Calgary was out of the question, but no four-wheeled vehicle could get through the deep drifts all the way to the highway.

He had hoped to get the jeep started by hooking it up to the cabin's hydroelectric grid, but that hadn't been possible because he was unable to find components or even rig them up for the connection to the battery. His little emergency charger had quit working last year with some of the components melting and he couldn't figure out a way to connect the hydroelectric current to the booster cables with the materials on hand. Of course, his specialty was not electronics or engineering, he was a doctor after all. His only hope was to get the car moving downhill and get it started that way. He didn't lack for slopes but needed a snow-free area to get it rolling.

Now that he'd made up his mind to go back to Calgary, the long wait was really getting to him. He hunted and took down an elk shortly after his trip to Dease Lake but just ate his stores of food and the elk meat, occasionally sharing with his sporadic companion. He varied his diet with the rabbits he caught.

The fox helped himself sometimes to the contents of his snares, but Lionel didn't begrudge him that, as long as he didn't damage them. Earlier in their association, the Arctic fox brought him a few offerings of squirrel and bat. Lionel had respectfully thanked him. He cooked the squirrel but couldn't manage to eat the bat. There were no offerings of late.

Lionel began to prepare himself for travel. He was going through the items he thought would be essential for survival in a hostile world. His Ranger .308, the .22 and ammo were essential, he was sure of that. He'd also bring his CZ 9mm handgun for protection. He was going to bring a couple of his snares as well. Since the nights were still quite cold and snow might fall again, his bear furs would come with him. His pack, too. He'd perfected that pack over the long winter nights. It was a marvel of pockets and slings, and he knew exactly what would go in each one. He had destroyed many of Janet's sewing needles and used a lot of canvas and leather in his pursuit of perfection. It was heavy when fully loaded but Lionel was strong. Of course, he may not need it, but if things were really bad, he might need to do some cross-country hiking. It was better to be prepared.

One cool evening, late in March, when the interminable snow was falling, Lionel went into the cabin and irritably slammed the door. He started rummaging through the shelves of the crowded bookcase next to the bed looking for a Foxfire book to distract himself. He pulled out two books and a worn volume without a title on the spine fell out. Lionel picked it up, opened it, and discovered it was Janet's prayer journal!

Feeling slightly like he was violating a confidence; he sat down and began to read. Janet had started the journal while he was in Guelph.

He read how she prayed for him and struggled to work enough hours to continue sending him money. He read about how lonely she was during his absences. He learned about her joy and happiness whenever he came home. Throughout this thread, he discovered that she prayed for neighbours and friends and even the animals she tended. She prayed for the children she taught in Sunday School, for the elders at their church. What a prayer warrior she was!

They say this China Virus is a pandemic, he read. *He says that's not true. He's so angry with the system: the masking they say is essential in spite of the studies that show it's ineffective, the social distancing that is stupid and arbitrary. I know he's right and he's trying so hard to use his knowledge and experience to wake up the authorities to the dishonesty they're showing and the damage it's doing to people. He wrote letters to the Alberta premier, the Minister of Health and the chief medical officer. I'm praying they will receive his advice. Oh God! Make them listen! Those poor children – those poor people walking around like zombies, dehumanized, avoiding each other as though they're terrified. It's like a nightmare – every day is like a nightmare. I can't believe this is happening.*

Lionel paused in his reading at this point, lost in a memory of an evening in the fall of the first year of the pandemic. That was when he still was delusional enough to think the chief medical officer of Alberta might be interested in advice from a highly qualified immunologist.

"She answered my letter," he snapped, padding sock-footed into their sunken living room from the foyer.

Janet was curled up reading a book on the country blue sofa with Ramona, their Shitsu, on her lap. The tableau he saw on entering was particularly stunning with her gorgeous silver-blond hair against the blue, the white of her shirt and the white dog and the black of her leggings and their very large black cat, Rico, on the back of the sofa.

Ramona jumped off Janet's lap and bounced excitedly over to him,

"I assume you're referring to the letter you sent the chief medical officer, since she's the only *she* and the other people you addressed your letters to were male,"

Lionel looked up from patting the wriggling thrilled dog. Her calm voice and the happy dog placated his annoyance somewhat, as did the sight of his beautiful wife.

"You assumed correctly." He straightened up and stalked over to his favourite easy chair by the unlit fireplace.

Ramona ran back to Janet, greetings finished, and jumped back onto her lap. Rico blinked his brilliant yellow eyes, uttered a rusty meow, stretched luxuriously, and stalked over to rub on his shins. Lionel picked up the heavy cat and flopped down in his favourite chair, stretching out his legs. Rico proceeded to knead his thighs, then gave a heavy cat sigh and curled up on his lap. Lionel scratched him behind the ears fondly.

"I gave her *scientific studies;* I gave her tons of *real* data about the ineffectiveness of masking and the futility of social distancing. *Social distancing.* There is not a *single study* that supports staying two metres apart as being effective against viral transmission. I gave her data that showed how damaging lockdowns are on children and how psychologically damaging it is to prevent children from interacting with each other. I explained to her how useless the PCR test is for this virus citing the very *inventor* of the PCR test. I pointed her to my YouTube channel where I go into even greater detail about these issues. I don't think she even read my letter!"

"Why do you think that?" Janet had placed her book face down on the sofa. She leaned back to look at him quizzically.

Lionel stopped patting Rico. He fumbled in his pocket under the heavy cat and pulled out the crumpled letter.

"See for yourself."

The cat continued his loud purring, eyes closed contentedly. Not wanting to disturb the happy animal by getting up, Lionel scrunched the offending paper into a ball and tossed it onto the sofa next to Janet. She picked it up and flattened it on her thigh then perused it quickly.

"Well," she set the letter back onto the sofa, "her tone is very similar to yours."

Lionel bristled slightly. "What does that mean?"

"I did suggest you tone it down a little and not be so arrogant and dismissive of her concerns. She was given the responsibility of providing health advice to everyone in the province. Her answer is arrogant and dismissive too."

"She could at least provide a response to my concerns. But, she can't, of course. She does not have science on her side." He resumed patting Rico. "It's the same on the government of Canada website. There are no scientific studies cited. It's gaslighting, that's what it is."

"You're right. Supper's in the oven. It should be ready in about 20 minutes. You hungry?"

Lionel reached for the remote, pointing it at the TV on the wall. "Starving!"

The screen cleared to show his nemesis, the very woman they had been discussing, behind a podium, making her daily update.

"... 387 new cases in Alberta with seven deaths. Halloween is coming, please do not gather in groups of more than five people and only family members. Remember, masking and social distancing saves lives. If you think you're sick, get tested. Stay home for 14 days. We're all in this together."

While her unctuous voice was inundating their gracious living room, Lionel's face was getting redder and redder, his wavy brown hair tumbling over his forehead as he yanked at it in his anger. He furiously clicked the tv off when the premier appeared on the screen, sprang to his feet spilling an indignant Rico onto the floor and began pacing back and forth shouting and raging against 'that stupid woman, that stupid, stupid woman who calls herself a doctor, clearly knows nothing about how the immune system works. We're all in this together – yeah right! Stupid, stupid woman!'

Lionel recalled that Janet had escaped to the kitchen to get away from his rage.

Now, sitting with Janet's journal on his lap in his remote cabin in the highlands of British Columbia, Lionel gave in to feelings of guilt and regret. So often she was the sympathetic absorber of his frustration and anger, listening and quietly murmuring comforting words when his battles grew difficult.

He remembered how the following year, he was invited by pastor James Coates to speak and explain the truth about the virus at the Grace Life Church in Edmonton. The police burst in on him when he was speaking in front of a congregation of more than 200 people. At the time, the arbitrary rule was that only 15% of the congregation could attend at one time and the auditorium was full. His arrest, along with Pastor Coates and some of the congregants, made headlines. The Justice Centre for Constitutional Freedoms negotiated his release along with that of the congregants, but in a gross miscarriage of justice, a judge had kept Pastor Coates in jail much longer.

Every page of Janet's prayer diary for more than a month included supplications to God for Pastor Coates. He remembered how she even became an activist herself, driving to Edmonton from Calgary to protest in front of the church. He was so proud of her and had the fine she received waived with help from the Justice Centre for Constitutional Freedom (JCCF). Tears he was holding back prickled in his eyes and he rubbed them away angrily.

Soon he read the entries she had written at the height of his battles in Calgary.

I miss Lionel terribly, he read. *He's spending so much of himself on this fight. Oh, God, is there any way he can win? I feel like we're strangers in the house. He comes in late and even when he's home, he spends hours on the phone with Viv, discussing battle strategies or cases. It's almost like he's married to her, not me. God, give me the grace to understand him and not get angry because I'm so frustrated.*

Another entry read, *I want a baby, but we haven't made love in more than a month. Does he even see me anymore? I don't think he hears me. God, help me not to be selfish.*

The familiar waves of guilt swept over Lionel. She loved him so much, and he hadn't loved her enough, and now there was nothing he could do.

The entries during the last months of her life tore his heart in two. He read how anguished she was about being ripped away from the world she had always known. She grew up in Calgary and spent all her life there. Other than holidays and her two visits to Guelph while he was doing his specialization, Calgary was her safe place, her familiar home. Selling their beautiful house and most of her lovely furniture and possessions had torn her apart. He remembered how her protests led to his gentle and repeated explanations about the move being for the best. Her words and the depths of her grief he largely ignored. He mansplained all of that away and didn't even try to be sensitive to the hurt she was feeling.

He remembered his gracious concessions to letting her bring her French press, some favourite books and photos and one chair. Rehoming her little Shitsu, Ramona, and two cats broke her heart. 'It's for the best,' he kept saying. Dear God, he'd been so arrogant, so sure that what he wanted was for the best and had swept her away, insensitive to her loss.

She was lonely and frightened, facing birthing and raising a child with a husband who had changed so much from the early years of their marriage. He read in those pages how much she had felt that he didn't love her in the same way he used to. He read how he never seemed to have conversations with her anymore, just mundane talk about the daily requirements of their rustic life. She ached for conversation, real conversation.

His tears streamed down his face into his beard as he read the very last entry. *Lionel has gone hunting. I'm so lonely and scared. God help me be happy. God keep my Butterfly. Deut. 31:8.*

He sat for a long time, his head in his hands. At last, he rose, pulled out his old worn Bible and opened it. He found the verse, then began to weep great choking sobs he had not been able to release those long torturous months of loss.

I turned away from God, I blamed my Saviour Jesus Christ, for my misfortunes. I was arrogant and certain I was doing God's will then when I lost my wife and child I became angry with God.

His churning mind turned to a beloved poem by Francis Thompson he had learned many years ago.

I fled Him, down the nights and down the days;
I fled Him, down the arches of the years;
I fled Him, down the labyrinthine ways
Of my own mind; and in the mist of tears
I hid from Him, and under running laughter.
Up vistaed hopes I sped;
And shot, precipitated,
Adown Titanic glooms of chasmèd fears,
From those strong Feet that followed, followed after.
But with unhurrying chase,
And unperturbèd pace,
Deliberate speed, majestic instancy,
They beat—and a Voice beat
More instant than the Feet—
'All things betray thee, who betrayest Me.'

I blamed God. I fled from Him, from the Saviour who was extending His hands to me and offering me comfort and had saved me from my sins. He never stopped loving me though I stopped looking to Him. I tried to do it all by myself. I thought I could save the world and in my arrogance, I fled from my responsibility and from Jesus Himself when things fell apart.

Now of that long pursuit
Comes on at hand the bruit;
That Voice is round me like a bursting sea:

'And is thy earth so marred,
Shattered in shard on shard?
Lo, all things fly thee, for thou fliest Me!
Strange, piteous, futile thing!
Wherefore should any set thee love apart?
Seeing none but I makes much of naught' (He said),
'And human love needs human meriting:
How hast thou merited—
Of all man's clotted clay the dingiest clot?
Alack, thou knowest not
How little worthy of any love thou art!
Whom wilt thou find to love ignoble thee,
Save Me, save only Me?
All which I took from thee I did but take,
Not for thy harms,
But just that thou might'st seek it in My arms.
All which thy child's mistake
Fancies as lost, I have stored for thee at home:
Rise, clasp My hand, and come!'
Halts by me that footfall:
Is my gloom, after all,
Shade of His hand, outstretched caressingly?
'Ah, fondest, blindest, weakest,
I am He Whom thou seekest!
Thou dravest love from thee, who dravest Me.'

Lionel fell to his knees by the table where he had been sitting. "Oh God," he prayed, his face supported by his clasped hands pressed to his forehead as tears continued to fall down his cheeks, "make me a better man. Help me to learn from my terrible mistakes. Hold Janet and Butterfly close to Your heart. Forgive me for my arrogance and never let me be that man again. Don't ever let me lose sight of what is really important. You are important and my family is important and I forgot that.

I forgot You are the only one who can save the world. I forgot I am Your clay, I am not the potter and I forgot that You gave me my beautiful wife. I have been so wrong. I have been so ungrateful. Help me, Lord, help me."

After three days of rain, the sun came out and shone brightly on April 2nd. Lionel went through his backpack, ensuring he had packed medical supplies he might need in an emergency, some herbs and salt for cooking, and sufficient ammo for his guns. He slipped Janet's journal in a side pocket. *It's like I'm bringing her with me and not abandoning her completely,* was his reflection.

Lionel was packing the jeep with the food supplies he had prepared when his friend the Arctic fox showed up with his mate and his 15 - yes, Lionel counted them - grey and brown kits. He checked his snares when he first went out that morning, planning to dismantle them to bring along with him. All of the snares were sprung, but there were no rabbits in them, just lots of tiny prints along with the bigger adult prints of the fox.

"Well, Brother Fox," Lionel said softly, hunkering down in the grass, "so this is your family. I can see why you needed so much food!"

His friend advanced closer to Lionel than he'd ever come before and sat down on his haunches exactly like a dog. The kits bounded into the clearing, yipping excitedly and nervously, while the female stayed shyly among the trees. The little foxes, who still had the small, rounded ears of a pup no more than six weeks old, milled around their dad and Lionel. A couple of the braver ones ventured to run up to Lionel and sniff his pants and boots then dash excitedly away.

"Did you know I'm leaving?" Lionel asked the fox. He slowly held out a hand, palm up. Two kits dashed up and sniffed it, then ran back to their dad. The Arctic fox, almost all grey now, moved slowly to Lionel's hand, sniffed it, then gave it a small lick. He allowed Lionel to scratch him briefly behind the ears before he moved away, the swarm of kits bouncing around him. He flicked his tail, gave a brief bark and the whole family faded into the bush.

Lionel had already decided to leave the next day. He was going to make one more try to speak to George that night before dismantling his ham radio antenna to bring it along on his voyage. He'd already rigged up his solar power bank onto the roof of the jeep and was prepared for using the ham radio as he travelled. There were also secure straps on the top of his pack where the solar unit could be fastened if he had to travel on foot.

He was just finishing his last meal in the cabin before an early start in the morning when he heard the ham radio crackle to life. He jumped up and hurried to the small desk which had held it for the last two years.

"Come in, Windy, Dark Mountain here!"

Another prolonged crackle.

"Come in, Windy. Over."

A voice that was definitely not George's interrupted by clicks came through the airwaves. "Oh darn, how do you use this thing?"

"Viv, is that you? Viv? Over."

A series of clicks. Then… "Lionel, can you hear me?"

"Yes!" Lionel leaned into the hand-held in his eagerness. He held down the button. Speaking slowly and clearly, he briefly explained how the ham radio operated.

Viv quickly caught on. "Lionel, I need to let you know what's going on here. Can you hear me?"

"Yes, Viv, please tell me, over."

"Oh darn, right, sorry, uh, I'll get the hang of this. George is failing, Lionel. His heart has been affected and also his brain and nerves. I'm suspecting it's the graphene oxide along with the effects of the proximity of 5G towers all over Calgary."

Viv rushed on, telling him about the increasingly prevalent military presence and the removal of civilians from their homes to an undisclosed location and the many suicides.

"I don't know where everybody is. The city feels so empty, now. There are military jeeps everywhere. So many deaths and disappearances and sick people. Meanwhile, the media is still pushing the jab. Can you imagine? They're still using the words 'safe and effective' and they're still saying there are a few 'rare' cases of heart problems and other 'rare' problems. I'm looking after George, for now, though I do worry about these soldiers, they're everywhere. Lionel, it's getting really bad. I'm having to go to food banks in churches to get food. They won't let us go to grocery stores. The digital ID is in effect now everywhere. We can't buy or sell without proof of the jab and social credits."

Lionel finally got a chance to interrupt her flow of words. "Viv, how are you? You're spending a lot of time with George. You know about shedding, don't you? Over."

"It's ok, Lionel, I'm taking precautions and lots of supplements. Will you come home? Calgary needs you. Be careful though, it's getting dangerous."

"I'm coming, Viv. I'll try to keep in touch, I'm bringing my radio. Tell George I'm coming, I miss you guys."

Long pause with just crackling noises. "I miss you too. Stay in touch. Bye."

Lionel was troubled when the radio fell silent. The military, 5G, people disappearing: it was all very alarming. Would he even be able to travel by jeep all the way to Calgary? Well, he would get there somehow.

He got up early the next morning. He headed up the mountain for the last time. At the carved wooden marker, he knelt silently and asked God to help him on his journey.

"Goodbye, Janet," he said quietly. "Thank you for the life you gave me. Thank you for the love you gave me. I will see you in heaven."

His jeep started after he coasted downhill. His voyage to Calgary began.

C H A P T E R 7

Heading South

Terrorism is the best political weapon, for nothing drives people harder than a fear of sudden death.

~ Adolf Hitler

Travelling old logging paths and overgrown hiking trails made the 20 km to Dease Lake more than a full day's journey. He could never accelerate above 40km/h, and the trails wound around hills and mountains and took him far to the north before turning south again. He had to backtrack a few times since the spring melt had extended the reach of the marshes. He had to winch himself out of a few deeper patches of mud and that slowed him down significantly as well. Small new trees were minor hazards to look out for as well; he didn't want damage to the undercarriage of his jeep.

There were still deep snowbanks beneath shading rocks and north faces of mountains. He stopped for his first meal by a pond glimmering between stands of partially submerged black spruce and willow. He sat down on a lichen-covered fallen tree and watched a family of hooded mergansers jumping off a log and diving for small fish. Somewhere he heard the high-pitched whistling of an osprey, and a muskrat swam busily across the pond. As he bit into his thick sandwich, a chipmunk darted by his feet.

Again, he experienced that sense of wonder at God's creation. Even while humans were destroying each other in the cities and towns of the world, these creatures of God continued on the seasonal cycle of their lives. He thought of the passage in Ecclesiastes he learned as a child:

> What do people gain from all their labours,
>   at which they toil under the sun?
> Generations come and generations go,
>   but the earth remains forever.
> The sun rises and the sun sets;
>   and hurries back to where it rises.
>
> The wind blows southward,
>   then turns northward;
> round and round it swirls,
>   ever returning on its course.
> All the rivers flow into the sea,
>   yet the sea is never full;
> to the place from which the streams come,
>   there again they flow.
>   in the ages before us.
>
> To everything, there is a season,
>   and a time for every purpose under heaven:
> a time to be born and a time to die,
> a time to plant and a time to uproot,
> a time to kill and a time to heal,
> a time to break down and a time to build,
> a time to weep and a time to laugh,
> a time to mourn and a time to dance,
> a time to cast away stones and a time to gather stones
>   together,

> a time to embrace and a time to refrain from
>   embracing,
> a time to search and a time to count as lost,
> a time to keep and a time to discard,
> a time to tear and a time to mend,
> a time to be silent and a time to speak,
> a time to love and a time to hate,
> a time for war and a time for peace.[1]

Lionel left the crumbs of his meal for the creatures to eat and continued his journey, again asking God for the ability to be a better, more humble man.

When the sun went down, Lionel found a clearing. He knew highway 37 wasn't far, however, to continue along the overgrown bush trail in the dark was a treacherous option. The temperature had dropped well below freezing, so a hot cup of coffee brewed in his small tin percolator and some left-over elk stew heated over his fire warmed him up.

Lying on his back wrapped in his bear furs, Lionel stared up through the black tree silhouettes painted against the reds and purples of the oncoming night. The brilliant, nearly full moon floated between wispy clouds. His mind was peaceful and calm as he listened to the crackling fire. Then a thought suddenly occurred to him: he had seen no planes and no contrails or chemtrails for months! How strange! Things must be really changing in the outside world! Oh, no, that wasn't true. There was that black helicopter... He fell asleep, wondering about it.

The clock on the jeep's dashboard showed it was approaching 9 o'clock when Lionel got to the highway. Weak sunlight struggled to shine in a grey sky and the road was empty to the north and to the south. His gas gauge was close to empty

---

[1] Ecclesiastes 3:1-8, BSB.

as well. He hoped he didn't have too far to drive to get to the gas station in Dease Lake.

He headed south and drove for nearly ten minutes without seeing any vehicles until he spotted a pickup truck in the marsh on the east side of the road. He thought he saw a human figure in the cab, so he pulled over to the side of the highway and put on his four-ways. He was about to plunge into the boggy ground through the thin ice that had formed overnight to see if he could help when he realized there was a fallen tree over the front end of the truck with a large grey owl sitting on it. Clearly, this truck and its driver had been here for some time. Lionel decided he would see if he could notify the authorities once he got to town.

Lionel saw two more vehicles in the ditch before he got to Dease Lake. One was a jack-knifed tractor-trailer without a driver, and the other was a VW Tiguan. That one was particularly distressing. The driver had smashed into a tree. It looked to have been a woman, though there was not much left of her for obvious reasons as a flock of crows rose into the air when he approached. Possibly there had been another passenger in the front as the airbag had deployed on that side too. In the back was a baby seat. It looked like a predator had removed the child through the broken back window. It had happened fairly recently since the blood had not been washed away by the rains of the previous week.

Lionel was troubled as he passed the Tahltan Nation Development Corporation. There were a number of trucks, some earth-moving equipment and a black helicopter there, but with no signs of life. There would likely be nobody here he could inform about these accidents since there was no smoke coming from the chimney. Would there be any gas available there? His gas gauge was now showing empty, and the warning light was on. He would likely have a better chance in Dease Lake.

When he got to the Petro-Canada in the town, he was running on fumes. In front of the Super A, an ancient woman was lying on the broken pavement. Her long grey hair straggled over her face and an empty bottle was gripped in one hand. Her head was pillowed on the other arm. He pulled up carefully to the gas pump on the opposite side of where she was lying. He thought she was dead until she sat up groggily, swiped her drooling sunken mouth with the back of the empty hand. She attempted to drink from the bottle then flipped it across the tarmac where it shattered, the pieces spinning to stillness. She got slowly and unsteadily to her feet and proceeded to stagger towards the swinging open door of the Super A.

Lionel opened his gas tank cover and unhooked and inserted the pump nozzle. Lionel heard no reassuring noises indicating fuel was flowing into the tank of the jeep. He repeatedly squeezed the valve lever in the nozzle to no avail.

Lionel got into his jeep, started it with a prayer, and moved it to the second gas dispenser.

"Don't waste your time, eh," the old woman was standing propped up by the doorway looking at him. "Ain't been no gas there for more'n a week, eh. No trucks been through here in a long time."

"Darn," Lionel said, "any idea where I can get some gas?"

"You tell me where I can get more booze, eh." The old woman didn't seem inclined to help, staring blackly at him and sucking slightly at her toothless gums.

"I'm sorry, I don't have any alcohol," Lionel answered. "I really do need gas. I'm Lionel, by the way." He stepped towards the woman, hand out.

"Bunch a cars around. Most people are dead or took off south, yah. You can probably siphon some from them cars." She limply shook his extended hand with her grimy one. "Joanne. Not that it matters, you know, ain't nobody much left to talk to me and say my name. All my kids and family dead or gone south, you know."

"I'm really sorry," Lionel said quietly. He sidled around the old woman and went into the store. There was no sign of Norm or his grandfather. The shelves were mostly empty, but he managed to find a new gas jerry can in the hardware section at the back. It took more rummaging in the attempt to locate a tube that would do to siphon gas. In the end, he cut a piece of yellow garden hose about a metre long with his hunting knife. He left a few bills on the glass cash desk even though currency was no longer in use because he didn't feel right just taking the items without paying for them.

Exiting the store, he looked around for Joanne, but she was gone.

He had to check quite a few cars to find gas. Many had already been drained of fuel. He struck it lucky at last with a newer car he found in the ditch in front of the Northway Motor Inn. He filled the gas can and walked back to his jeep. After pouring the gas into his tank, he drove back to the car and finished siphoning the gas into the jeep's tank and his canister.

Exiting Dease Lake, he saw people on three ATVs stopped on the side of the road. They were dressed in a motley array of clothing. It looked like they'd been looting and had found some expensive items. The one woman in the group seemed to be having some trouble with her facial muscles, especially on one side of her face. Lionel waved and began his journey south down the Stewart-Cassiar Highway.

He didn't see Joanne standing under a tree, talking to a man all dressed in black.

C H A P T E R   8

Nass River Bridge

Be strong and courageous. Do not be afraid or terrified because of them, for the LORD your God goes with you; he will never leave you nor forsake you.

~ Deuteronomy 31:6 NIV

Soaring mountains, majestic forests, rushing streams, and sparkling lakes soothed Lionel's eyes as he travelled south. In a marsh, where vegetation was reviving from the winter cold and snow, he spotted a cow moose and her very young calf.

Everywhere, the fresh young green buds were showing on the balsam poplar, black cottonwood, and mountain alder. The mountains were still snow-covered, and banks of snow could still be seen in shaded areas of the forests, along north-facing slopes, and along the road, but spring was definitely coming.

Very few vehicles were on the road. In the first 100 km of his travels, he saw only one car, and the driver and passenger wore masks and gave him furtive glances as they rushed north. He saw that they had four jerry cans on a carrier at the back of their RAV4 and the rear seat and trunk area of the car were fully packed with personal items. They also had a storage container strapped to the roof.

"Preppers," Lionel said out loud, then, "I wonder why there are so few people anywhere?"

There was nobody to answer his query, just a family of mallards, and a few busy buffleheads diving and resurfacing on the pond off to the west of the road.

In Iskut, a small aboriginal town, two motorcyclists were siphoning gas from an older truck. One was a male, the other a female. Both turned to look at him as he drove by. Lionel waved and continued on his way.

Coming over the crest of a hill, he had to swerve to avoid two vehicles that had collided in the southbound lane. Both were pickup trucks hauling trailers. The southbound trailer was a U-Haul that had spilled onto the side ejecting household goods. The other was a holiday trailer. It looked to have been a head-on collision. The drivers of the two vehicles were dead and were preyed upon by local carrion-eaters; there was not much left of them. Another couple of kilometres down the road, there was a partly eaten human body, quite likely another casualty of the collision. Passing slowly, Lionel's medical eye could see that the victim had a fractured collar bone and was probably female. She may have sustained other injuries, but the evidence was no longer visible.

Lionel passed a resort decorated with moose antlers and boasting gas and diesel availability. He opted not to stop as his gauge showed more than half full and there was the gas canister to fall back on.

Beside an endless lake off to the west of the highway, Lionel stopped for a break and something to eat. He'd packed some sandwiches he'd made with the last of the bread that would keep him going for a couple of days. A GMC SUV and a RAM 2500 passed him, headed south. Both were travelling fast and Lionel thought he might see them on the way by the side of the road since they were both fuel hogs. Unless, of course, they were carrying extra supplies of fuel.

Lionel left his little picnic spot and was gathering up his things when a helicopter passed overhead. Astonished, he stopped and stared upwards. The helicopter swung southwards, then turned and passed overhead again.

"What are you looking for?" Lionel murmured and finished packing the jeep, climbed in and drove back out onto the road. The helicopter followed him for a couple more minutes, then disappeared leaving Lionel with a slight feeling of uneasiness which quickly dissipated.

Back on the road, it was more endless forests and magnificent snow-covered mountains. It started raining quite heavily, so Lionel slowed down slightly as some of the curves in the road were quite sharp. Three more hours of driving, and all he saw was a rusting Ford Escort with the hood open and nobody around and a Camaro in a marsh with skid marks on the pavement beyond a sharp turn in the road.

Cresting a fairly high hill, Lionel saw an eruption of black smoke off to the southeast.

"Too early for forest fires," Lionel mused out loud, "too much rain and snow, too, hopefully."

It was just past Meziadin Junction that his trip encountered real difficulty and he discovered the cause of the smoke he'd noted earlier. On the Nass River bridge, a northbound b-train tanker that appeared to have been loaded with a combustible and explosive chemical or gas had jack-knifed after colliding with the RAM he'd seen earlier. The bridge surface was still smoldering from the fuel spill, the asphalt still hot and bubbling. The pickup truck was crumpled and deformed and the lead tanker appeared to have exploded when the RAM had smashed into its side.

Lionel stopped his jeep and got out. Walking onto the bridge, he assessed the situation. The entire bridge was blocked, that was clear. The west lane was still on fire and looked to have enough fuel to keep the surface of the deck molten for quite some time. In the northbound lane, the lead unit had collapsed to the surface of the tarmac as the landing gear had completely given out. Even if his small jeep could push the tractor off the bridge into the swollen river – and that was highly unlikely – there was no room for him to get by as the lead tanker was only a little over a metre away from the cement barrier on the east side of the bridge.

How did this bizarre accident happen? The tractor of the northbound b-train had ended up facing south completely detached with the smashed nose protruding out beyond the edge of the bridge. Perhaps the driver had attempted to avoid the RAM and had jack-knifed? It was likely when the tractor had jack-knifed that the kingpin on the fifth wheel of the Kenworth tractor had broken, separating it from the tankers, and the momentum had rammed it up against the guardrail.

Standing on the west side lane, Lionel spotted the source of the fuel pooling on the deck of the bridge. The severed end of the guard rail had perforated the second unit in the b-train low down. It had not exploded when the RAM collided with the lead unit but a slow, steady seeping of fuel onto the bridge deck was serving to keep the fire burning.

Approaching the wreck, Lionel could feel the heat of the fire still bubbling in the asphalt. There was absolutely no way to get under or over the two units in the b-train until that cooled off, which would likely take days, and he didn't really want to spare the time. He walked over to the once classy-looking dark blue Kenworth tractor and assessed the possibility of getting by that way. It now became clear that the only way to cross this bridge would be to do it on foot and even that would be difficult.

Standing with his hands on his hips, Lionel considered his options. Returning to his jeep, he pulled out the map of British Columbia from the side pocket of the door. Consulting it, he saw that highway 37A was not an option since the road petered out once it entered the boundary of Alaska and there was no other bridge or road for hundreds of kilometres.

Lionel looked at the sun; he would have time to cross before nightfall if he moved quickly. He would have to load his backpack with essential food supplies and conceal the jeep. If he ever came back this way, he would like to know he had transportation on this side of the burned bridge as well as some gas. He concealed his jeep deep in some undergrowth well off the road and covered it with branches and other fallen debris.

Regretfully he sorted through his supplies. He wouldn't be able to bring any of his canned food with him as it was too heavy. From now on, he would be eating dried meat and peas and rice or any game he was able to catch. Maybe he could gather some dandelion greens or some other herbs. Fiddleheads would be a bonus and he knew it was almost the season to gather them.

He would have to leave his bear furs behind, that was evident. He put on a heavy sweatshirt under his weatherproof leather jacket and pulled on a woolen tuque and his lined leather gloves, hiked his heavy pack onto his back, buckling the waist strap securely around his middle.

Lionel had to wend his way around chunks of unidentifiable debris from the exploded tanker. There was no way to get by the tractor on the right side since the still smoldering exploded tanker was jammed up against the passenger door on that side. He would have to find a means of getting over the tractor after working his way down the driver's side.

Lionel eyed the catwalk, wondering if there would be possible to swing himself from the catwalk at the back of the tractor past the Studio Sleeper to the step. Unfortunately, there was nothing to grip for more than two metres and nowhere to wedge his boots to sidle along to the step since the fairing around the fuel tank on the Kenworth was level with the bunk and the gap between the two was minimal.

The only way to get to the step would be to climb onto the guardrail and inch his way along the double bars to where it protruded beyond the edge of the bridge and get onto the step from there.

Moving along the guardrail was treacherous since he was bent almost double as he slid his feet carefully along the bottom rail while gripping the top bar with his gloved hands. He had to avoid looking down into the spring-swollen rushing river far below him in the gorge. One misstep would send him plummeting into the icy waters.

At the severed end of the guardrail, he braced himself then made the leap to the step. For a split second, it felt like he wouldn't make it with his heavy pack pulling on his shoulders. His hands scrabbled desperately for the grab handle and one boot landed precariously on the edge of the bottom step.

A tremor shook the tractor and Lionel noted with alarm that the two sets of drive tandems at the back of the tractor were over the edge of the bridge deck and the only thing that was holding the rear of the tractor in place was the guardrail that he had just left and the friction of the undercarriage on the broken cement at the edge of the bridge. If the guardrail gave out, the tractor could very well plummet into the cold waters of the Nass River.

Moving as smoothly as he could, Lionel reached for the mirror. A faint smell of cooked meat reached him, and he glanced through the broken window and then wished he hadn't. The heat of the explosion of the lead tanker had apparently barbecued the driver. Gulping back nausea, Lionel averted his eyes, searching for something to climb onto at the front of the tractor.

This was not easy. The hood of the tractor was tipped forward, hanging precariously by the left hinge, leaving what remained of the engine exposed. The nose of the tractor was seriously damaged on both sides from impact with the cement lip of the bridge. The right side of the nose had likely struck the cement first causing the jack-knife when the cement broke under the impact. The driver had to have been going very fast to have swung the tractor right around. When it spun, the left end of the nose had finished breaking the cement, smashing the radiator, and leaving the tractor perched treacherously on the edge.

There was nothing to climb onto since the left front tire was gone. Reaching around the mirror Lionel groped for something to hold onto in order to facilitate his climb over the engine. Grasping the metal brace for the power steering fluid receptacle with his left hand, he ducked under the mirror, still holding it with his right. This left him hanging precariously over the void, the heavy pack hauling at his shoulders.

He extended his left foot and scrabbled for footing on one of the coolant lines or wiring with his boot. It was time to let go of the mirror and try to get over the engine block.

A gasp and a heave later and Lionel was lying full length on top of the engine. Panting, he extended his left foot feeling for something to step onto. A juddering went through the surface under him and a prolonged groaning somewhere beneath the tractor accelerated his heartbeat as the entire mangled structure slid forward, closer to the edge. The hanging hood swung twice, then broke loose and plummeted into the icy water below. Lionel's foot slipped.

"God, help me! Help me!" Lionel whispered. Would this be how it would end for him? The fall to the churning water might kill him since it was at least 30 metres. If the fall didn't kill him, the shock from the cold would, or his pack pulling him down into the depths. That was if he didn't strike a chunk of floating ice. Then his final moments would be excruciating.

Right hand clinging desperately to the cowl at the base of the windshield, Lionel shifted the grip of his left, grasped the air outlet, then slowly shifted his weight towards the left. Groping with his foot, he found the right tire. He released the cowl and eased down onto the tire. A final twist of his body and lunge over a section of the bubbling pavement and Lionel regained the surface of the bridge beyond the catastrophic tangled shambles.

It was none too soon. A screech from the guardrail announced its release of the metal wreck it was holding in place. An ear-splitting shriek of metal and crashing noise and the entire dark blue broken monstrosity plummeted from the edge of the bridge into the frigid maelstrom below.

When Lionel got back onto the unburnt surface of the bridge next to the smashed pickup truck, he let his shaking body fall to the asphalt. He panted and trembled for a couple of minutes until his wildly pounding heart slowed and he was able to get back on his feet. A look back told him that he couldn't retrieve his jeep in spite of the tractor having fallen into the river because the pavement was still molten and too broken to navigate. He shrugged his pack tighter on his back and decided to continue his journey on foot.

He walked while light flakes began to fall. By then the pale sun was low in the sky leaving only a ribbon of light on the horizon. He stopped and ate his last sandwich by the Nass River that still rushed along beside the highway. He took a long drink after running the river water through his carbon filter purifier and stored a bottle-full in the secure pocket he'd rigged up on his pack. The flakes of snow had now turned to a light drizzle.

CHAPTER 9

Totems and Teachings

It is a quite special secret pleasure how the people around us fail to realize what is really happening to them.

~ Adolf Hitler

After a chilly night on the damp ground wrapped in his lightweight waterproof sleeping roll, Lionel made a quick breakfast of dried meat. He'd only been walking for about three hours along the sunlit highway when an older pickup truck pulled up beside him. An Aboriginal man with two long black braids rolled down the window and called out to him.

"You're going my way, eh? Can I give you a ride?"

"Thanks, that would be great!" Lionel opened the back door and swung his pack onto the narrow back seat of the extended cab, then climbed in beside the man. "Where are you coming from? I had to abandon my vehicle north of the Nass bridge because it's blocked. Is there another way across the Nass that I don't know about?"

"No, no, I didn't come from there," the man responded. "You seen that dirt road a bit north of here? My daughter lived up there with her husband. I just came from there. She died, you know. Bleeding from her woman's parts. She'd been bleeding for months."

"I'm sorry," Lionel said quietly, "she got the vaccine, didn't she?"

"Yeah. Me too. I'm gonna die soon too. Ain't nobody much left in her wilp, many left to go south in the middle of the winter. They thought they could get help if they complained to the government about being sick. Some of them believed that a booster shot would make them better because the government said so on the TV. Nobody came back, though."

Lionel's mind leapt to a couple of questions. "Excuse me, I'm not sure what you mean by 'wilp'. What is that?"

His companion laughed comfortably. "That's just like a territory of the Gitxsan People where I come from. It's just a traditional way of describing our family group."

Lionel's medical eye roved over the man. His breathing was fine, so clearly his lungs had not been affected nor his heart. His mind also seemed alert. Lionel asked his second question since the first did not seem to have discomfited his new friend.

"You seem well, why do you think you're going to die?"

"I dreamed my death, sometimes I dream true dreams." The man's black eyes turned to fix Lionel's ice blue ones. "I know who you are, too," his eyes went back to the road and he swerved to avoid a skunk and her three kits. "You're Bear Heart and you have a mission from God to save the children. Will you come to my wilp with me? I'm Tyrone Rush of the frog clan." He extended his right hand to Lionel, who gripped it with his own.

Lionel was too astonished to speak. How could Tyrone know about the words of the old man in Deese Lake?

Clouds were gathering, and a light rain began to fall.

"It's funny, you know," Tyrone continued, "they're committing genocide against their own people, out there. They come and shoot us all up with their lies and their poison, but they did it to the white man, too. I heard that from my cousin who went to Prince George for supplies last month. He said there's lots of sick people there too. White people and Chinese people and everybody, doesn't matter the colour of their skin. Killing them all off. I know that from my true dreaming. At the vaccine clinic, people are still walking in and getting their shot or a booster because on the news they keep saying if people are sick it's the China virus, you know. They keep saying it's variants and they need another shot to keep them safe. It's not just on the news, it's on every program, in the commercials, everywhere. Nobody in Gitanyow believes that now, but it's too late, you know."

While the wipers on the elderly F150 swished back and forth, Tyrone told Lionel of the proud Adawaak traditions of the Gitxsan people in Gitanyow, his home. He spoke of the Lax'yip and their protection of the traditional land, of their respect for nature. He described their partnership with nature to protect the animals and the fish and harvest the natural healing plants.

"Now the Huwilp and the Gitanyow people will soon be gone." The man's face was sad. "You will come, won't you? You love this land. We have to give you our memories."

Lionel sat silent while the man spoke, gazing out at the lowering clouds, the forest, the rivers and the lakes they passed and listening to the rhythmic swishing of the wipers. He didn't answer right away, his mind struggling with the need to get to Calgary and see George and Viv and help in any way he could. Here was another need. This man said he'd dreamed he would come. What could he do for these Indigenous people? What did they expect from him? But Tyrone had dreamed he'd come. Was it God that kept telling these dreamers about him? How could he refuse a summons from God? He sure would like to know what these dreams meant, though. If they were dreaming about him and a task he had to do, why didn't God speak to him?

Lionel nodded. Decision made. "I'll come."

Tyrone was not a fast driver, so it was dusk when the elderly truck made a right turn onto a dirt road. The rain had stopped and the skies had cleared at last. About one and a half kilometres of rutted road full of puddles brought them into the village of Gitanyow where Lionel saw before him, in the dim light of the setting sun, a whole series of majestic totem poles, perhaps two dozen, intricately carved.

Tyrone stopped the truck and Lionel got out. Without speaking he made his way reverently to the closest pole. He gently ran his hand over the carved wood and looked upwards. Moving slowly down the row he saw squirrel and wolf, bear, raven, frog and human figures carved in whimsical poses.

Lionel walked through the village in silent marvel, trying to discern the figures through the gloom. Tyrone hunkered down by a hut and lit a pipe, watching him silently.

"Totem poles," Returning to him, Lionel spoke softly, "I never thought I'd see such an amazing artistic wonder in such great numbers. While my people etched our history on linen paper with black marks, your people carved it in the ancient red cedar of your forests. Your people created beauty and images to tell your tales. I can't help but envy you your ancestry."

As he was moving through the totem poles, a small group of people had gathered around Tyrone Rush. They, too, had hunkered down, sitting on their heels in the dusk. One man had lit a fire in the centre of the village.

No longer able to see the intricate carvings on the poles in the dim light, Lionel accompanied Tyrone to the fire where all the people were dressed in traditional clothing. A drummer began drumming and the singing started. Tyrone settled next to Lionel, legs crossed, pipe smoke seeping from his mouth.

"Listen to the heartbeat of Mother Earth," he said. "This is our last dance. It is our final li'ligit. You know this as a potlatch or feast. Today we will feast on Salmon, thanking the salmon for our food. We will eat Bear, thanking the bear for his sacrifice. We will share the gifts of Mother Earth, thanking her for them. We will dance for you. Tomorrow, you will learn of the totems, our stories and our history. We are the people of the river mist."

The dancing, drumming and singing continued. Lionel shared Tyrone's pipe and entered a dream-like state. At one point, he found himself dancing in a line with his arms looped into those of two young dancers on either side. Later, he ate with them, then the stories began. He heard stories of Raven the trickster, of Frog the curious, and of the Thunderbird.

Early the next morning he woke in a smoky longhouse. A few people were moving about and speaking quietly to each other. Tyrone, seeing him sit up, greeted him warmly.

"Good. Now we begin our time of learning," he said, drawing Lionel to the fire and handing him a mug of steaming herbal tea.

Lionel noted that some of the people who had danced so well the night before and seemed so healthy were not. He saw an older woman, one of the cooks from the evening before, who seemed to have had a stroke and dragged one leg, the arm on the same side bound to her body and the side of her face drooping. Another man was missing the lower part of his leg and his fingertips were gangrenous likely from blood clotting. A middle-aged woman had misshapen breasts, likely an advanced case of breast cancer. A young woman was very pale and Lionel had good reason to suspect that she was previously pregnant and was now losing a significant amount of blood. There were no children visible.

That day, Tyrone led Lionel through the village and talked to him about the tradition of the totem poles. He named them all and gave their history and meaning. Over the next week, he took Lionel to different locations around the traditional lands or lax'yip of the Gitanyow people. He taught about their care of these lands. They sat with an elder and Lionel learned about weaving and mask carving. Lionel's guide to each of these places was none other than the shaman of the wilp, whom he discovered, was Tyrone.

Each evening, they sat by the fire and someone shared the Adawaak or oral history. It was usually Tyrone since he was a shaman. Lionel felt intensely happy among these people of the land. They had so much beauty, such a wealth of knowledge and respect for all the inhabitants of the land. They had learned to coexist in peace and harmony with nature. The more Lionel learned, the more he felt a sense of loss as not only this Indigenous nation but so many others would vanish from the earth.

"You have so many healing herbs," Lionel asked one day, after having received detailed lessons about the uses of the watercress, the bergamot, the sow thistle and the shepherd's purse. "Isn't there anything that can heal you from the damage caused by the injection?"

"Many of us still live, I am still alive, because we use the herbs we have, but there is nothing that will stop the rot spreading through our bodies. You are safe from us because you are drinking the tea I give you many times a day. Our death is delayed, but not stopped. Even now, Nayeli lies dying. She was young and joyful with her husband Ellis, waiting for the birth of her child. Ellis died soon after the vaccine and Nayeli's child fell from her womb and she bled from that time. Now, she can no longer make the blood she needs to keep her alive. She will be gone soon. The last of our hereditary chiefs, Chief Williams, went to his ancestors when the last moon was full. I am the last of the shamans, I will be gone by the next full moon."

They were sitting by the fire again, in the village centre after dusk. Crickets were chirping in the forest and there was the distant sound of the river over the stones. Lionel leaned back on his elbows to contemplate the starry sky. A bat swooped overhead and Lionel tracked its progress until it obscured the moon. It was a sudden sense of unreality that roused him from his contemplation.

"How long have I been here?" Lionel sat up abruptly upon seeing the slender crescent of a new moon where there'd been a nearly full moon when he left his mountain retreat.

"Long enough," Tyrone laughed, "you're ready to go, eh? There's a truck ready for you with gas in three cans in the back. You can leave when the sun rises."

Very early the following day Lionel ended his sojourn in Gitanyow. All the people had gathered to bid him farewell. One young man approached him and handed him a carved wooden object. When Lionel looked at it, he realized it was a butterfly.

Lionel turned the small carving around in his hands, tracing the fine cuts in the wood.

"Thank you," he said sincerely, and slipped it into his pack. It would remind him of his daughter who had not lived to see a butterfly.

In the distance over the rushing of the water, he heard the whomping of a helicopter and he raised his head to look. The small group of Natives shifted uneasily, then the sound vanished.

As he gripped Shaman Tyrone's arm in farewell, he asked him the question that was burning in his mind since he arrived in Gitanyow.

"Why me?"

Tyrone laughed merrily. "You ask questions that none of us ever get answers to until the right time comes. Do we ask the sun why it rises or the fire why it burns? We can't ask the Creator why he decides something for us. When it's time, you'll know."

C H A P T E R   1 0

Hungry Hazelton

"Human kindness has never weakened the stamina or softened the fibre of a free people. A nation does not have to be cruel to be tough."

~ Franklin D. Roosevelt

"Communists disdain to conceal their views and aims. They openly declare that their ends can be attained only by the forcible overthrow of all existing social conditions. Let the ruling classes tremble at a Communist revolution. The proletarians have nothing to lose but their chains. They have a world to win. Working men of all countries, unite!"

~ Karl Marx

Passing through Kitwanga, Lionel was soon on Highway 16, the Trans-Canada Highway east. He ignored the friendly invitation on a sign inviting him to go through Kitwanga. He saw a few people, here and there, but was deeply disturbed by how untended this once busy junction town had become. He remembered coming through the town on the way to his mountain refuge and stopping at the National Historic site with Janet. There had been tourists everywhere, August was one of their busiest months. Now, there were a few furtive people, masked, with darting anxious eyes. The campaign of fear had worked. Those who were still alive in Kitwanga lived in constant fear. Lionel was sure most, if not all, had taken the vax.

At one point, in the town limits of Kitwanga, he saw a GMC pickup hauling an Outback heading north. He waved vigorously, wanting to warn them of the bridge outage over the Nass River. The driver glared suspiciously at him, avoided his gaze and continued on his way north.

"You'll be back," Lionel muttered.

Arriving at the outskirts of Hazelton, Lionel recognized the name. That was where he and Janet had stopped for lunch on the way north to the mountain. Where was it they had stopped? Yes! It was Zelda's!

Lionel decided to see if there were any shops open where he could get a few canned goods and maybe some fresh bread. The people of Gitanyow had stocked him up thoroughly with dried meats and bannock and he even had fresh watercress and other leafy greens he could eat. However, it was a long time since he'd had a beef hamburger with one of those puffy white buns. And fries! Lionel realized he missed fries!

Going through the centre of town, Lionel's longing for a hamburger and fries vanished. The town looked abandoned. The windows of the Red Apple and the gas station were smashed, and the places looked looted. He saw a few people, but they looked frightened and furtive.

There were a couple of burned-out cars on the road and he saw two vacant-eyed adults. One was sitting on the bench in front of the deli, swaying back and forth. He was dressed in a suit that was crumpled and ripped and there was blood running down his face from a cut on his forehead. The woman was pushing an empty baby carriage shuffling slowly down the road. She looked dully at him as he passed, then continued on her aimless journey.

Societal collapse seems well on its way, Lionel reflected as he absorbed the decaying town. *Is this a fulfillment of Karl*

Marx's dream? A complete teardown of everything? What will be the next step?

There was likely no food to be had here, at least not legally, he concluded. Lionel wasn't sure he was prepared to join the looters and help himself - if there was anything left to be had.

He had his window rolled down and was slowly cruising down the highway when a succulent odour reached his nostrils. *Steak? Someone is cooking steak? OK, I've had moose and deer recently — but steak? That smells like a marvelous beef steak, and I haven't had any of that for ages!*

Following his nose, fairly drooling with anticipation, Lionel followed the succulent scent past a few silent, closed restaurants to Laurier Street which intersected with the highway. Picnic tables had been set up in a parking lot outside a vandalized motel. A few vehicles were parked along the street, and most of the tables were filled with groups of diners busily wielding steak knives and forks.

They're eating fries! How long has it been since I had fries? Steak and fries sound divine right about now!

Four barbecues lined the parking lot with a red-faced fat man wearing a blood-stained apron tending the sizzling grills. A woman who looked like she was wearing a brown tent and was even fatter than the man was tending two large turkey fryers filled with sizzling fries. Two girls in matching blue dresses sat at a nearby picnic table peeling and slicing potatoes into fries and dumping the potatoes into large buckets from which the fat woman scooped. Another dangerously thin woman was dashing around carrying plates of steak and fries to diners as they joined at empty spots on the tables. Lionel noticed people holding tickets sitting in the cars lining the streets. Nearby a younger man with a 30-06 rifle was ensconced on a bar stool keeping a close eye on the diners and shouting numbers as diners finished eating and departed.

Lionel pulled his truck over to the shoulder of the road and rested his arm on the edge of the open window, his eyes roving over the scene.

That's an odd lot, shouldn't they be laughing and chatting? Some kind of interaction? They're barely talking to eat other, quite strange. But – steak and fries! It's been so long!

The group was so quiet he could hear the meat sizzling on the barbecue and the knives and forks clinking on the plates. There was no conversation between the girls chopping potatoes and only an occasional shout from the fat man to the thin woman about orders and the rifle wielding man shouting numbers.

Lionel slowly got out of the truck. The clunk of his door closing woke echoes in the oddly quiet scene. He sauntered across the road to the parking lot, feeling eyes on him from the parked vehicles, the click of his boot heels loud on the tarmac. The man with the rifle tracked him, gripping the weapon tighter and turning the barrel toward him.

Diners at the tables also eyed him with no change in the intensity of their eating. *Not used to strangers, I guess. Maybe I should have brought my own weapon with me. Yeah, no, probably best not.*

"Good morning," Lionel didn't have to raise his voice at all. More heads bent over steak and fries lifted and turned toward the sound of his voice. "How much for a meal?" He was addressing the fat man at the hot grills who was almost the only person ignoring his approach.

"Read the sign." It was the harsh voice of the mountainous woman sweating over the sizzling fries who responded. One jiggling arm pointed to an easel stand by the potato choppers. Lionel hadn't noticed it as it was sideways and quite small.

The fat man slammed the barbecue fork onto the side extension of one of the grills and wiped his hands on his stained apron turning a furious face in his direction. The shout he let out was not directed at Lionel, however. "Hey, Johnny, git me that bucket a charcoal ova there. Make it snappy!"

A teenager who was carrying an armload of dirty dishes and clearing the tables as the diners were leaving yelled back, "Gimme a minute Pa, I'll be just a sec!" He vanished into an open door at the back of the building.

Lionel ambled over to the sign. *Guess I'm not having a steak dinner after all.*

Hand-lettered on the tattered green Bristol board were the words:

Steak 'n fries – well-done only
Adults 35 Socdits
Kids under 8 years 20 Socdits
No Socdits, no steak

This is one strange bunch. Guess they all took the jab. Odd though. None of them look diseased or sick, just anemic. They were indeed an anemic bunch – other than the fat man and woman, that is. All the diners were pale with an unhealthy hue to their faces. *Funny how they almost look guilty about eating that steak. Shifty eyes, keep looking at the other diners…*

Lionel gave a mental shrug, turned and began sauntering back towards his vehicle. The bright amused eyes, buried in a deep network of lines, of a man leaning against the speed limit sign caught his attention. Lionel raised his eyebrows at him quizzically and, when the man jerked his head to indicate he should come closer, changed direction and headed towards him.

"Weird lot, huh?" the man said when Lionel was still halfway across the street.

"Yeah, what's with them?" Lionel encouraged.

"They're vegetarians, 'spec they feelin' guilty about eatin' that meat. Some of it's maybe pig, too, cause Hodges raises hogs, and they're kinda scared it is. Kinda smell pig – but who knows. Not 'spost to eat pig, that lot. Unclean, yuh know."

"They're Jewish? Not Muslim, they don't look Arab – but Jews are allowed to eat meat, as long as it's clean…" Lionel's stood next to the man, looking at the odd group in the parking lot. "I'm Lionel, by the way. Just passing through and smelled the barbecue."

"Name's Trent. They ain't Jewish, they all go to a church out in Two Mile – Saturdays only – they're seventh day somethin'-or-other. They was all gettin' sick cause they can't get the soy 'n shit they usually eat – no truck comin' through to keep 'em stocked up. A doctor in their lot said it's cause they ain't gettin' enough iron and stuff. Pastor told 'em they could have a feed of red meat once a month. Hodges – that's the fat guy at the barbecue – he knows a good deal when he sees one. Chargin' 'em the price of gold for a mess of steak and fries."

"He's charging them Socdits. Are they all vaccinated? I understand you can't get Socdits unless you're vaccinated."

"Where you been? Livin' in the bush?" Trent laughed, revealing a gapped array of worn yellow teeth.

"Well, yeah, actually," Lionel chuckled, watching a group of children in the overgrown park across from the barbecue parking lot who were tossing a ball back and forth. *First kids I've seen in a long time,* he reflected. *I wonder why there were none in Gitanyow. Tyrone always avoided the question when I asked.*

"Bush, huh?" Trent shot him a sideways glance and returned to his narrative. Lionel turned his attention back to the old man. "Don't think they got the jab. Guess you don't know that socdit system's real easy to hack. Just gotta know somebody who can do it. Most of 'em got their Socdits by payin' some guy. He charges gold 'n silver for 'em - gettin' super rich.

Guess they were smart, them people, stocked up on gold 'n silver. I got the jab, don't got no gold to buy hacked Socdits. Hodges there's gettin' rich on Socdits cause he's got a bunch a beef cows 'n hogs and a bunch a kids with guns to guard 'em from gettin' stolen..."

"You took the jab? How is your health?" Lionel's medical mind prompted the question. He turned his eyes back to Trent.

"I ain't got no problems from the jab. My wife, Dolly now, 'course she's always been kinda sickly and she ain't as young as she used ta be, but she's been complainin' a lot about headaches 'n stuff she never complained about before. Started droppin' stuff and says she hears like a screamin' noise in her ears all the time. Could be just cause she's gettin' older, dunno."

"Has she seen a doctor?"

"Doctor? Nah, she got no use for doctors. She says if it's time fer her to go, she'll just go."

Lionel's attention was now fully on the man, diverted from the barbecue scene and the playing children. "Listen, I'm a doctor, but I have no medicine to offer, however from what you're telling me, those are the symptoms that could very well be related to the jab." He then proceeded to share some of the herbal lore he had gleaned from his stay in Gitanyow.

The conversation between Lionel and Trent was interrupted by the sobbing wail of a child, the roar of a speeding car engine, and a piercing scream. "My baby! She took my baby! Help me!"

The ball-playing kids in the park had scattered, some crying, all seeking out their parents. A woman in a blue and white gingham dress was frantically scrabbling under a small grey car after a set of keys just beyond her reach, sobbing and begging for help. Two other vehicles that had been parked with their prospective diners waiting for their numbers to be called now roared to life and tore off after the receding cloud of dust heading around the corner and west back down the Yellowhead.

Lionel sprinted to his truck and was soon speeding through the noon sun in pursuit of the other vehicles. Behind him, the sepulchral silence of the diners was broken by an excited babble of voices as many sprang to their feet and hurried towards their cars, abandoning their plates. Women surrounded the sobbing distraught mother and helped her retrieve the keys from under her car. Other vehicles departed in the same direction of the chase.

Lionel, gripping his steering wheel tight, pressed hard on the accelerator. His truck was not built for speed, and it was also an older model Silverado that had seen better days. "C'mon, baby, faster," he gritted, then seeing the sleek black Impala ahead of him swerve into a northbound side street, slammed on his brakes. He took the corner at a more moderate speed, then accelerated again. The Impala was pulling ahead on the heels of the red Camry at the head of the pursuit.

Lionel began mentally questioning why he was even getting involved. He did not have a fast vehicle, and the kidnapper was driving a powerful SUV. *Those guys will likely catch up and get the kid back, what's the point?* Going around a sharp curve in the road by a lumber yard, suddenly the Camry began swerving wildly. The Impala slowed to avoid a collision and Lionel drew up behind the Camry. The driver vigorously waved the Impala driver and him on as he gained control of his car and pulled over, and Lionel realized the man had a flat tire. The Impala driver and Lionel accelerated and returned to the pursuit.

Another sharp curve in the road took the Impala, with Lionel trailing further and further behind, over a breathtakingly high single-lane suspension bridge. Teeth gritted, foot slammed on the accelerator all the way to the floor, Lionel struggled to keep up with the two newer and more powerful vehicles. He sailed over the bridge, sparing a fleeting thought for the beauties of the canyon that yawned far below his truck tires. He lost sight of the other vehicles briefly around a curve in the narrow highway cut through a dense forested area. The highway straightened out by an abandoned auto shop and a brief series of modest homes and overgrown fields.

The driver of the SUV suddenly slammed its brakes and made a sharp right turn to head up an even narrower road through a small neighbourhood with a few houses. The Impala driver almost missed the turn, careened into a sideways drift, then recovered and shot north after the SUV.

Lionel was more than 500 metres behind and had time to take the turn more sedately. Rounding the corner, he realized that the other two vehicles were nowhere to be seen. He slowed down, scanning the few small houses and the silent side streets, his windows down. There was no sign of the chase in the quiet sunlit village of modest homes and crumbling pavement. *Ok, what am I doing here, Lord? Should I go back?*

He spotted a stooped old man hoeing some weeds in a tiny garden behind a peeling white fence. Lionel pulled his truck over and called out the window. "Excuse me, sir, did you see an SUV and a black car go by here at a high speed?"

The man continued hoeing, not acknowledging Lionel's question. *Is he deaf?* Lionel repeated the question in a louder voice.

The old man stopped poking at the weeds and leaned on his hoe. Sucking at his gums, he eyed Lionel. "I ain't deaf," he said. There was a pause. Lionel prepared to speak when the sunken mouth opened again, "Mebbe I seen 'em, mebbe I didn't."

"Sir, this is urgent, a child from your community has been kidnapped. I'm trying to help find this child." Lionel kept his voice loud, wondering if the man understood him.

The filmy eyes turned away from Lionel and the ancient man went back to hoeing slowly and laboriously. Ready to give up, Lionel was putting the truck back into drive when he saw the thin stringy arm point and heard the dim words of the rheumy old voice, "They went thata way."

Shaking his head, Lionel pulled back out onto the road he was already on. *I'll probably never find them now. Lord, You're going to have to help!*

A couple more side streets opened up to the right and left. *Dear God, this is impossible! They could have turned down any of these streets!* The area was somewhat commercial now: a trucking company, signs for a quarry. *I don't think they can be here.* Lionel continued along the road, scanning on both sides, windows down. Steering around a sharp curve, Lionel was on a dirt road now, the deteriorating pavement had ended. There were signs of tires skidding sideways on the dusty surface, exposing darker dirt. *Good, that's fresh. Thank you, Lord.*

Lionel accelerated, eyes still scanning from side to side for other evidence of where his quarry had gone. The road began to rise steeply in front of him as he climbed the shoulder of the mountain. Forests closed in on the narrow dirt road. A deer accompanied by a spotted fawn eyed him from the shadows of a dense stand of Western hemlock. A rabbit broke from the undergrowth and sped down the path ahead of him for a short distance, then vanished down a hidden burrow. Through the open windows of his truck, Lionel could hear a veritable symphony of bird song in the forest.

Suddenly he came to a fork in the dirt path. Lionel stopped the truck and walked around to the front. The road to the left looked wider and more travelled. A sign, almost hidden behind tall grasses and young saplings advertised a lookout point. Another sign with the writing almost weathered away, was nailed to a tree to his right. As far as Lionel could make out, it was indicating that there was a mine somewhere down the right-hand fork. This path was essentially tire ruts with tall grass growing down the centre. *I think the Impala would have problems following this trail, the grass doesn't look disturbed either.*

Feeling like a tracker in a western movie, Lionel paced a short distance up the road to the left, scanning the dirt for evidence of the passage of the other vehicles. He grunted with satisfaction at the sight of freshly torn grass on the side of the steep path then loped back to his truck.

The route climbed steadily, then abruptly looped back at a sharp angle. Lionel was coming out of the tight curve when he heard the distant sounds of screams and viciously barking dogs. He accelerated and soon came to another tight curve with a narrow path opening off to the left of the road. He slowed, trying to determine if he should turn down this track or continue along the main road. Flattened grass on the edge of the side path galvanized him into action. He steered into the heavily shaded narrow trail, while fumbling to open the top of his backpack and extricate his CZ 9mm.

A short jerky ride that challenged the suspension of the truck brought him to a small clearing and a scene of utter chaos.

Three large dogs that looked to be Rottweiler crossed with monster were barking and snarling and lunging at a man who had sequestered himself in the narrow opening between two ramshackle outbuildings next to what looked like a large hunting cabin. From all the blood on the man's clothing and even in the patchy grass by the Impala, it was evident that the man had been injured quite badly though he was still on his feet and trying to fend off the savage, slavering animals with a stick.

On the veranda of the cabin, a black-haired woman wearing a bedraggled scarlet evening gown was clinging with her red-tipped claws to a screaming, struggling girl of around eight years, trying to drag her through the door into the cabin. The little girl's hands scrabbled desperately to maintain their grip on the door frame while kicking frantically at the woman.

Taking in the scene, Lionel did not hesitate. He pulled the 9mm from the open backpack next to him, quickly found the clip and inserted it. He took down the dog closest to him with one shot, opened the truck door, and stepped out.

"You bastard! Don't you shoot my dogs!" the woman stopped trying to drag the girl into the house and turned on Lionel.

Profiting from her distraction, the little girl twisted free of the furious woman's clutch and fled to Lionel's truck. Sobbing and gasping, she hunkered down next to him. "I want my mom, please, I want my mom," she hiccoughed into her arms clasped around her knees.

"Get in the truck," Lionel ordered, to which the child quickly complied, scrambling through the driver's side door to the passenger side to sit next to his backpack, huddled in a little heap, still sobbing and calling for her mom.

Lionel closed the door of the pickup and turned to the woman, "Call off your dogs, now!"

Oblivious to the death of their companion, the two other dogs had continued their assault on the bleeding man. Ignoring Lionel's command, the raging woman, who had continued to scream imprecations at Lionel, disappeared into the house nearly catching the swirling tail of her long gown, slamming the door behind her.

Lionel swung back to the snarling mayhem and sighted down the barrel of his gun. A second shot missed the twisting lunging dog he had aimed at. Striding closer, another shot struck one of them in the back. The dog screamed and turned on him but was unable to charge at him because of its now useless hind legs. A final squeeze of the trigger dispatched the injured animal, leaving one still savagely ravening with bared fangs at the bleeding man.

Because the ferocious leaping beast was directly between himself and its quarry, Lionel hesitated to risk a shot to take it down, fearing to hit the man. He thrust the 9mm into the back of his pants, unsnapped the sheath for the hunting knife he always carried on his belt, slid it out, and threw himself onto the enormous gleaming back of the enraged dog.

In moments, the animal dropped lifeless in a massive bleeding heap to the ground. Lionel's knife, which he always kept razor sharp, had severed its throat all the way to the cervical vertebrae.

"I'm Lionel, I'm a doctor. Where did you get bitten?" he asked, wiping his knife on the gleaming hide of the now inert animal and trying to calm his panting breaths. He eyed his bloody right hand thoughtfully, then settled on wiping it on the dog's hide then on his pants.

The beleaguered man now exited his flimsy sanctuary and dropped the broken stick he'd been using as a weapon. He ignored Lionel's question, though he was bleeding quite profusely from deep gashes in his forearm visible through the shredded sleeve of his shirt. Blood also trickled from a wound on his scalp, and he appeared to have sustained bites on his left leg.

"Roger Martin. There's more kids in the house, I think. Is my niece safe?"

"She's in the pickup…"

A wail emanating from inside the cabin confirmed Roger's suspicions.

Lionel gave a quick scan of Roger's wounds to ascertain that it was not arterial damage he had sustained and that there was no sign of spurting blood. Satisfied that this was the case and Roger would not bleed out imminently, Lionel turned and sprinted toward the building, slipping the hunting knife back into its sheath and extricating his 9mm again. He paused at the door to snap the clip from his gun and check his ammo, rammed it back in, then tried the handle. Finding it locked he resolved the problem with a couple of violent kicks then he eased his way through the now broken door into the dim interior of the cabin, gun at the ready. Smells of urine and feces assaulted his nostrils, and the sound of harsh breathing and quiet sobbing filtered through the murk.

His left hand groped for a light switch on the wall. Finding none, he sidled quickly to the window and yanked at the moldering curtain which fell apart in his hand. Sunlight flooded the room.

Somewhere in the recesses of the house another door banged open.

"No, please, no, please." It was the distant trembling whimper of a child followed by what sounded like a slap and a harsh "shut up!"

Simultaneously Lionel let out a gasp and a muttered "Oh, my God!" On the far wall of the room was a gurney with a small child strapped to it. The child's dull dark eyes were open, but did not turn toward him, gasping breaths the only sign of life. A phlebotomy needle and tube in the right arm of the child trickled drops of blood to the floor. There was very little blood on the floor, evidence that a pouch which should have been collecting the blood was recently removed. In a nearby corner sat a boy with a chain around a lacerated ankle, black hair falling over his dirty bruised face. Flies swarmed a 5-gallon bucket next to him from which the noisome odour of human waste emanated.

At the same time as Lionel was absorbing this horrific sight, a shout came from outside. "Lionel! She's getting away! You have to stop her!"

The roar of an engine nearly drowned out the plea of the small boy, "Please, mister, she's got my sister."

Lionel took an indecisive step towards the child. *Oh God! What do I do?*

"Lionel!" It was Roger again.

Lionel swung around and dashed out the door he had entered so precipitously just moments before. The little girl that had been in Lionel's truck was clinging to Roger's undamaged leg. Roger had wrapped his shirt around his injured arm. The black SUV was disappearing down the narrow path.

"Take my car, it's faster!" Roger shouted, "the keys are on the console!"

"The backpack on the front seat, there's a first aid kit there! Look after the kids in the house!" Lionel redirected his rush toward the Impala, slid behind the wheel and fumbled the keys into the ignition. The powerful motor roared to life. In moments, he was in pursuit of the SUV, careening down the path doing his best to avoid the jutting rocks in the uneven surface of the road.

Dappled sunlight filtered through the trees as Lionel accelerated through the forest – light – dark – light – dark. The lurching, thumping of the car over the raw trail cut through the towering firs, hemlocks and spruce and the roar of the engine found Lionel praying out loud. *Lord, help those kids, Lord, I have to stop that woman, Lord, don't let this car hit a rock, don't let Roger bleed out, Lord, help!*

Back on the gravelled road, SUV disappearing around the sharp bend of the path, Lionel accelerated even more. Sideways drifting, taking the curve with gravel spitting under the tires, back onto a straight-away, down the steep stretch back to the dividing track – another sight of the SUV – foot to the floorboards. *How am I going to stop her if I catch up?*

Down, down, down the track, wrestling with the steering wheel, eyes straining for sights of the SUV, past another divide, signs for the lookout and the silver mine – was he getting closer? Gas – he couldn't run out of gas – no, there was half a tank, good!

Back on pot-holed pavement, through the silent village, old man gone from the weedy garden, skidding around the corner onto the main road for Two Mile. Lionel was right on the tail of the SUV now.

The bridge – the single-lane bridge was up ahead – what was on the other side? It was a veritable barricade of vehicles blocking the exit to the bridge. *Those other pursuers that followed me, that must be them! Don't let her through!*

At the entrance to the bridge, the SUV skidded abruptly to a stop. Lionel slowed the labouring Impala and pulled over. He removed the revolver from the back of his pants where he'd stowed it. Carrying it by his side, safety off, bullet chambered, he approached the other vehicle. The door flew open. Elegant sandaled feet appeared; then long finely molded legs followed by the tattered red evening gown-clad figure of the black-haired woman.

Close up, it appeared she was not so young as she hoped. Though heavily made-up with layers of foundation, rouge, facial contouring powder, mascara and lipstick among other artificial beautifying agents, the wrinkles and decay of a woman well past her prime screamed through the mask.

"Hello, handsome," her voice was composed, far from sounding like someone who had fled by high-speed chase through a forest after kidnapping a child and severely harming – and who knew what else she had done – several other children.

"Where is the girl?" Lionel's tone was harsh.

Her red lips emitted a trill of laughter though her rigid features barely moved. "Loosen up, sweetie, she's fine!"

Lionel grasped the rear door handle of the SUV and risked a quick glance inside. The terrified eyes of a small girl met his from where she huddled on the floor behind the driver's seat. By now people were streaming across the bridge led by the woman in the blue and white gingham dress. Even from that distance her wail could be heard, "My baby, what did you do with my baby?"

Distracted by the scene across the bridge, Lionel did not immediately realize that the woman had begun to chant in a low voice that began to gradually increase in volume.

"Time draws nigh
For Jackal's son
To take his share

We are the Watch
Helping the rise
Of god's demise

He'll unleash the demons
And extinguish the light
Unleashing legions unto the sky

We are the Watch..."

As the words vomited from her blood-red lips, she was running toward the bridge, the tail of the shimmering scarlet gown flowing behind her. Momentarily stunned, Lionel took off in pursuit. By the time she was on the bridge, the sound of her voice filled the canyon, rebounding over and over in a tumult of noise, off the rock walls and seething river far below.

"...From the final times
Helping the unholy
Reach his prime

He'll send them plague
And grant us power
The path is set
For the final hour

We are the Watch
We'll usher in doom
All who oppose
His victory tune."[2]

Across the bridge the mother in the blue and white gingham stopped as though she hit a brick wall. The surging mass of townsfolk behind her also halted.

The scarlet figure clambered like a possessed monkey, up, up the steel suspension cable at an inhuman speed until she reached the top of the tower closest to Lionel. There she stood, impossibly balanced and she laughed and the laughter shrieked and thundered and all the people on the bridge would remember that laughter in dreams years later and awaken sweating and trembling.

"Lionel!" she howled, "Lionel, come and get me!"

The sound of his name in her mouth sickened Lionel. How could she possibly know his name?

"Lionel," she bellowed again, her voice reverberating, wrapping her audience in cloying strands of noise and pain and sickness, pale faces lifted to a darkened sky, eyes blinded by the slash of scarlet far above them on the tower. "Lionel, the black bird is coming for you. Joanne will destroy you."

She spread out her arms and it seemed black wings enveloped her. "You can't get me," she howled, then emitted a final scream, "my Prince will save me!" Then, she leapt from the tower to plummet in utter silence far, far down. In the vacuum of sound, every soul on the bridge watched the falling crimson streak and heard the crunch of the body striking the rocks. There were long seconds of shocked immobility, then the crowd rushed as one person to the edge of the deck to gaze, still without a word, at the tiny, crumpled form so far below.

---

[2] https://occultist.net/satanic-prayers/

"Her prince didn't save her," a voice said into the silence after several long minutes. It was the mother. She released her grip on the guardrail to look at Lionel. "Where is my baby?"

Lionel did not need to answer. Just then, his truck pulled up behind the Impala and Roger exited with the little girl in his arms. The child leapt down and ran to her mother who met her halfway.

Roger limped over to stand next to Lionel who was still staring at the motionless scarlet blot on the rocks far below. "That her?"

"Yeah," Lionel swallowed to control the sickness he still felt from the interaction. "Where are the children that were in the house?"

"Truck. A bunch of the guys are going back to the shack to see if they can find any evidence of other kids. I dunno, I left pretty quick."

The local doctor, after checking Roger's niece and ensuring she was uninjured, joined Lionel where he laboured over the silent inert body of the exsanguinated child, trying to determine vitals and warm the limp form. Roger had had the presence of mind to remove the phlebotomy needle and apply gauze to the injection site. Lionel opted not to disturb the blood-soaked gauze, trusting the doctor to know what to do. The harsh breathing of the small pallid form continued, reassuring Lionel that the child still lived, though the eyes were now closed.

"Dr. Phillips," he greeted Lionel, "I take it you have medical training? Let's get that poor kid to the hospital."

Wrinch Memorial Hospital was silent, sporting broken windows, overgrown grass covered in dead leaves from the previous autumn, and an ambulance still in the ambulance bay with four flat tires. Lionel, who was following the doctor's car, climbed out of his pickup to greet the doctor who was removing the limp body of the child from his back seat.

"This doesn't look good," he commented, nodding at the decaying medical building.

"Grab the bags in the trunk," Dr. Phillips instructed. He'd already popped the lid. "What do you mean, 'doesn't look good'? That's what happened after the so-called 'vaccine' was rolled out and the death toll rose. The chief medical officer for British Columbia mandated the mRNA jab for all medical personnel as soon as it came out. Same thing everywhere, not just here."

Full of questions, Lionel hurried to the back of the Lincoln, however people from the convoy that had followed them to the hospital were already collecting the large bags and following the doctor through the broken front door of the emergency entrance.

Bemused, Lionel caught up with Dr. Phillips. "Room three," he was saying, "I think the lighting is intact there." A flurry of activity ensued with a crew carrying buckets and cleaning supplies returning the treatment room to pristine condition. Phillips laid the child on the clean stretcher. "I need O neg. Find me someone who's O neg." A nurse in scrubs appeared, nodded and dashed to the waiting room where members of the convoy were milling about, calling for O neg.

Within minutes, a blood transfusion began for the silent victim on the stretcher, warming blankets wrapped around the small form. Lionel and Phillips did a thorough inventory of the child's injuries, shaking their heads and muttering imprecations under their breath. The tiny skinny body had been severely abused over a period of time with poorly healed fractures in both arms, some cracked ribs, and various partly healed wounds along with evidence of severe sexual abuse. At times, as they ministered to the victim, Lionel's suppressed rage burst out of him.

"God has a very hot place in hell for those monsters that did this to her! Eternity won't be long enough to punish them!"

Dr. Phillips, who remained calm throughout the examination, merely responded, "I wish!" to Lionel's amazement.

Some time later, stretching his aching back, Lionel wandered into the waiting area to find a gathering of community members. The buzz of conversation stopped immediately upon his entrance and all eyes turned to him.

"How's that poor kid doing?" Roger was the first to speak. His wounds had been tended, and he was sporting an assortment of white bandages on various parts of his anatomy.

Seeing the entire group was waiting on his verdict, Lionel shrugged. "It's touch and go. She's in pretty rough shape. She'll need more blood by morning. Dr. Phillips will be looking for more donors." He opted not to share the extent of the child's injuries.

"My friend, you came at the right time," Roger said, "God knows if you hadn't come I'd probably be dead, all those kids – including Lisa, my niece, would be too. I'd like you to meet Sabrina, my sister and her husband Elmer. They're Lisa's parents."

Upon inquiry, Lionel learned that Waubun, the young boy rescued from the shack, and his sister Winona had spent some time with another community member who was a social worker.

"We fed them first, of course. And the nurse checked them over. They're malnourished and show signs of some significant abuse, but no broken bones," Dixie, a thin older woman with grey hair informed Lionel while handing him a thick egg sandwich. "They were sexually abused, though," she said in softer, sickened tones. That did not surprise Lionel.

"We were discussing the witch's reasons for wanting to kidnap and abuse all those kids," Roger said. "We wondered who all was involved and where they are now? There had to be men involved, not just the witch, that's clear. But why would she take them out to that cabin and – well, do what she did – I mean, apart from being a member of a pedophile ring, of course? Some people suggested it was for adrenochrome, what do you think?"

"Adrenochrome, I thought it's the adrenal gland that's eaten?" queried Sabrina, still hugging her now sleeping daughter to her. "Oh God, imagine! What if she'd done that to my baby? Plus, what did she want their blood for – oh, that is so horrible! Just thinking about it makes me sick!"

"I have no idea. I know pedophile rings had a lot to do with trafficking in adrenochrome, but I hadn't heard much about it before – well, before I became a prepper..." Lionel took a big bite of his egg sandwich, discovering that in spite of the nausea he'd been feeling since his interactions with the witch and discovering the extent of her abuse, he was indeed quite hungry.

"Aha! Thought so! You had the look of a guy that's kind of out-of-touch. What brought you back to our crumbling world..."

The reappearance of the social worker, who was Sabrina's cousin Kathy, rejoining them in the hospital waiting room spared Lionel from having to answer Roger's question.

It was much later that Lionel, while lying in a comfortable bed in Sabrina and Elmer's spare bedroom, was able to sort out the horrifying events and revelations of the day. Kathy revealed that Waubun, Winona, and Namid – the dying child still in the hospital fighting for her life – had all been systematically sexually abused while in captivity in another location. The witch – the children had been told to call her Queen Jezebel – had stolen them away for satanic rituals of her own. The children said Queen Jezebel was very old and stayed young with the help of children's blood. A jumbled tale of bizarre rites that involved using the blood of the children, chanting, black symbols and naked dances spilled through the children's narrative leaving Kathy sickened and nauseated.

"The poor little things, they've been through so much!" Kathy had said, vowing to take them under her care. "We have no idea where they come from – they're obviously Aboriginal children, but how long they have been exploited and where they were stolen from is not clear."

Hearing that Queen Jezebel would eat part of the children after she killed them confirmed the suspicion that adrenochrome was involved.

"Adrenochrome is supposed to give long life to the person who consumes it," one well-informed listener commented. "Maximizing the tortures inflicted on the victim prior to killing the child and consuming the adrenal gland enhances the effects."

Lying in the dark in the comfortable guest bed, Lionel's restless mind was full of questions: *are these the kids I'm supposed to save, Lord? Queen Jezebel? Who was she and who is Joanne?* He thought of the woman in Dease Lake by that name but dismissed her. *What is going on in the world now? I wonder if things are as crazy in Calgary. Are George and Viv OK?*

Lionel's thoughts turned to the group of men that had gone to the hunting cabin on the mountain. They had returned from their mission, not having found anymore living children, only gnawed bones, evidence that more had died and been fed to the dogs.

"We burnt the place down," they reported, charcoal smudged faces full of horror, "found bones. Brought 'em back, no way to tell much but thought they should be buried properly in a grave."

Another group of men with even paler faces, also smelling of smoke also rejoined the gathering in the moldering hospital some time later. "Burned the witch's corpse. Lou here had a tiger torch. Horrible, smelled like pork."

The exhaustion of the day's events finally closed off Lionel's jumbled thoughts and he slept.

C H A P T E R   1 1

Meeting in Burns Lake

Although images of perfection in people's personal lives can cause unhappiness, images of perfect societies - utopian images - can cause monstrous evil. In fact, forcefully changing society to conform to societal images was the greatest cause of evil in the twentieth century.

~ Dennis Prager

Everything the State says is a lie, and everything it has it has stolen.

~ Friedrich Nietzsche

It was late morning before Lionel was back on the road, heading south after a modest breakfast of eggs and grainy toast. He had an interesting discussion with Elmer about his opinion on whether the world was ending. Elmer held the Seventh Day Adventist belief that the reason the world was imploding was that they were in end times and that it was the papacy that was behind all the chaos in the world.

"There are Jesuits at every level of government and power in the world, it's a cabal and they're all connected," Elmer averred. He also firmly opined that a Sunday law would soon be passed forcing everyone to attend church on Sunday

Lionel had so little knowledge of what had been happening over the last few years that he wasn't prepared with a developed opinion about who or what was behind everything, He did have some questions, though.

"Interesting idea about the papacy – I can see that the Jesuits have had a real influence in many spheres of power... But, why would Muslims agree to attending mosque on Sunday – I assume they could still attend mosque? Four years ago there were some two billion Muslims in the world. They do their worshipping on Friday. Hindus – they don't even go to church – there's probably nearly as many of them as Muslims. I really don't think that's possible. ."

Elmer pulled out a bible and a catechism and plunged into a lengthy and convoluted defense of his beliefs. He did not have an answer to why likely more than half the population of the world would, as a result of such a decree, modify their usual practices to attend a place of worship on a Sunday.

Lionel was grateful when Roger appeared with news about the children.

"Kathy is doing her best to care for Wabun and Winona, they're pretty traumatized. Dr. Phillips says the other little kid's organs are shutting down. He doesn't think she'll make it."

After thanking Sabrina and Elmer for their hospitality, Lionel stopped in at the hospital where Phillips had spent the night in a cot by Namid's bed.

"Poor kid, she really didn't have a chance. She's jaundiced now and has no kidney function. I was able to rescue a lot of supplies before the hospital was abandoned, but I'm afraid I don't have anything that can save her other than giving her some peace. I put her into a coma and I'm giving her fluids. Best I can do."

Roger, who had accompanied Lionel to the hospital, insisted on filling up Lionel's gas tank in spite of his protests. He shook his hand as he left. "Thanks, Lionel, for what you did for our community. We had no idea such evil was festering so close to us and you helped us get rid of it. Maybe you couldn't save Namid, but you saved my niece, you saved those two little kids with Kathy and you probably saved a bunch of other kids that witch may have caught and abused too!"

The sun was high in the sky by the time Lionel was back on the highway. Beyond New Hazelton, a tractor-trailer that had been loaded with Molson Canadian beer had gone off the road, plunging up the embankment into the bush. It looked like it was there a while because the looters had partied quite happily on the embankment and left a heap of empty Molson cases and well over a hundred empty bottles littered around the truck and trailer.

"Looks like somebody had fun," Lionel smiled.

Continuing down the Yellowhead Highway, Lionel passed small town after small town. All looked similar to Hazelton, mostly looted and very few people around. It was after passing through a small looted town called Lake Kathlyn, by the sign saying 'Welcome to Smithers' that Lionel encountered a group of armed civilians and a barricade.

It's never taken me so long to get anywhere, Lionel reflected. *What is it now?*

He slowed the truck to a stop and rolled down the window. "What's the problem?" he asked the bearded man holding a .308 rifle who seemed to be in charge.

"Get out of your vehicle," the man barked, eyes suspicious.

Lionel got out slowly, holding his hands away from his body. The last thing he needed was the boy with the AR on the roof of the garage nearby losing his cool and squeezing the trigger.

A woman hurried forward and patted him down professionally. She was wearing an RCMP jacket, Lionel was happy to note. Perhaps there was some law in this town.

"What's your business here? We don't need no vandals in our town. We seen what they been doing along the

Yellowhead. You part of that gang we saw rolling through here?" The man's voice was harsh.

"I'm Lionel Goudreault," Lionel stepped forward gently extending his hand in greeting. "I'm just passing through. No, I do not belong to any gang."

"Who are you?" Another woman spoke up from behind a couple of younger men who were also heavily armed. "How come you look so familiar?" She came closer, scrutinizing him closely.

"Yeah, you do." The bearded leader nodded his head, "I seen that too! You a politician or somebody from TV?"

"No, I'm a doctor."

"That's it!" The woman's voice was triumphant. "I seen you on YouTube. You're that Awaken doctor! Man, I'd know those eyes anywhere! Shit, your videos were awesome - until they took them down. My cousin," she turned to the other people, "she took one jab, then I told her to watch this guy. She never took another."

The other people at the barricade began shifting and relaxing and talking to each other. One of the men that was standing back stepped forward with his hand extended. "I want to thank you. My two kids were going to take the jab, but when I told them to watch your videos, they decided not to. I'm Allan Fortin, the local Fire Chief."

Lionel shook his hand. "I'm glad you told me this," he said. "Sometimes I felt nobody was listening and my voice was just resounding in some echo chamber of the converted. Every life I saved makes it worthwhile."

"Yeah, lots of us haven't been vaxxed," one of the younger guys said, "we don't welcome vaxxed people neither."

"Also, none of us got a digital ID!" a tall man interjected. "Do you have one?" He eyed Lionel's hands speculatively.

Lionel's head shake reassured him and he gave a short grunt of satisfaction. Lionel told them briefly where he'd been for the last few years and received some sympathetic nods.

"Will you stay and have lunch with us? We got a bit of gas we can give you, too." The leader spoke, extending his hand. "Aaron Plouffe," he said.

"Fries," the word burst from Lionel and he laughed, "I've been away from civilization for more than two years and now I'm obsessing about fries, especially since I saw a bunch of people eating them in Hazelton. I would be glad to have lunch with you." His smallish breakfast had long abandoned him, and his rumbling stomach was telling him to accept the invitation. "No need for fries, of course, I'm joking. I am heading to Calgary, but it cheers me to know that there are still some sane people around. Ran into some weirdness in Hazelton, looks like things are getting pretty crazy. Anyways, I should be all right for gas, for now, please keep it."

They had lunch together in the Community Centre. Dozens of tables were set up and it looked like they ate together as a community on a regular basis. When Lionel asked about their communal way of living, Aaron Plouffe explained they simply shared what they had and worked together to provide food.

"As I re-enter society," Lionel commented, "I've noticed that the communities that survive the collapse of the post-modern world are the ones that work together." He had already briefly explained his absence for the last few years.

"Funny how that works, isn't it?" interjected an older stocky woman who had joined their group. "Sylvia, former teacher," she added, then elaborated. "Communism puts collectivism over the individual; forced participation, that is. Superficially, that looks like what we have here, the utopia socialists and communists dreamed of. It's not, though. We still respect individual ownership but require participation in the pursuit of survival."

"Reminds me of the early Christian church outlined in Acts," Lionel commented. He was sitting at one of the long tables in the community centre. All the tables were filling up quickly and tantalizing scents were coming from the kitchen at the other end of the large hall. He had already locked his truck and left it in the care of the guards who remained at the barricade. "The believers in the resurrection of the Son of God had all things in common."

"Well, I don't know about that," responded Sylvia, who was sitting across from Lionel. "I'm no Bible scholar, but it works. The difference between what we have here and communism is choice. People can choose to participate. Our leader," she nodded at Aaron who was now at the other end of the hall, "we elected him. He'll stay as leader – we don't call him mayor because that position is surrounded in bureaucracy – and he'll continue in that position until a majority decide they want someone else."

Sylvia was interrupted by the arrival of steaming dishes heaped with food. For lunch, there were fries. Hot, salty, crispy, delicious fries. Lionel burst into laughter when he saw the enormous plateful set in front of him. Heaven! There were also hamburgers! The buns were homemade but light and delicious. The burgers were thick and juicy with homemade ketchup and French's mustard.

Replete, Lionel looked around at the group. There were at least one hundred and fifty people present. Lionel could easily pick out ones he thought were vaxxed. They were the ones with the yellow faces, likely from liver failure due to the accumulation of the spike protein. They were the ones with blue lips, clearly experiencing heart problems. *The folks in Hazelton just looked anemic, nothing like this.* Lionels eyes wandered through the group, happy to note that many looked healthy.

Lionel had already met Dr. Haskins, a physician working in Smithers. He knew the sick people were getting what care was available under the circumstances. He was just sorry to note a couple of the sicker people were in their late teens.

"Were a lot of the teens vaxxed?" he asked Haskins quietly.

"Yes. We lost three in the first two months. Myocarditis. The kids you see here, I can't do much for them. We sent the sickest off to Prince George a few months ago, but the ambulances never came back. We haven't been able to reach any medical service outside the town for at least a month. We have three doctors and several nurses here; we're doing what we can."

"Why are there so few people?"

Dr. Haskins sighed. "I guess you've been out of the loop for a while. I know Sylvia explained that people can join our group by choice. Some chose to survive on their own. We don't really know how they're doing. Others left. You see, what they did was send out a notice when people started getting sick, saying it was because of a viral variant - I forget which Greek letter it was, maybe epsilon or omicron or a variation thereof. They led people to believe that if they were ill, it was the variant and that they needed boosters. We were also told that vaccines were getting rare and would now only be offered in major centres like Prince George. People left Smithers in droves to get the boosters – they called them the bivalent vaccine by then – or medical help. Even a lot of medical staff went. Nobody ever came back."

Lionel shook his head in disbelief. "It's like a mass psychosis, there's absolutely no reason to any of this."

Sylvia put down her fork with a clink. "Hair worms," she said decisively. When Haskins and Lionel turned surprised faces in her direction, she elucidated. "Yes, I said hair worms. I'm thinking about a book I read a few years ago by a Lebanese man. Gad Saad – S-a-a-d – not sad. He's an evolutionary biologist that equated the insane human behaviour of the last few years with all its wokism and postmodern suicidal tendencies including abortion, homosexuality, transgenderism, breakdown of the family, refusal to reproduce for fear of climate change, you name it."

Haskins interrupted her flow of talk. "Sylvia, where do hair worms come in?

"I'm getting to that," Sylvia picked up her fork and started fiddling with it, "so this Dr. Saad wrote this book called – I think – Parasitic Mind. He talked about how these woke ideologies are like mind parasites and equated it to the wood crickets that get a parasite called a hair worm that invades the brain of the wood cricket and changes its behaviour. Wood crickets hate water. Hair worms need water to reproduce. When they invade the brain of the cricket, the cricket loses its fear of water, jumps in the water and drowns. Anyways, these woke ideologies – or hair worms - were leading to a dangerous decrease in birth rate in western societies. It wasn't happening fast enough, so they brought in fear as another hair worm. Blinded by fear and utter belief in the righteousness of governments to govern and unable to conceive of the possibility that media and the medical leaders are lying, they are plunging to their own destruction and that of society as a whole."

"Mind parasites, makes a lot of sense to me," Lionel nodded thoughtfully.

"That's why they refuse to believe the vax is killing people. It's like this mind parasite has kept them from noticing." Sylvia picked up her plate and cutlery. "I'll be back, just getting some tea."

Lionel turned his attention to Haskins. "Did you lose many to the actual China virus?"

Dr. Haskins snorted into his cup of herbal tea. "They kept talking about how many were dying on the news. You know what was really weird and the virus believers didn't pick up on?" He paused for effect, looking expectantly at Lionel. Lionel, concluding it was a rhetorical question, did not respond. Haskins continued after taking a sip of his tea, "nobody died at home. Everybody who died, died in the hospital. Those who didn't go to the hospital survived. Sounds fishy, wouldn't you say?"

Lionel nodded. "Definitely fishy." He changed the subject abruptly. "I didn't see any 5G towers here in the town."

"You know about that? You never did a video on 5G and the vaccine, I think?"

"No," Lionel shook his head. "I just recently became aware of the link, just in the last few weeks. Don't forget, I've been out of the loop for a bit."

"Right. Anyways, they put up a 5G tower over by the town hall. We took it down and unhooked everything. We believe that is how the OGOA will control people - the vaxxed, of course."

"The OGOA? What is that?"

"Ah, of course you don't know about that. It's an acronym for the One Government Over All. It took over from the United Nations a while back. They didn't like the term 'nations' because they deny the existence of sovereign nations."

"I see." Lionel frowned. "Who do you think is behind all this? Do you think it's a co-ordinated attack on national sovereignty by a secret cabal?" He thought of the discussion he'd had with Elmer back in Two Mile. "Somebody recently suggested it was a plot by Jesuits – I thought of the Rothschilds, Bloomberg, Kochs. What do you think?"

"I tend to agree. I'd add that software engineer that's involved in vaccines – probably put him at the top of the list." Haskins nodded.

"Don't forget all the corporate giants!" Sylvia was back across the table. "There's Blackrock, Vanguard, a bunch others. They all want a piece of the pie."

Well, it sure seems like end times no matter who is behind it all, Lionel thought. *The one-world government is officially in place now.* "Do we have a one-world religion yet?"

"I'm not sure. I know Chrislam is spreading and there's a huge push to unite Catholics and Protestants, but I don't know if it's officially the religion of the OGOA or if there's some other version being brought in. We don't follow world events much now, we have enough to deal with around here." Dr. Haskins poured himself another cup of tea. Sylvia had brought an entire pot of tea with her. "For example, depression. There's been a serious increase in suicides even in our small town. People get sick or they develop rampant systemic cancers, or serious liver disease or hepatitis, then they can't go for the 'booster' they think they need because they don't have transportation, or they just lose hope. We help the ones we can."

"I'm sorry to hear that," Lionel said. "Do you have any who lost their cognitive abilities? You know - the ones who were affected in their brains."

"Yes. We have round-the-clock care for them. Some recover with reduced cognitive function or permanent brain fog. Others complain of persistent tinnitis. Obviously, the mRNA injection crossed the blood-brain barrier and we know neurons, once destroyed, do not regenerate. We care for them at the medical centre. Not much hope for them, though."

Sylvia, who was following the conversation with interest added, "My cousin Ruth started hearing voices. It was the weirdest thing. She ended up killing herself, poor thing. She said voices were telling her to do it."

Lionel took a gulp of tea. "I'm sorry to hear that, Sylvia. Have you heard of prion disease?" He directed his question to Haskins. "Ever since I left my retreat, I've been trying to figure out why some people lost their cognitive abilities or developed what appeared to be early onset Alzheimer's. I was thinking about prion disease as related to the China virus injections. I wondered if the mRNA injections' effects could trigger prion disease. Specifically Creutzfeldt-Jacob disease in susceptible individuals. I wrote a paper on Creutzfeldt-Jacob disease while I was studying in Guelph with Byram Bridle."

Haskins cleared his throat. "I don't know much about prion disease. We covered it briefly at a conference I attended back in 2019. It's plausible, though. I did discuss it with some colleagues when we started having an unusual number of cases of premature Alzheimer's even in people in their late 20s and early 30s."

"What are you doing about the shedding from the vaxxed?"

"We're doing the only thing we can, making sure people get enough protein to eat in the hopes they can create enough of their own glutathione and fight it off. Some good hunters here. That burger," he nodded at Lionel's empty plate, "that was deer."

"Nice. Pretty much what I've been eating for the last few years. Clean wild meat – the best! Pine needle tea can help," Lionel said, returning to the previous topic. He explained how to make it and why it was important. "Be sure everybody drinks at least three cups daily. It may also help the vaxxed, so have them drink it too."

After eating his fill, Lionel regretfully took his leave, shaking the hands of Aaron and Allan and thanking the cooks for a wonderful meal. "Protect your kids," he warned in parting. He had already provided a succinct narrative of his experiences with the witch in Two Mile. "It could be the gangs that are kidnapping kids, but it can also be single males or females."

By 3:30, Lionel was back on the Yellowhead. More forests, lakes, mountains and rivers. A few more looted and mainly abandoned villages. He stopped once at a rest stop to refuel from his gas canisters.

Around 5 pm, Lionel passed a burned area that looked like numerous propane tanks had exploded. Many shards of metal from the blasted tanks littered the road, and he had to drive carefully to get around them. Shortly after, he entered a small town. He slowed to circle a pickup and car that had collided. Coming around the wreck, he spotted two skinny bigger kids, maybe 10 or 11 years old, that appeared to be fighting with a small wild-haired dark girl and a blond-haired toddler!

More kids! Seems I'm destined to having a lot to do with them!

Stopping the truck and approaching the group on foot, Lionel noted that it was a green shopping basket with some cans of food they appeared to be fighting over. The little girl with a wild thatch of curly black hair was hitting at the bigger kids with a stick and the tiny boy had attached himself like a limpet to the leg of the bigger girl. There was also an Asian girl sitting on the long grass by the road sobbing.

"What's going on here, then!" Lionel used his sternest voice.

The four combatants stopped immediately and turned to stare at him.

"Whadda ya want!" the boy, who was at least twice the size of the little girl with the wild hair, put his skinny fist on his hips. "That's our food these stupid kids are stealing."

"That's a lie!" the little wild-haired girl swung her stick at the boy again. Lionel caught it in midair and removed it gently from her grasp.

"Dat's a lie!" echoed the tiny limpet boy, putting his own little fists on his hips. He had released the bigger girl's leg.

The Asian girl on the grass had stopped crying and was watching with interest.

The big boy pulled up the hood on his ragged sweatshirt, reached out and grasped the handle of the green basket. "Get lost, old man, we're taking our food and leaving."

"No, you're not," Lionel answered calmly and removed the boy's hand from the basket. "Where did this food come from? Whose basket is this?"

"It's MY basket and I've been using it for ages!" the little dark girl exclaimed vehemently. "Me and Matt and Abi got the food somewhere secret and I'm not telling anybody where we got it. We never steal food, we always ask if there's anybody around. Jesus says it's bad to steal!"

Matt and Abi nodded solemnly. The little girl continued, "These are bad kids and they steal our food sometimes."

The game was up, and the two bigger kids knew it. Swearing and uttering threats, they ran off.

"Yeah, get lost!" the little wild-haired girl picked up the stick that Lionel had dropped on the ground and threw it after them. She was still fairly hopping with anger.

Lionel hunkered down and held out his hand to the little boy. "Hi Matt, I'm Lionel," he said gently. The big blue eyes of the tiny boy gazed solemnly at him.

"Hi, 'Ionel," he said. He put out his minature hand and Lionel gently pressed it with his thumb and forefinger.

The Asian girl still looked skitterish, so Lionel turned to the hopping little dark girl, "I'm Lionel, what's your name?"

She approached warily, still tense with emotion. "I'm Rachel. Is that your truck? How come you're alive?"

"Pleased to meet you, Rachel. Yes, it's my truck. Why are you surprised I'm alive?"

Rachel ran to look in the truck. She climbed onto the running board and standing on her tiptoes, looked inside. "You have a lot of stuff in there. Is that a gun? What do you have in the back?"

"Wow! That's a lot of questions!" Lionel followed her over to the truck. "Where do you kids live?"

Rachel eyed him suspiciously from her elevated position on the wheel-well she had just clambered onto. "At my house," she answered cautiously. "Can you open the black lid and show us what's inside?"

"Where's your mom - or moms," Lionel asked, acknowledging that, from the looks of things, they weren't from the same family.

"None of us have moms or dads anymore," Rachel responded. "Where are you going?"

Lionel started to laugh. "You ask a lot of questions, but you never stop to listen to answers. I'm going to Calgary; I have some friends there."

"Are they grown-up friends?" Rachel was sitting on the hard tonneau cover now, her legs hanging over the side of the truck. "Please show me what's inside. I want to see."

Grinning through his beard, Lionel unlocked the cover and helped her to stand on the back bumper. He lifted the lid and showed her the camping gear, his tent, and some split firewood the Aboriginals had put there for him as well as the canisters of gas. It was in huge disarray due to his pursuit on the mountain in Two Mile. "Not very interesting, is it?" he grinned.

"Do you have food? Your truck is really messy! How come you're not sick? Most of the grown-ups are sick or dead now - or they went away a long long time ago." Rachel hopped down while Lionel re-locked the tonneau cover.

Lionel nodded at the green basket, "Do you want me to drive you home in my truck? I can make sure those kids don't come back and steal your food."

Rachel had skipped over to the green basket. She eyed him suspiciously again. "My mom says - my mom used to say," she corrected herself, "that I'm not supposed to get in cars with strangers."

"Good advice," Lionel agreed, "but we're not really strangers anymore. We all know each other's names and I just saved you from some bad kids. Also, I think we have a mutual friend."

"What's a mutual friend?" Rachel asked.

"We both have the same friend. I'm talking about Jesus. I think he's your friend. He's mine too."

"Ohh, OK then. I guess we're friends." Rachel skipped over to the passenger side of the truck. "C'mon, Matt, c'mon, Abi!"

They all scrambled into the passenger seat, the three little children sitting happily in the one seat, while Lionel started the truck.

"Tell me where to go," Lionel said.

While Rachel directed, Lionel drove slowly, looking around. Things were pretty bad in this town. He marvelled that the children had survived on their own with no adults to help them. He saw quite a few partly eaten human bodies; it was worse than almost any of the other towns up the Yellowhead. Likely a particularly virulent version of the vax had been used here to kill off so many. There were burned-out vehicles right on the main road, either from vandals or from collisions. He only saw two living adult humans. They were in rough shape; eyes empty, clothing unkempt and ragged. He was astonished to see vultures. He didn't know that they ranged this far north. The abundance of food likely was causing a significant increase in their numbers, and they had moved into the area. Crows were also everywhere. Carrion-eaters were doing well around here.

When they drew up at the little blue house where the children lived, Lionel saw that the windows were broken, and the door was ajar.

Rachel flung herself out of the passenger side over Matt and Abi and dashed up to the front door. "Oh, those bad, bad kids. They came into our house." Tears of anger were in her eyes.

Lionel and the two other children followed her in. She was standing in the middle of chaos. Some of the chaos looked far from fresh. The house hadn't been cleaned in quite some time and there was litter everywhere. The fridge lying, door ajar on its side on the floor of the kitchen and the smashed dishes were fresh, though.

"Oh, my doll!" Abi spoke for the first time. She was holding the head of a Chinese figurine, the rest of it was in shattered bits on the floor. Matt had found a teddy that was obviously a beloved toy. The stuffing was ripped out of it and the head was partially severed. His blue eyes were overflowing with tears.

Every room in the house was looted and destroyed and it looked like someone had urinated on the double bed in the main bedroom. A trek into the basement where the playroom was, showed the same vicious destruction.

"Who wants to have a barbecue?" Lionel said, cheerily. In his mind, he ran quickly through the supplies in his truck and recalled a precious package of hotdogs the people of Smithers had given him. He also had two greenhouse tomatoes and some fresh buns.

The children cheered up considerably after eating until they were bursting. Lionel suspected it was a long time since they had enough to eat.

"That was yummy!" Rachel declared, picking up a crumb of bread she found on the table Lionel had hauled outside. She put it in her mouth, then looked speculatively at Lionel. "Can we come with you? To that place you're going where there's other alive grown-ups." She ran inside and came back out with the green basket of food. "We have food, we don't have to eat yours. I know where we can get a bit more before we go. It's a secret, but I'll tell you."

Lionel shook his head. "It's dangerous out there, Rachel. I can't bring you into danger. I will see if there is something else we can do."

Are there any good grownups in this town? Should I bring them to Smithers? Lord, what should I do?

"Please take us with you," Rachel repeated. She skipped over to Matt and Abi and brought them with her to stand in front of Lionel. She whispered loudly in their ears, *"Tell him you want to go with him."*

In a chorus, all three children repeated her words, "Please take us with you!"

Lionel sighed, considering all the dangers he would see out there. "I'm sorry, I can't. We have to find a different solution."

There was a short pause while Rachel considered him thoughtfully.

In the silence, Lionel stood up from the table. "Who would like to camp in a tent tonight?"

"Me!"

"Me!"

"Me too!"

They got the tent set up in the backyard. The children were more of a hindrance than a help. Lionel just grinned and retrieved the tent poles that had stopped being swords and were abandoned when the kids discovered the fun of going under the tent.

It took some time, but the tent was finally erected, and everybody retreated inside away from the various biting insects of a spring evening. They had hauled the cleanest blankets and pillows from the house, so everybody had a comfortable place to sleep. Lionel left the waterproof flap open on the side so he could see outside through the screening. The children were laughing and rolling around without a care in the world while Lionel lay on his back, his arms crossed under his head. He was trying to figure out what he could do with the children. It was clear they couldn't live in this house anymore.

"Oomph," he grunted. Rachel had just done a handstand and landed on his stomach. "Hey kid," he said quietly, "do you ever stop moving?"

"Not much," Rachel giggled. "That's why my mom always calls ... called me Butterfly." She was back in motion again, hiding under a blanket and jumping out, pretending she was some animal or other.

Lionel rolled over abruptly. In his mind, he was back in a dark storeroom in Dease Lake and an old man was telling him he had to save the butterfly, save the children. Was Rachel the butterfly? Were these the children? Why was his destiny being mapped out for him like this with riddles to solve and tasks to do?

The children soon settled and fell asleep, huddled together in the blankets. Lionel groped in his pack and pulled out the small intricately carved butterfly. He lay awake for a while fidgeting with it, prayed, then he slept too.

CHAPTER 12

New Friends

We are seeing, right now, the highest death rates we have seen in the history of this business. The data is consistent across every player in that business. It's not elderly people who are dying, but primarily working-age people 18 to 64 who are the employees of companies that have group life insurance plans through OneAmerica.

And what we saw just in third quarter, we're seeing it continue into fourth quarter, is that death rates are up 40% over what they were pre-pandemic.

Just to give you an idea of how bad that is, a three-sigma or a one-in-200-year catastrophe would be 10% increase over pre-pandemic, so 40% is just unheard of.

~ Scott Davison, CEO

Breakfast the next morning was the half dozen eggs Lionel had received as a gift in Smithers and the last of the homemade buns. Lionel cooked the eggs in his little metal pan over a fire beside the tent. Rachel and Matt ate with gusto, but Abi just picked at her food.

"I'm not going to be able to always feed you this well," Lionel said to Abi.

"I like noodles," Abi responded. "My ba always gives me noodles to eat with my eggs."

"It's OK," Rachel broke in, "Abi's ba is her grandma. Her grandma was a really good cook. Abi's just used to eating nice cooked food. She's starting to eat some of our stuff cause she's hungry. She'll eat when she wants to."

Rachel took the last bite of her toasted bun topped with egg, then the meaning of Lionel's words dawned on her. She choked and started coughing and dancing around.

Matt, seeing her dancing, got up and danced too, smiling happily and waving his tiny hands.

"We're going with you! You're taking us with you to Clag - Clagy - to that place where there's other living grown-ups!" She danced and made a song with it once Lionel corrected her pronunciation.

"We're going to Calgry, we're going to Calgry!"

Abi lost her natural reticence and danced and clapped her hands too. Rachel's joy was very infectious, and Lionel found himself grinning and clapping as the children danced.

After breakfast, Lionel packed up the tent while the children went into the house and collected some personal items. Rachel came out hauling a huge suitcase, panting and puffing as she pulled it to the stairs. Arrived at the stairs, she gave it a push and it trundled down, thumping and banging.

"What on earth do you have in there?" Lionel queried. He opened it and discovered that she had packed all the undamaged toys she could find, the food from the green basket and some items of clothing for herself and the other kids. There were also a few items that had no possible use such as a clock that didn't work, a bag of pretty stones and shells, and the head of Abi's Chinese figurine.

"Sorry, kids," Lionel said. He went up the stairs back into the house with the huge suitcase and dumped it onto the messy floor. "You guys each need a change of clothes, a few pairs of underwear, and food. That's all. We'll find some sleeping bags for you somewhere."

He looked at Abi, whose eyes were full of tears, and relented. "You can bring the head of your doll. Matt, you can bring your teddy bear. I'll fix it for you. Rachel, you can bring one little toy. That's it."

Lionel rummaged around in the closets of the house and found an old gym bag. He packed the kids' personal items in the bag and put the food items back in the green basket. He put everything into the back seat of the truck with his backpack and left the green basket by the road.

"OK, now we need to find some food that will last us for the next week," he told the children.

Rachel told him where her secret store of food was. It was in the Key-Oh Lodge. She'd found a store of food in one of the rooms. It was almost completely gone. There were a few cans of soup and vegetables and a 6-pack of beer. Rachel didn't know what it was, so she'd opened one can experimentally and decided it was very nasty and left it there. They took the last of the food, Lionel reflecting that they'd need more than that.

They drove slowly up and down the streets. Lionel stopped at a couple of places.

At one place Rachel refused to go in with him, which was unusual. Entering the house on Hill St., Lionel understood the reason for her refusal. There were the remains of four kids and one female in the living room. All had bullet holes in their foreheads. Lionel found the remains of a man hanging in the hallway under the stairs going to the second floor. He had hung himself by the neck. All the bodies were partially consumed by mice or rats.

"Why didn't you warn me?" Lionel asked Rachel when he went out to the truck.

She looked uncomfortable. "I didn't remember what I saw here, I just remembered something bad happened."

Lionel marvelled at the ability of a child to block out bad things. Maybe that was why this little girl was so resilient.

A couple of houses down from the tragic scene, Lionel abruptly stopped the truck. "There's food here," he said with absolute certainty. He pulled into the driveway, got out and opened the gate, which was only partly open, then drove into the private walled garden.

"I already came here," Rachel told Lionel. She did remember that this place was already looted when she came, and she didn't get much.

All the children got out of the truck to go see where this food was that Lionel was so sure about. Rachel didn't think he would find anything, but she was willing to check with him.

Lionel surprised her. She was an expert forager, she thought, so why was Lionel going into the basement? Food was in pantries and cupboards and fridges, not basements. She already knew the pantry was empty as was the fridge. She'd searched all the cupboards as well.

In the basement, Rachel was astonished to discover another kitchen! There was a door at the back of the basement that led out to the back garden. In the basement kitchen, there was no fridge, just a big stove. On shelves were boxes of empty tin cans, big pots, strange machines, and empty glass jars.

Lionel stood and surveyed the open area in the basement thoughtfully. He opened one door. Nope, it was the furnace room. Ah, here it was. The door was barely discernable in the wall. Only the handle showed that there was a door. The handle was also very difficult to see since the whole wall had glued jigsaw puzzles of gardens and flowers and animals dispersed all over. Somebody had put a lot of time into putting together and gluing those puzzles.

Lionel grasped the ring that closed the door and pulled. The door was heavy and moved reluctantly. He continued pulling while the children inched forward to try to see inside the hidden room. It was completely dark and quite cold in there. When the door was fully open, Lionel stepped inside and fumbled on the wall on both sides of the door. Nothing. He stepped further in and swung his arm in the air above his head.

"Ah," he grunted and pulled downwards.

The light sprang on and before the children's astonished eyes were shelves and shelves and shelves and more shelves of FOOD!

"Wow!" the children spoke simultaneously, turning in circles. Labelled cans and bottles, dried fruits and vegetables, herbs, bottles of soup and stew, boxes of cereal and crackers, bags of rice and flour, so much FOOD!

Rachel flung her arms around Matt and Abi. They hugged, turning in ecstatic circles.

"We can fill up the truck and tie some food on the roof and put some in the back..." Rachel was already planning what to do.

"No, Rachel," Lionel interrupted her plans. "We'll take enough for a week, that's all."

"But, there's so much food! We never have to be hungry again!" Rachel was shouting because she was so annoyed with Lionel's obtuseness. She stamped her foot angrily.

Lionel hunkered down. "Listen, Rachel, I know you've been taking care of yourself for a while, but now I'm in charge. I happen to know that it will only take a few more days to get to Calgary. What I have to worry about is gas. I have to keep from over-loading the truck and hope I have enough gas, or I can find enough gas to get to Calgary. Please don't question my decisions all the time."

Quelled by Lionel's calm tone of authority, Rachel subsided. She watched while he moved through the room thoughtfully. He found a big freezer at the back and triumphantly held up a loaf of frozen bread. He went back out into the main part of the basement and returned with a crate.

He filled it with a selection of bottles, cans, dry goods and the loaf of bread. He ushered the kids out, turned off the light and closed the door.

He looked around the room, then he pushed a big table in front of the door handle and completely hid it by putting some big pots on the table.

"How did you know that there was food here?" Rachel asked curiously.

"Come with me," Lionel responded. He led the way back out to the garden. "Now really look around you."

It was too early in the year for anything to be producing yet, but there were raspberry and blackberry bushes, elderberry and currant bushes, cherry trees, peach trees and strawberry plants. Behind the house, there was a cleared space where a garden was planted every year.

"See those bushes and trees? They produce fruit. That garden grows food. If somebody has something like that, it's because they preserve it." Lionel walked through the back garden naming the bushes and trees.

The three children trailed behind Lionel. Matt stopped briefly to point at a passing helicopter with his tiny finger, his big blue eyes round with interest since he hadn't seen many of those in his short life.

The distance whump of the helicopter was forgotten when, suddenly, everybody jumped at a loud smashing sound close by.

Lionel abandoned his lesson and sprinted around the house. "Hey you!" he roared when he saw the cause. A figure in a green hoodie froze in place at his shout, then turned and dashed away.

Lionel didn't pursue the person. He stopped beside his truck and surveyed the damage. The vandal had just managed to break the passenger side window but hadn't had time to take anything. There was glass everywhere on the passenger seat and some on the supplies in the back seat. That, however, wasn't the worst of the damage.

Before breaking the window, the vandal had slashed the two back tires of the truck. Lionel put his hands on his hips looking at the mess. Now, what to do? He only had one spare tire. He couldn't walk through town looking for another tire, the vandal would probably be back and clean out the truck of everything he could carry. The kids were too small to protect the truck.

During his glum meditations, he didn't notice that the children had joined him and were all standing in line next to him. Matt even took up the same stance, with his hands on his hips and a frown on his little baby face.

"Only one thing to do," he said finally with a little smile for Matt, "we have to find another car or truck. It has to be nearby; I can't go too far in case that bad person comes back."

"We'll help!" Rachel said cheerily. "C'mon, Abi, let's go look for a car."

"I know where there's a car," Abi said carefully. "Down the road I saw a red car. It looks ok."

"The little Honda?" Lionel queried. He remembered seeing the Accord while cruising slowly up the hill. He looked at the three children and thought about how he could pack them in and what he'd have to leave behind. It would be better on gas than a truck, so his fuel supplies would last longer.

"OK, let's go see if we can find the keys in that house," Lionel decided.

Meanwhile, Matt had wandered off from the group and was somewhere calling what sounded like, "Cow! Cow!"

About to sprint off down the road to the red Honda, Rachel paused to look where Matt was pointing. He was standing in front of the two-car garage of the house where they were and pointing at the garage door.

"Matt says there's a car in there. How can we get in to check?" Rachel said excitedly.

"There's a door into the garage from the basement where we were," Lionel said, wondering why Matt thought a car was in there. He remembered seeing the door but hadn't checked behind it because he was focusing on finding the cold cellar. They all trouped back into the house.

Rachel and Abi ran ahead, down the stairs into the basement. Lionel went more slowly looking around for somewhere there might be a set of keys for a vehicle that *may* be in the garage. He had never learned the skill of hot-wiring a car, so keys would be essential.

"There IS a car, come, come quick!" Rachel's voice came up from the basement. "It's bigger than the red car, too!"

Lionel scooped up Matt who was doing his slow going down backwards thing on the stairs. "C'mon, kid, let's go see what you found."

Arriving in front of the garage door which, indeed, had a window through which you could see a vehicle, Lionel started to laugh. The utter incongruity of the idea of driving this vehicle struck him as hilarious. It was an older model white Dodge Caravan. He, Dr. Lionel Goudreault, an eminent immunologist, would be driving a Soccer Mom minivan! Since achieving his eminent status, he'd never driven anything less than a Lexus! OK, he'd driven his jeep and a truck, but a minivan, that was priceless! But it was perfect. Low gas mileage and lots of room!

"Why are you laughing?" Rachel, who could never keep quiet, wanted to know.

Lionel scooped up Matt again and set him on his shoulders. "Let's go look for some keys. It's perfect!" Still chortling, he climbed the stairs back to the front hallway.

"You smell like you need a bath," he commented. "I guess we all do."

He rummaged through the drawers of the table in the front hallway. No car keys, but he found a few keys that might unlock house doors or padlocks. Hopefully one of them would unlock the garage door.

"There's keys here!" Abi called. The girls had followed them up the stairs and started rummaging around too. Abi had opened the hall closet and discovered a key rack on the inside of the door.

Sure enough, there was one key fob with the Dodge logo that was most definitely for the minivan.

"Good job, kid," Lionel said, pocketing the fob. Abi glowed with happiness.

One of the keys Lionel found did open the garage door in the basement. The children helped Lionel transfer his things from the truck to the minivan after they opened the automatic garage door to the driveway.

Abi was particularly interested in Lionel's guns.

"My mom had a gun," she said, "it was to shoot people who tried to steal our stuff. Why don't you shoot the people who tried to steal your stuff?"

"That's not my job," Lionel answered, "it's the job of the law to decide who should live and who should die. I don't think your mom would have shot anybody unless she thought you were in danger."

Abi regarded him thoughtfully. "Is there any police left?"

"Not many," Lionel looked at her with his eyebrows raised. "I still won't shoot somebody unless they're threatening the lives of other people who don't deserve to be hurt."

"I'll be the law someday," Abi said, "then I'll shoot all the bad people."

Lionel insisted that everybody have a bath in the big upstairs bathroom. He had closed the garage door on the minivan, just to be certain nobody tried to slash its tires too. All three kids piled into the nice big tub, Matt insisting on bubbles.

Bubbles were duly found, and they played in the tub for half an hour before Lionel scooted them out and took a quick shower.

It was early afternoon before they were on the road, minivan loaded with all three kids happily sitting in the front passenger seat. They had a quick lunch before leaving. Lionel heated up a bottle of soup from the hidden room so they wouldn't have to use any of their supplies.

"Goodbye, goodbye," the children called to the town as Lionel circled the truck of stripped pig carcasses and headed east on the Yellowhead.

CHAPTER 13

The Gangs of Prince George

When you see that trading is done, not by consent, but by compulsion - when you see that in order to produce, you need to obtain permission from men who produce nothing - when you see that money is flowing to those who deal, not in goods, but in favors - when you see that men get richer by graft and by pull than by work, and your laws don't protect you against them, but protect them against you - when you see corruption being rewarded and honesty becoming a self-sacrifice - you may know that your society is doomed.

~Ayn Rand

After a quick scan of his map, Lionel became hopeful of getting beyond Prince George that day. They'd only been on the road for a little over an hour when Abi announced that she needed to pee.

"Can you wait a bit?" Lionel asked, hoping he could get in another hour of travel. Abi subsided, though she became somewhat fidgety.

Lionel tried to remember some car games he played as a child. 'I spy with my little eye' he mentally ruled out since the scene was mostly uniformly forests, mountains and water - other than an increasing number of crashed and abandoned vehicles. Lionel didn't want to draw the children's attention to these. Especially since there were human casualties visible occasionally.

"How many black animals can you name?" he finally decided on. They went through as many colours, features and associated animals as they could. That kept the children interested and they forgot the urgency of a bathroom visit.

By the time they were getting close to Prince George, the number of vehicles and casualties could no longer be ignored. The vandalism was getting worse, too. Many of the abandoned vehicles on the side of the road and even on the pavement had broken windows and flattened tires. There was graffiti all over signs and buildings and on the cars and trucks.

"Government kills." "Jab kills." "Run riot." "Shoot the bastards." "Kill the cops." These were some of the less profane slogans. The images were violent and bloody. Many had stylized needles killing people. Skulls and screaming faces were everywhere as well as zombies and human corpses. Red was heavily used along with images of soldiers dying bloody deaths.

"Wow!" Lionel exclaimed quietly at one point, "this sure isn't a thriving community like Smithers, or even Two Mile!"

"What do you mean?" Rachel wanted to know.

Lionel merely grunted in response.

The children soon subsided into silence, gazing wide-eyed around them. Abi was moving her lips, sounding out the words.

Lionel was relieved that they had stopped talking. He needed to focus on the road. Here and there were a few people, some quite severely incapacitated, many seemed to be suffering from nerve tremors. Others looked to be in rough shape with different health issues. All seemed furtive and frightened. The crows and vultures and other carrion-eaters were clearly well-fed.

Lionel had to drive slowly and wend his way through obstacles, many of which would damage the minivan if he passed over them. Garbage and broken household goods were everywhere scattered in the street. Most of the restaurants and shops were vandalized. All had graffiti of some kind. They passed the familiar McDonald's sign, broken now and unlit. Lionel took a left there, hoping that was correct, but it was hard to tell.

They drove slowly along for maybe twenty minutes through the chaos of the city and Lionel had a creeping suspicion that he was going to have problems finding the Yellowhead Highway again. He knew he had to turn right at some point, but with so many signs missing, damaged and painted over, he no longer was sure where he would have to make his turn.

He drove past a smashed-up Tim Hortons and then a bank. A cavernous hole suggested someone used a bomb to gain access to the vault.

Spotting three motorcyclists moving through the debris towards him about 300 metres down the road, Lionel made an abrupt decision to turn right. He did not like the look of those people and he would rather not get too close to them. He drove two blocks and made a left turn to conceal the vehicle from the main road, then he stopped the car and reached in the back for his pack.

"Lionel, Lionel, please, can we go into the restaurant?" Abi was using her best pleading voice.

"What restaurant?" he lifted his head and followed her pointing finger. It was a small place on the corner bearing a damaged sign: W..s Sushi. Some of the letters were obscured. Interestingly, it looked like vandals had attempted to enter but were unsuccessful because of the steel bars around the place. Some windows were broken and one bar was slightly bent, but clearly, nobody had succeeded in penetrating the restaurant.

"How are you going to get in?" he asked from his adult obtuseness. At least it was obvious that Rachel thought he was obtuse.

"That's easy!" spoke the expert. "I can finish breaking the window where the bar is bent and get in there, then I'll let you guys in. Abi wants to eat noodles and we all need to go to the bathroom."

Lionel grunted assent as he fished around in the top of his pack. He found his map of British Columbia and his CZ Shadow 9 mm. Abi looked with interest at the handgun, but the siren call of the noodles - and likely the bathroom - was too strong. She followed Rachel and, using a crumbling piece of cement from the sidewalk, helped her finish breaking the window. When Rachel opened the door and the children disappeared inside, Lionel absently stuck the revolver into the back of his pants and unfolded the map.

While perusing the map, he kept an eye on the road. He did not want trouble with those bikers. This city didn't feel safe at all. He was worried about the children more than anything. They were so vulnerable. He had to get out of this place quickly and back on the east and south trek to Calgary. *Was I wrong to bring them with me instead of driving back to Smithers? Maybe they wouldn't have taken them, they already had a lot on their plates.* His eyes perused the map. *Great*, he thought, *there's a lovely map here of Victoria and Vancouver, but none of Prince George.*

He followed the Yellowhead with his finger on the map. He could see that it intersected with Highway 97 north to Dawson Creek, but he was pretty sure he passed that intersection already. *The left turn I made at the McDonald's was also correct*, he thought uncertainly, *but where would I meet up with the Yellowhead again? It's not that street that looked like a boulevard a ways back, no...*

"Lionel, Lionel, come quick!" Rachel was standing in the open door of the restaurant, her face a mask of terror. Lionel flung the map onto the passenger seat and shot out of the minivan like a bullet. He could hear Abi screaming too. He charged into the restaurant.

"Oh, Lionel, oh Lionel, something's wrong with Matt!" Abi was frantic, slapping the little boy on the back. "I don't know what's wrong, oh Lionel, help him, help him!" She was almost incoherent with fear.

Lionel scooped up the child and laid him on a table. This wasn't choking, slapping him wouldn't help, nor would the Heimlich manoeuvre.

"What did he eat?" he said harshly to the distraught little girls.

He grabbed one of the plates with partly eaten food. "Stop screaming, girls," he commanded. From a quick glance at the plate, he saw Abi had found her noodles and had mixed them with... "Is that shrimp?" he asked.

"Yes," Abi was sobbing so hard her whole body was shaking. "I'm not sick and Rachel's not sick, why is Matt sick?"

"He's allergic," his voice was terse. He tipped the little boy's head back and looked into his mouth. Matt was clearly in respiratory distress, wheezing badly. His airway was partially closed, and his tongue was swelling. His face was bright red as were his hands and arms. The tiny boy's eyes were frightened but trusting.

"Oh Lionel, can you make him better?" Rachel burst out.

"We have to find a hospital," Lionel answered. Carrying the child, he ran back to the minivan. The girls scrambled into the passenger seat. Lionel continued holding Matt in his left arm. "Did either of you girls see a sign for a hospital?"

"I don't know what that looks like," Rachel's voice was very small now, her cheeks streaked with tears. Abi was too incoherent to help.

"It's a big H," he said, then, "Oh, you don't know the alphabet."

Lionel opened the glove compartment. He saw a pen in there earlier - yes, there it was! He scribbled a big H on the dash of the minivan. "It's usually white on a blue sign and looks like this."

Still gasping with sobs, Abi spoke up. "I saw one, it was back down the road a bit." Her sobs subsided and she managed to explain that it was near a Save-On-Foods.

Lionel started the van and drove as quickly as he could through the debris back to the main road. There was no sign of the bikers. He continued to hold the small wheezing boy on his lap. Matt's breathing was not improving, if anything it was getting worse.

He began to pray, "Lord, please save this little boy, Lord, please don't let him die." He discovered he was saying this out loud when he noticed the wide-eyed stares of the two little girls who were still gasping and sobbing. He attempted some CPR breathing for Matt. Trying to keep the child's legs elevated, his head back and do CPR breathing while driving meant he couldn't watch the road very well.

"Lionel! Watch out!" His head jerked up and he saw that he almost ran over a ragged middle-aged man with his head hanging down standing in the middle of the road. Rachel had screamed just in time. He swerved and heard a thump and the sound of metal ripping under the car. They jerked and thumped some more, and the motor raced when one wheel left the pavement. They had run over something. As they drove forwards, he heard a dragging sound.

"What did I run over? Did you see?" he asked the girls. They shook their heads mutely, with tears still running down their cheeks. Whatever it was, now their muffler was dragging.

At the Save-On-Foods, Lionel made a right turn onto the boulevard he noticed earlier. Sure enough, there was a hospital just a couple of blocks down.

But it was surrounded by military vehicles and soldiers with UN badges. As they pulled up, a black helicopter landed on a grassy slope nearby. Lionel pulled up to where a group of UN soldiers were in a tight formation on both sides of the road. The hospital itself was completely barricaded with heavy-duty mesh fencing. There were UN military Jeeps and vans all over the hospital green.

Lionel rolled down the window. A corporal approached him. "Vaht do you vant?" the man asked, speaking with a heavy foreign accent.

"I need to get help, I have a little boy here with anaphylaxis," Lionel was seriously worried now. Matt's heart rate was slowing and, even with the air Lionel was attempting to force down into his swollen bronchials, he wasn't getting enough air. There could be permanent brain damage if he didn't get oxygen and relief from his body's allergic reaction.

A thin man with a moustache wearing a black uniform but no insignia strolled over and spoke in an undertone to the sergeant who had not yet spoken. The sergeant saluted and strode over to the vehicle.

"Go avay, go now. You are not authorized to be here. Go!" The soldiers tightened their formation and came closer to the minivan.

"You don't understand. This little boy might die! I just need some medicine for him!" Lionel went to open the door, thinking if they didn't want him to drive in, maybe he could carry Matt into the emergency room.

"If you do not go now, ve vill shoot you!" All the soldiers raised their weapons and took aim at Lionel. The sergeant's Glock was pointed directly at Lionel's forehead. The man in the black uniform didn't move, he merely clasped his hands behind his back.

Lionel released the door handle and didn't exit the van. He breathed into Matt's slack mouth a couple more forceful breaths, then put the van in reverse and left the scene. As he reversed, a ripping sound announced that the muffler was gone.

What was he going to do now? He drove slowly down the road. The chuff-chuff of a helicopter rising into the air followed them. A strong smell of urine filled the van and he realized that at least one of the little girls had wet her pants.

Lionel felt a deep sense of despair and helplessness. Here he was, in the middle of a city full of hostile people. He had three kids depending on him and one would die if he didn't get him help soon. The tiny boy, lying nearly inert in his arms, would need an epinephrine injection and some diphenhydramine in the next few minutes.

"Lionel," Rachel's voice was small and anxious. "Can you find the medicine you need for Matt in a store? There's a bunch of stores over there, maybe there's some medicine there that you can use to help Matt?"

Lionel slammed on the brakes, almost sending the two little girls through the windshield. *She's right! Looters wouldn't probably be focussing on those medications; they would go for Percocet and other opiates!* And there was a London Drugs in the mall Rachel was indicating, and a Save-On-Foods that might have a pharmacy! *Why didn't I think of that!*

He veered sharply into the parking lot, almost running over a mangy dog. He steered rapidly around the shopping carts, abandoned vehicles and other debris that was littered everywhere and pulled up in front of London Drugs. The two little girls were bracing themselves by now and didn't go flying when he slammed on the brakes.

Lionel was out of the van and into the store in a flash, still holding the wheezing little boy in his arms and trying to get some air into his airway. It was easy getting into the store, the doors hung ajar with broken windows.

The interior was chaos. Everything was trashed, empty packaging and boxes, broken glass and ceramic, fallen shelves and shelving units were everywhere. There were feces in corners and trashed food littering the floor.

Lionel ignored all of that and rushed to the pharmacy area. Chaos reigned here as well. He scrabbled desperately through the debris behind the counter. Surely there would be just one epinephrine auto-injector somewhere! Surely!

"Abi!" he shouted, "where are you?"

The little Asian girl approached timidly.

"Help me! I need to find an EpiPen!" He grabbed a lipstick off the floor and wrote the word for her on the end of one shelving unit. He went back to frantically sifting through the debris of rejected medication. Under his breath, he was chanting supplications to God, while doing breathing every 15 seconds for the little boy who was fading fast.

It felt like an eternity, but it was likely only a minute when his eye fell on exactly the item he was looking for - it was a 2-pack of EpiPens! He ripped the box open and administered the injection into the tiny slack thigh of the little boy. Was it too late?

Lionel continued breathing into Matt's mouth, gazing anxiously into his face between every pair of breaths. Rachel and Abi silently approached and stood next to where Lionel crouched with the little boy on his lap.

It was like a miracle. Matt's colour started to turn to normal at about the same time as the swelling in his face and tongue began to diminish. When he started coughing and his eyes opened, Rachel and Abi started sobbing again, though possibly it was out of relief. Lionel gave them an exasperated look. Girls cried too much, he decided.

Still holding the boy, he went back to rifling through the debris of medication. He found some prednisone and the diphenhydramine he'd been hoping to find as well as a couple more packs of EpiPens. Matt was still wheezing, so he would need an antihistamine and possibly the steroid. Having the extra EpiPens might come in handy in the future as well. He would have to see.

"Matt's OK now?" Abi asked, almost whispering. "I'm really sorry I made him sick. I didn't know. We didn't have any shrimp left in my restaurant when he was there. I'm really really sorry."

"Matt is fine," Lionel hunkered down in front of her, still holding Matt. "No, you didn't know. How could you know that he is allergic to shrimp? It's not your fault."

Abi's face cleared a little and she attempted a smile. Lionel gave her a one-armed hug which reassured her even further.

Matt began wriggling on his hip where Lionel had set him. Lionel cleared a spot on the counter, then sat him there to have another look.

"Open your mouth," he told the boy. "Stick out your tongue."

Matt obediently stuck out his tongue. There was still some visible swelling, but he was much better.

"Girls, see if you can find a bottle of water somewhere."

When Abi ran excitedly back with a bottle of water, Lionel got Matt to take a small dose of both meds. Rachel's discovery of a bag of chips that was intact and only a bit crushed was also really exciting and soon all three children were dancing around again. Matt was still a bit shaky and wheezy, but he was young and healthy and recovering well.

Lionel sent Abi off to look for some fresh pants and underwear since she smelled quite strongly. He was foraging around, hoping to find an intact map of Prince George, when he heard a crashing sound from outside.

A quick look out the window sent Lionel to the back of the store, hauling the children into the storeroom behind the pharmacy.

"Stay here and don't make a sound!" he commanded. He dashed out again and through the open front door.

There was a souped-up car with horns on the hood pulled up beside the minivan. It was heavily armoured with a black iron grille guard protruding from the front. The zenith of the grille guard was shaped like a plough with a convex angled front end. Three people were smashing at the minivan with metal bars to break the windows. They had already slashed the tires.

A fourth person who was very large and tattooed was rifling through the contents of the van. The back door was ajar and he had already thrown the tent on the ground. As Lionel dashed outside, the large man with a spider tattoo on his face was hauling out Lionel's backpack and howling with joy. He'd found the guns.

"Don't touch that!" Lionel shouted. He did his best football tackle at the large man's waist. They both went down hard, rolling across the littered parking lot pummelling at each other.

Lionel managed to get on top of the big man and administer a couple of good blows to his face. The spiky-haired woman of the group was on Lionel in seconds, striking him viciously with the metal bar she was holding. Lionel howled, rolled off the man on the ground and attempted to get up. His right arm was numb from the blow the woman had struck. He flailed with his left arm at the two other men who were coming at him with their metal bars. A heavily scarred man with a missing ear struck the first blow in his abdomen. The second man, wearing a Hell's Angels jacket, hit him almost immediately afterwards at the back of his thighs. He was down in moments and the men proceeded to kick him with their boots.

"Git 'im, git 'im!" the woman cackled, dancing around and shouting, showing a mouthful of blackened teeth. "Git 'im good, he's a feckin' muffa!"

The big man was on his feet now, swearing and joined the other two men, kicking Lionel and grunting. "Take that, you muffa, take that!" He was bleeding from his ear and there was swelling around one eye.

The whole group continued to kick and strike at Lionel, swearing and laughing.

"We run this place, you muffa, everybody knows that!" The big, tattooed man had the biggest boots and the biggest need for revenge. "We gonna kill you like we kill any muffa tries to give us trouble."

Lionel was dazed with pain, trying to protect his head from the kicks. He attempted scrambling to his feet a few times to get away, but the woman would dash back in and strike him again with her metal bar. *The 9 mm*, he thought, *why didn't I use that? Stupid, stupid.* He'd forgotten all about it and now it was too late. All he could do was make sure they didn't get that too. The only way he was able to conceal its presence in the back of his heavy, lined jeans was to make sure they didn't feel it when they kicked him. There was no way he could get it; his right arm was still numb from the elbow. So he continued trying to protect his head and keep his back to the pavement as much as possible.

When Lionel was inert, bleeding and motionless in the parking lot, they lost interest. They finished stealing everything they wanted from the minivan and damaged and destroyed the rest. Within five minutes they were gone, roaring away in the armoured car with the horns.

Across the boulevard, a black-uniformed man with a moustache climbed back into the helicopter with spinning rotors. It lifted off and vanished into the late afternoon sky.

C H A P T E R 1 4

Loss and Rebellion

What you allow is what will continue.

~ Unknown

A government big enough to give you everything you want is strong enough to take everything you have.

~ Thomas Jefferson

Viv rolled over in the big king-sized bed. It still felt strange to sleep alone even though it was months since George fell sick.

Five am. Why did she always wake up at 5 am? She sat up, groaned, and stretched her arms out and did some yoga stretches.

It was chilly in the room. When she opened the curtains, she discovered that it had snowed and was still snowing. *Welcome to spring showers,* she thought glumly. She wouldn't go for a run today, but she'd have to go out before 10 to get to one of those churches up by 17th Ave. Hopefully, they had some food. It was Sunday, so they should be open. If the snow stopped and there wasn't too much accumulation, she could take her mountain bike. She had run out of gas for her Highlander a couple of weeks ago and wasn't able to get any more at any of the local gas stations. They were all closed.

Oh, yeah, even if they have gas, she reflected morosely, *I can't buy any because of the criminal vaccine passport and digital ID law and I can't use George's credits if he's not there.*

She sighed. She had to go look after George soon. It was getting increasingly difficult. The improvements in physical health a few weeks ago had been only temporary as his mind became more confused. Though his body was shrunken and thinner, he still had so much strength. Now she had to put restraints on him.

The last time he went into a frenzy trying to leave the house in obedience to a siren call only he could hear; he knocked her across the room with one blow. She was only able to subdue him by hitting him in the back of the knees with the poker from the fireplace. Her ribs were all bruised from that incident.

Viv pulled on a pair of black leggings and a long-sleeved t-shirt, squared her shoulders, and headed downstairs.

That morning when she entered the small room at the front of the house, it was more of the same. George was panting and chanting in a rasping voice, "get me out of here, get me out of here," when she entered the room. He looked like he had barely slept. His eyes were wild and frantic, his wrists raw and chafed from trying to escape the restraints.

"You bitch!" he screamed when he saw her, spittle flying from his twisted mouth. "You bitch you bitch you bitch! You did this! This is all your fault! Get me out of here!"

He writhed and wrenched furiously at his restrained wrists and ankles.

Viv approached slowly making calming noises like she was soothing a wild animal.

"Hey, honey, it's me, it's your Viv! Sshh, it's OK, please calm down, it's me!"

George's thrashing eased though he continued to glare suspiciously at her with distended bloodshot eyes. She carried a bowl of hot cereal with raisins the way he liked it. There was no milk, but she made it thin enough so that he might not notice.

"Here," she said, sitting down cautiously beside him and placing the bowl on the side table. "I brought your breakfast."

George abruptly began to scream, his whole body arching up from the bed. His head thrashed from side to side and he emitted blood-curdling shrieks. Viv sprang to her feet and leapt onto the bed, trying to hold him down. He began to snap at her with his teeth and dreadful words poured out of his mouth.

"You bitch, damn you, damn you, you bitch you bitch you bitch!" Then the obscenities started.

Viv was panting on top of him, trying to rouse him out of his violent paroxysms. "George, stop, George, you're still there, George, please!" then she prayed out loud, gasping her words out. "Please God, please help George, I can't help him, he needs you now! Please God, please God, please, oh God oh God oh God. Oh Jesus, help George, oh Jesus, oh Jesus I need your help!" She was sobbing, trying to stroke his face and his hair. His convulsions continued and she was thrown from side to side, desperately trying to bring him back to himself. He began roaring like an animal, foam pouring from the corners of his gaping mouth. His body was like a massive volcano under her and she was heaved wildly into the air again and again.

Suddenly there was a snapping sound. George's furious thrashing succeeded in breaking one of his wrist restraints. Flailing wildly with his freed hand, he struck her violently in the chest. The blow threw her off the bed and sent her skidding across the floor to slam into the wall. She lay on the floor momentarily stunned, trying to get air back into her lungs. The bowl of cereal smashed to the floor into shards spilling its sad contents and the spoon spun off under the bed.

George didn't notice that his arm was free, nor that he'd struck her. He was in a full-blown convulsion, his eyes rolled up in his head. The screaming had stopped. His teeth were locked together, and he was making an inhuman grunting noise that sounded like "Unh, unh, unh." Suddenly it stopped and a powerful scent of urine and feces filled the room.

Viv picked herself up off the floor, still wheezing and rubbing her aching chest. Approaching the bed slowly, she could see only the whites of George's bulging eyes. His expression was a horrible rictus of pain and he wasn't breathing.

"George, George," she said quietly. No response. Taking his freed wrist she checked for a pulse. There was none. Cautiously extending her hand she felt for the carotid pulse. Nothing. She collapsed onto the chair by the bed and held her head in her two hands.

I will not do CPR to revive him, I asked Jesus for help and now he's dead. I can't do CPR to revive him, it won't do any good, this isn't George anymore. Viv wrapped her arms around her head and prayed.

Gradually the feeling that she wasn't alone crept over her and words came gently and peacefully into her ears. It was almost like a quiet, calm voice speaking to her. She heard someone say, "Behold, I am with you always, to the end of the age."

Finally, peace came upon her and her mind calmed. Whispering a prayer of thanks, she began the difficult task of preparing her deceased husband for burial.

It was only 10:30 in the morning when she finished digging a shallow hole in the back garden and laid George to rest. The sun was shining long enough to melt the snow that had fallen. She felt furtive and guilty at the thought of burying her husband in the back yard, it was almost like a murder mystery novel: a wife burying her husband like this. She was grateful for the rain and the early thaw last month, otherwise, she wouldn't even have been able to dig a grave for him.

She was pretty sure there would never be any inquiry. The houses on both sides of hers were uninhabited for a few weeks now. When she tried to call a mortuary before digging the grave, she discovered there was no phone service. Oddly enough, the internet was still working as was the electricity, but she was unable to reach anybody in emergency services by internet, so she resorted to sending a couple of emails to mortuaries.

She sat by the grave and prayed for a while. She thought about her marriage; the joy and laughter of the first few years. George had always been able to make her laugh. She marvelled at how things had changed with the China virus pandemic. It was like a huge divide had arisen between them. So much love and laughter and now it was over.

Finally, she rose and went into the house, leaving her husband in the cold spring ground by the winter-bare rose bushes. She didn't think she'd be using her back patio much anymore.

Viv stood wearily by the window, rubbing her bruised and aching breastbone, unsure of her next move. Her mind was in turmoil. These last couple of months had been devoted to George. She gave very little thought to planning her future in the eventuality that George died. When she had time to herself, she would chat with contacts in the freedom fighters' group. Things were even worse in Ontario if that were possible. The non-vaxxed were in hiding now because the military didn't stop at collecting the homeless and the people suffering from severe adverse vaccine events. They were also collecting everybody who didn't have a vaccine passport or digital ID, and they were trying to force the digital ID on the entire population - the surviving population, that is...

Viv hadn't been able to contact anybody from the freedom fighters' group for nearly a week. Today was no exception. Tired and sad, she snapped her laptop closed and turned on the TV. It was airing a panel of celebrities discussing the vaccine passport that had been incorporated into the digital ID, and how it was the only thing keeping people safe. They spoke with smiling positivity about the wonders of the digital ID and its convenience now that Socdits were attached to the chip which could be scanned to award or spend with ease. They questioned why so many people were stupid enough to not recognize the convenience of having a chip scanned on their wrist or even on their forehead. It made everything so ridiculously simple! One panellist ventured to ask, with a nervous giggle, why so many people who were vaxxed were getting ill. The others leapt on her arguing that it was because there were still unvaxxed people out there spreading the China virus everywhere and that it was time these germ-infested rats got collected and forcibly vaccinated and chipped. They were a public health disaster waiting to happen.

Viv sighed, too tired to feel enraged at their folly. She flicked off the TV.

At lunchtime, she wandered into the kitchen to get something to eat. She didn't feel hungry and her ribs and chest still ached from the blows she received over the last couple of days. She opened the fridge and found that all she had was part of a bottle of mayo, a partial pack of cheese slices and a container of thin soup she made the day before. Her freezer looked just as empty with one chicken thigh and half a bag of frozen peas. She moved wearily to the pantry and saw the same desultory emptiness with only a few cans of assorted goods, some lentils and quinoa, the remains of the oatmeal and part of a bag of flour. In one canister, there were a few lonely raisins left. Maybe she had to make that trip downtown to the churches and see if there was anything to be had. Maybe then she would feel less dreary.

The bicycle ride did not cheer her up. This was not the Calgary she'd known when she moved here with George less than five years ago. It was depressed due to the willful destruction of the once-thriving oil industry by the Canadian government. Many people moved away from Calgary before she came, but it never was like this before! It was a beautiful city even then, in spite of the many homes for sale. There were families walking dogs and pushing strollers. There were high-end pickup trucks jostling for position with the Teslas and SUVs, there were busy shoppers and businesspeople moving through the city with purpose. The C-train was usually full of people reading newspapers, playing games on their smartphones, or talking on their cell phones.

That was before the scamdemic. Now there were few cars on the roads. The few vehicles that still moved were mainly electric vehicles, but those were rare since the power grid was becoming unreliable. She saw the occasional person, but their movements were fearful, their behaviour was furtive. The C-train sat, silent, empty and unmoving when she cycled by.

Viv spotted a few military jeeps and some roadblocks. Approaching the downtown core, she started to see more people. They were moving purposefully towards the centre of the city. Why? Where were they going?

Abandoning her plan temporarily of finding a church that had food, she dismounted and, pushing her bike, she followed a group of three men carrying signboards. More people gathered, streaming in from side streets or from apartment buildings until there was a throng of at least 1000 people. The crowd was agitated, excited. More and more people had protest signs with slogans. One man wearing a baseball cap bearing the slogan #MakeCanadaGreatAgain chanted in a loud rhythmic voice as he marched, waving his arms to encourage others to chime in:

Your vax pass can kiss my ass.

People everywhere started picking up the chant as more and more streamed in from all the side streets. As far as the eye could see, down this main thoroughfare, there were signboards by the hundreds with slogans like: "YOU LIE WE DIE," "OUR CHILDREN ARE STARVING," "YOU CAN KEEP YOUR DIGITAL ID," "MY MOTHER'S DEATH IS ON YOU," "WE ARE CANADIAN, NO UNITED NATIONS NO OGOA," "BLOOD CLOTS TOOK MY FOOT, GIVE IT BACK" "SADS AND SIDS=MURDER" and "DEPOPULATION IS HERE." Canadian and Alberta flags waved everywhere with defaced UN flags and OGOA emblems interspersed, covered with black and red null signs.

Along the north side of the street, the most agitated group was carrying signboards that told the most tragic tale of all. "WHERE IS MY DAUGHTER?" "YOU STOLE MY KIDS," "WHERE IS MY TOMMY?" were some of the slogans. Others read "MY BABY'S DEATH IS ON YOU" or "MYOCARDITIS WAS NOT RARE."

Military wearing riot gear were everywhere, but they were outnumbered as more and more people gathered.

One group marching down the street took up 'Onward Christian Soldiers'. They even had a drum and were marching in formation. Many of them carried signs saying things like "THE VAX IS THE MARK OF THE BEAST" and "WHEN WE DIE WE'RE GOING TO JESUS, YOU'RE GOING TO HELL."

The crowd was getting bigger, swelling to the thousands as more people gathered. The furtive ones had found their courage and the sick ones were there too. There were so many sick. Everywhere Viv saw signs of illness likely caused by the jab. Heart problems, dull-eyed sick towed along by family members, Bell's Palsy, Guillain-Barré Syndrome, skin growths, stroke, so many sick people. There were even people with missing limbs, probably from blood clots. But they were here, and they were fighting!

Watching the crowd, Viv felt her heart swell with pride. These protesters had been terrorized and fed fear in daily doses by the media and the government but were starting to fight back. By now she was marching along with the crowd, her bike abandoned by the side of the road. She completely forgot about going to get some food.

She turned to a thin young woman stumbling along nearby. *Bell's Palsy,* said Viv's diagnostic mind, noting her drooping facial muscles.

"Excuse me," she called to her.

The woman shakily turned her head to Viv. She gestured to herself with her trembling hand. "You talking to me?"

"Yes, yes please." She approached the woman. "How did people know to come today to a protest? I didn't know anything about it."

A large man who was wheezing badly moved closer and protectively put an arm around the woman. "You didn't get the flyer?"

"Yeah, there were flyers about this dropped off all over the city," the woman said.

Flyers? What flyers? She thought she remembered a paper thrust into the front door handle several days ago, but she wasn't sure.

She smiled broadly at the couple. "It's really great that people are starting to fight back."

They were by City Hall now and the crowd was getting louder and louder. Different groups were taking up different chants. Viv heard one group while marching with linked arms, singing 'We Shall Overcome'.

We shall overcome

We shall overcome
We shall overcome, someday

Oh, deep in my heart
I do believe
We shall overcome, someday

We'll walk hand in hand
We'll walk hand in hand
We'll walk hand in hand, someday

Oh, deep in my heart
I do believe
We shall overcome, someday

We shall live in peace
We shall live in peace
We shall live in peace, someday

Oh, deep in my heart
I do believe
We shall overcome, someday

We are not afraid
We are not afraid
We are not afraid, today.

Viv wanted to laugh, she wanted to hug everybody. This was so great! This morning her husband had died, but now in the early afternoon, she was so happy and proud of these Canadians! The lost feeling had vanished, she wanted to climb onto a podium and tell them how proud she felt.

Somebody did climb onto a podium in front of City Hall. A fat Indian man waddled up the stairs while a military detachment surrounded him protectively.

"Go home!" he boomed once an obsequious young man had handed him a mike. "Go home! This gathering is against the law! Go home now!"

"Boooo! Booo! Shut up! You're a killer! You're a murderer!" Yells erupted and people waved their fists in the air.

The fat man tried again. "Public gatherings are against the law! You will be punished if you don't disperse to your homes now!"

Once again he was drowned out by the loud shouts and heckling. "Pig! Shut up! You're kissing the ass of the killers! Go away! You did this, you murderer!"

The man on the podium turned to the UN military man standing next to him. From the stripes, it was apparent he was high in command. They consulted briefly, then the fat man turned back to the mike.

"You have five minutes to disperse or we will take action! Go home now, or the soldiers are authorized to begin firing!"

The crowd just got angrier, yelling and chanting. One woman threw what looked like an empty pop can at the man and he was hustled off the podium as a rain of debris from the street flew through the air in his general direction.

At a gesture from the general, the UN soldiers in riot gear took action. They raised their rifles and began shooting. Others wearing gas masks launched cannisters of tear gas into the crowd. People began pushing and shoving at the riot shields of the military. Screams erupted as the rubber bullets struck and sloughed off skin on faces and bodies or left deep impact marks. Some of the soldiers in riot gear were knocked over by the sheer weight of the people and then trampled. A few backed away. More projectiles flew through the air, but now it was pieces of pavement, rocks, sticks and metal objects. Now signboards were being used as weapons to attack the soldiers.

The fat Indian man was gone, and a tall, thin grizzled black man forced his way onto the podium. He picked up the abandoned mike. More people joined him on the podium: a girl with spiked purple hair, an older man with glasses, three powerfully built men that looked like boxers and a stocky woman carrying a baseball bat.

The thin man now spoke. "TODAY….IS THE FIRST DAY OF THE WAR. TODAY…. IS THE FIRST DAY THAT WE STAND UP AND REFUSE TO COMPLY ANYMORE. TODAY…WE REJECT WITH FINALITY THE WORLD ECONOMIC FORUM DICTATORSHIP. TODAY…. WE SHAKE OUR FISTS AT THE OGOA! NO WORLD GOVERNMENT FOR US! TODAY WE REMEMBER THAT WE WERE BORN FREE UNDER GOD. TODAY WE TELL YOU ELITE THAT ARE PLOTTING OUR DESTRUCTION THAT *WE WON'T TAKE IT ANYMORE!*"

The crowd pushed forward, screaming with rage and took up his cry. *"We won't take it anymore!"*

Many had eyes streaming from the tear gas, some were bleeding from the impact of the rubber bullets. But all screamed again and began the chant, "WHAT DO WE WANT? FREEDOM! WHEN DO WE WANT IT? WE WANT IT NOW!"

Somewhere at the back of the crowd that had now swelled to over 5000 protesters, a group broke into a new version of U2's song "Bloody Sunday." Voices rose, singing the chorus and the words,

> Broken bottles under children's feet
> Bodies strewn across the dead-end street
> And I will heed the battle call
> It puts my back up
> Puts my back up against the wall.

The military had not been inactive. They formed a barricade with their riot shields and began forcing their way through the middle of the crowd, shooting their rubber bullets steadily at them. The UN general was back, standing on a balcony overlooking the street. He held a megaphone to his mouth. "Disperse! Go home!" He repeated that several times, then he roared through the megaphone, "This is your final warning! We will begin to use live ammo on you! Go home now!"

A group of soldiers had begun raining bullets at the people on the podium. The three large men and the stocky woman leapt off the podium and responded with blows using fists and sticks. It was enough to allow the spokesman to escape off the podium with the other members of the group.

Suddenly a huge blast erupted down the street and three military vehicles exploded from the pavement and shards of metal and glass rained far and wide. The screams intensified as the soldiers reloaded with clips of real bullets and began firing. People began falling to the ground, bleeding profusely or dead.

Another blast went off at the other end of the street where the military had set up a barricade. Chunks of cement hurtled up, smashing windows and injuring the soldiers from behind. Some fell to the ground, wounded.

The black man was back, standing in the middle of the seething screaming crowd. Somehow, he managed to be heard above the bedlam. "YOU WERE WARNED! THE WAR HAS BEGUN!"

After this dire warning, he turned to the crowd, "Go home, we won this battle. There will be more battles to fight."

His words passed through the throng, but people were already dispersing. That day's battle was indeed over.

C H A P T E R   1 5

Small Refuge

God is our refuge and strength, a very present help in trouble. Therefore will not we fear, though the earth be removed, and though the mountains be carried into the midst of the sea; Though the waters thereof roar and be troubled, though the mountains shake with the swelling thereof. Selah.

~ Psalm 46:1-3 KJV

"Lionel, wake up! Lionel! Please don't be dead!" Small hands patting his battered face brought him slowly back to painful consciousness. Lionel attempted to open his eyes and discovered that one of them wouldn't open. He squinted up at the children from his prone position on the filthy pavement.

"Hey," he mumbled through his battered mouth. He lay for an indefinite time wondering if he should pass out again or try to sit up. Every part of his body was a massive throbbing agony.

More face-patting and pleas in children's voices roused him again from his lengthy meditation on whether he should just lay there until he felt better. It seemed those little kids didn't want him to rest. Gradually his wandering thoughts returned to him. He let out a long groan which stopped the face-patting, He squinted at the kids again.

"Gimme a sec," he said. His words sounded slushy.

Using his left hand, he cautiously explored his face. His right eye was hugely swollen and he had a gash in his forehead and cheek, just above where the hair of his beard started. There was also something wrong with his scalp. He would have to investigate that later. He moved his nose experimentally and discovered it was broken and steadily seeping blood into the back of his throat and down his face. No wonder he was mouth-breathing. Two of his teeth were loose, but still present and accounted for, though he seemed to have bitten his tongue rather badly. Ok, so far so good.

Another long groan precluded an attempt to lever himself up to a sitting position. Eager little hands helped to push him up. That led him to discover that he likely had some cracked ribs, but none of them seemed to be broken. What did seem to be broken was his right arm, it certainly wasn't working properly.

Lionel slowly struggled to stand up, with several false starts, stumbling back to the pavement in a jarring fall. Every single part of his body throbbed agonizingly and he had a horrible headache. He suspected it might be a concussion since he felt quite nauseated.

Finally upright, shuffling like an old man, escorted by anxious small hands, he made his way slowly back into the London Drugs cradling his right arm. He spotted an overturned chair with an armrest that people used to use to take their blood pressure.

"Hey," he mumbled, his thick tongue flopping in his mouth, "can one of you sit that chair up?"

Rachel and Abi dashed to set it upright and hurried back. He realized that they were using their tiny strength to help him walk.

Once seated, he looked vaguely around, trying to decide what to do. He had to clean his wounds somehow and suture them. His bag was gone so he didn't have any type of medical kit, there had to be something here he could use that hadn't been stolen or damaged. And dear God, he would kill for some Tylenol!

"What should we do, Lionel? Lionel, please be OK," Rachel asked after a long minute of silence and put her little hand on his skinned left hand.

"Ah," he grunted, "gimme a minute." His mind was sluggish and weary. He looked at the three little children that were depending on him and he felt so inadequate. This world was such a dangerous place and he had nothing left to protect them with. He had no food to feed them. He'd seen the mess that was strewn around the destroyed minivan. All the bannock and dried meat and vegetables had been scorned and trashed by the vandals. All the preserves they found in that basement were stolen or the jars broken. He had no shelter, the tent was ripped and trashed as was his sleeping roll and the blankets and pillows for the kids. Worst of all, his guns, and his bag with the ham radio, Janet's journal, the carved butterfly, and so many essentials were gone.

I was wrong to bring these children with me. I can't protect them. Oh God, I don't know what to do. Please help me!

That was when he remembered why there was such a pressure at his back. Lionel reached around experimentally with his skinned left hand and found he still had the 9 mm!

"You have a gun!" Abi said excitedly when he slowly and clumsily pulled it out.

He checked the clip one-handed, then returned it to the back of his pants. *Two bullets.* His mind grappled with this discovery. *Two bullets between these children and unimaginable horror.* Had his hubris doomed them? *I have to decide what to do. Lord, what can I do? I need Your help to protect these little kids because I haven't even got my own strength left.*

He slowly levered himself to his feet.

"Abi, can you go to behind the desk where we found the medicine for Matt and see if there is a bottle of Tylenol or something like that left? Aspirin or Advil works too. Rachel, can you go look in the back and try to find something that looks like a red suitcase with a white cross on it?" It was hard to speak around the thickness of his tongue, but the girls understood. They ran off, Matt toddling behind Rachel. Lionel spared a thought of gratitude that Matt looked like he was almost back to normal.

With the help of the little girls, Lionel found what he needed to do some repairs on his face and scalp. After packing his broken nose with gauze from the first aid kit and cleaning the blood from his face and beard, he resorted to a straight needle from a small sewing kit since there was no suture needle in the first aid kit Rachel found. It was a painful procedure with his left hand, done in front of a piece of the bathroom mirror that was left in its frame and Lionel threw up twice during the process with the children looking on anxiously.

Lionel and the two girls were searching for anything edible in the disaster that was their supplies when the sun dropped low on the horizon. Abi was standing as a lookout at the front of the store while Lionel and Rachel searched. Matt fell asleep behind the counter of the London Drugs on a package of sheets and pillowcases. Lionel used a corner of one of the sheets to make a sling for his right arm.

He was relieved to discover that it wasn't broken after doing some experimental prodding. He figured his elbow probably had a chip out of it, but that would heal faster than a broken bone.

The swelling in his right arm and various parts of his face and body would likely go down within a few days with the help of the Advil Abi had discovered. His headache was easing as well, thankfully. He would sport some nice bruises for a good while, but there was nothing he could do about that. He could only hope there would be no infection in his wounds, but he was happy to discover a couple of boxes of undamaged amoxicillin and one of azithromycin, so he was prepared.

Everybody was really excited when Rachel found an unharmed package of dried meat in the side pocket of the front passenger door of the van. They'd snacked on some of it on the way and stuck it in there and the vandals hadn't found it. After the bits of glass were carefully shaken out of the bag, there was a nice amount left. The discovery of a bag of freezer-burned peas and a small pot promised a bit of supper if they could find some way to boil everything together.

Lionel went to the front of the store in the gathering darkness, looked out of the window and wondered if he could risk a fire in the parking lot. He still felt nauseated, but he knew the kids had to eat. He bent from side to side cautiously, wincing from the jabs of pain in various parts of his anatomy. It could have been a lot worse; he reflected, sighed, and went back into the darkened store where he heard excited children's voices.

When he limped hurriedly into the lit backroom, he saw the kids were not alone. An older black woman was with them. She looked like someone who had once been fatter and had lost a lot of weight recently. When she saw Lionel, she moved quickly towards him.

"Sorry, I let myself in the back, I have the key, I'm … I was the manager here. I'm Louise Parent."

Rachel spoke excitedly, "It's ok, she's a good person. She wants to help us."

Lionel squinted at her; he had no time for niceties. "Why do you want to help? How did you know we were here?" His words were slurred but intelligible since he was speaking slowly and forcefully.

"Look, sir, I'm just trying to show you a kindness. I'm alone here, Phil my man is dead - and he didn't die of no jab neither. Both of us didn't want nothin' to do with that crap. Phil had diabetes and no meds, I got him what I could after they looted the stores but he needed insulin and that was all gone. Now, I just do what I can to help people. I seen you guys when you were going to that hospital. I saw the kids and I knew it wasn't going to turn out good. There's no kids left here. Don't know what happened to them after they started collecting them. I knew you wasn't from here, that's how. I seen you come in here and I wanted to warn you, but those gang people – I think that guy in the helicopter sent them here after you. Not sure about that, though. I had to wait until dark to come in the back. I'm pretty good at sneaking around by now."

Louise Parent ran out of steam and looked expectantly at Lionel.

Lionel was mutely staring at her. *Can I trust this woman? Are there any trustworthy people left? Why would a guy in a helicopter send the gang after me? I needed help. God, is this the help You sent me? Is she trustworthy?*

Rachel went to him and slipped her little hand in his left one. "Lionel, she's *good!* I just know she's good."

Lionel patted her on the back. OK, he would trust this woman for now. He shuffled over to a stool in the corner. "If you can feed the kids and give us a place to sleep tonight, that would be appreciated." He leaned forward, using his left arm to support his exhausted and agonized body on his aching legs.

"I can do that. Like I said, I'm pretty good at sneaking around, so I got food. It's three blocks from here. Can you walk?" Louise eyed him doubtfully. "We gotta go fast across the boulevard and nip in by the Value Village behind them stores. We can't be seen by the gang or the military. Can you run a bit?"

"I can run," Lionel said, though he wasn't sure. But he had to so he would.

He sent the girls off to scrounge up a bag of some kind for his antibiotics and the medicine for Matt. Matt was still sleeping, so he went over and gently roused him and led him by the hand into the back where there was some light to check him out. Matt sleepily rubbed his eyes then looked round-eyed at Louise.

"I expect that kid's yours, I don't think those little girls are, though," Louise commented.

"No, he's not mine..." Lionel began, but Rachel was back beside him and cut in.

"He's my dad now, I decided that. He can be Matt's dad and Abi's dad too but he's mine."

"I just kinda inherited them," Lionel mumbled.

"Well, the way them kids is with you tells me you're no child trafficker, so you're probably doing right by them. What was wrong with that little guy?"

"He was all - allgeric or something to shrimp. I fed him shrimp and he got sick," Abi piped up. She had just come in with a bag containing the food they'd found.

It was full dark outside now. They left through the shattered front door since going by the back door would be a longer walk and Lionel did not look well at all. They walked quickly, wending their way cautiously through the abandoned vehicles in the parking lot, the girls holding hands with Rachel's hand in Lionel's left. Louise, after asking Matt if he'd mind, scooped him up and carried him. He clung trustingly around her neck. Nobody looked at the destroyed Caravan as they passed, they had to move on now.

Lionel quickly discovered why Louise had survived for so long. She had to have the keenest eyesight and hearing of anyone he'd ever met before.

They were sheltering beside the paint store by the road after their careful trek through the debris-covered parking lot. Everything seemed to be dark and silent, and Lionel was grateful that the vandals had seen fit to smash most of the streetlights along the boulevard. Lionel thought it was all clear and figured they were going to make a dash for it.

"Wait, somebody is coming," Louise hissed, just as Lionel braced himself for a dash across the road.

Sure enough, less than a minute later a 250-cc motorcycle buzzed by with two gang members on the back.

"OK, let's go," Louise whispered once the motorcycle had disappeared around a curve.

The dash across the road was the slowest dash Lionel had ever made and when they got to the Value Village on the opposite side, he had to lean over and throw up again.

"Sorry, concussion," he explained as they made another slow dash across another narrower road to the back of a small strip mall.

Lionel was deeply grateful when Louise turned into the driveway of a house just a block and a half beyond the stores.

The house looked like the other ones on the street, dark and vandalized. There were even the remains of a corpse half on the overgrown lawn, half on the driveway.

"Don't mind old Tom there, he won't bother you," Louise said offhandedly as they shuffled by. The children did not look reassured and Lionel started to question his decision to come with Louise. They followed her up the steps of the front veranda and into the swinging open door of the house. Cold air blew in the broken front window and the house looked trashed.

"It's a mess, I know. I trashed it myself," Louise told them. "That way they didn't come and trash and steal my stuff, they thought someone had already hit it."

Lionel, leaning against the dirty sink in the kitchen because he had no more strength left, looked at her with surprise. That was amazingly astute on her part, however, how did she live in such a mess?

Louise put Matt down on the floor and pushed the door partly shut. "Tom out there is part of the cover-up. My Phil I buried out back. I hauled old Tom out of the road when I seen him lying there. He was one of those people that lost their minds. I seen it happen, like his brain started to melt and soon he couldn't even talk anymore. Weirdest thing. Anyways somebody shot him and left him there, so I used him as a camouflage. He used to work at the Save-On-Foods 'til he lost his marbles from the jab."

Some people can't talk and do anything, and Louise was one of them. The children were hungry and exhausted, and Lionel was ready to collapse, but Louise hadn't talked to anyone for so long, she seemed to not see their condition.

"Broke the windows myself, too." An expressive arm with loose flesh made an expansive gesture that was visible in the light of the flashlight Louise had produced. "Did it back when it was cold and snowing so it got darn cold in here. But nobody came, so I guess that was a win!" She suddenly noticed the exhaustion of her guests. "C'mon, let's get you guys something to eat and somewhere to sit!"

Louise bustled over to a door in the kitchen partially concealed by coat hooks on which hung a motley array of dusty ragged clothing. She opened it and led the way down the stairs into the basement. Abi followed her and Rachel took Matt's hand and helped him downstairs. Lionel followed slowly and painfully.

The basement was a surprise. Louise had made herself a cozy nest down there. There was a fully equipped self-contained kitchen, a pantry, a double bed, sofa and rocking recliner. The three windows were covered with dark fabric.

The children quickly decided the recliner was a really cool toy and were soon ensconced on it with the footrest up, rocking back and forth. Lionel fought the urge to collapse on the sofa since it looked very soft and he didn't think he would be able to get up again. He sat down gingerly on one of the old metal chairs with stuffed plastic seats next to the Formica table. Louise began heating up some tomato soup.

After a hot meal of soup and crackers, the children began to droop.

"I'll sleep on the sofa, Lionel," Louise said briskly, "you take the bed and the kids can sleep right there on that recliner. I've got blankets for them."

Lionel didn't protest. When Louise produced some expired Toradol, he took it gratefully.

When the Toradol wore off, he did wake up. He slept fitfully after that and kept waking up with pain in various parts of his body. He did have time to think, though. They would need a vehicle. He considered asking Louise if the kids could stay with her, but Prince George was a dangerous place and definitely not somewhere kids could grow up in safety. He would need a vehicle and food supplies and he was increasingly convinced that he would have to get his guns back or find weapons somewhere. Even his hunting knife had been taken by his aggressors in the parking lot, though they had not found his almost useless revolver. He could not protect the kids, hunt for food, or feel even slightly safe without weapons and ammo in this post-apocalyptic world. His heart also grieved for Janet's lost journal and the tiny carved butterfly. And he definitely needed his radio to keep in touch with George in Calgary.

In the morning when the others started stirring, Lionel painfully swung his legs off the bed. His body felt even worse than it had yesterday if that was remotely possible.

He stumbled and caught himself on a chair.

"You ain't goin' nowhere today, mister," Louise said briskly. "I got enough food here to keep you folks until you're feelin' better. Lie down again after breakfast. I got more Toradol if that helps. You got some Advil, maybe you can get some of that swelling down."

In the end, Lionel had to put plans to leave on hold for several days. Louise kept the kids entertained with books and some toys she scrounged up at a house down the street that used to have kids. She even found some puzzles.

Matt was back to full health by the time three days were up and Lionel's right arm started to work better once some of the swelling went down. His bruises were very colourful and Lionel figured he'd probably have a permanent bump on his thin nose. Both eyes were fiercely black, the right one especially. He had a look at the bruises on his body when he stood naked in front of the mirror in the little basement bathroom. *Lucky I had so much muscle from living in the wild*, he reflected, *it could be much worse.*

It was on the third day that Lionel was awake enough and his tongue wasn't so swollen anymore that he started to pick her brain about the situation.

"How long has that UN army detachment been here in Prince George?"

"Oh, I dunno, probably around the time they shut down all the mobile clinics up north and in the towns and reservations around here and told everybody who was sick that the University Hospital was the only place to get a booster to save their life. You shouda seen it. It was last spring it started, I think. People came by the dozen, then by the hundreds. Maybe even thousands. The military had already shut down the doors of the hospital and put up that orange fence and only let people in if they had two vaxes. No vax or no way to prove it, they sent them away. Told 'em to get the vax or no service. Crap, if you asked me. People lined up for days and days. They died in the streets and them soldiers just carted them off I dunno where. If people got in, I don't know if they ever got out again. You seen all them parking lots with cars just sitting there. Well, you should see the back of that hospital. I took a walk around there one time. There's thousands of cars and trucks just sitting there. They kept coming for months. There were kids...I saw them gang people collecting them in school buses, now they're all gone. I'll never forget those parents crying and calling for their kids and the kids with their scared faces being pushed into the buses, it was so horrible..." Louise's voice trailed off.

Lionel dozed a bit, thinking about the dreadful scene she'd just painted. *They took the kids. Where did they take the kids?* His mind drifted to his experiences in Hazelton. *Child traffickers. Are they the ones that trafficked those little Aboriginal kids? Is this where the witch got the kids? What should I do? What CAN I do?* Again, the voice of the old man in Dease Lake came to him: "Save the children." But, his hubris had already gotten him to this point: three helpless little kids in his care and only two bullets between them and the horror little Winona and Wabun had experienced. He forcibly wrenched his mind to an earlier conversation.

"When was the digital ID implemented?" he asked gently after a bit.

"Yeah, that digital ID. It started with a vaccine passport. It was probably a couple of years ago they brought that in. They said nobody without proof of the jab could go to restaurants or movie theatres. After that it was no non-essential services for the unvaxxed. Soon they started with the digital ID. My Phil said it was the mark of the beast and only the beginning. He was right. You know, it's only because of him that I know anything about this dirty crap the government - well, I don't know who because it's not just that fool PM of Canada, so it has to go higher since it was everywhere." She picked up Matt who had fallen asleep on the floor and gently placed him on the sofa for his nap. Abi was reading a picture book to Rachel in her schoolgirl reading, following the words with her finger.

"In every country, I mean. In the US some states held out longer, but they finally caved, I don't know why. Then it was vouchers with that digital ID - you know, they were calling them Socdits - money doled out for doing what the government wanted. Anyways, Phil told me what was going on way back when they started talking about the China virus. He'd say stuff like 'we're in a war and it's the worst kind of war 'cause nobody realizes we're being attacked, not by enemies from outside, but by enemies inside our gates'. Enemies inside our gates, he said that a lot. The government, the so-called universal health care system - run by Big Pharma, he said. Heck, even all the fake news media in on it, pushing the lies. 'We're fighting a war and we can't back down. We gotta never comply,' he said.

"My Phil was always checking into this stuff. He wanted to know why it was all happening. He found out about the Jesuits and Freemasons and how they're behind a lot of this garbage. They were behind ISIS and Mosaad – you know, the Israeli fighters. They just *pretended* to be fighting each other. They were behind 9/11. That wasn't real, Phil called it a false flag. They play both sides of every war, even the ones going on now. They do that to take control of everything. Of course, every world leader is a member of the Freemasons or Jesuits or controlled by them now. People thought for years that voting made a difference. It didn't really. The Jesuits were behind all the people they were voting for."

Lionel eyed her thoughtfully, thinking her opinion was very similar to Elmer's in Two Mile. The discussion he'd had on the topic in Smithers had made him think otherwise, but he decided not to debate the question and just let her talk.

Talk she did: "I told my family about some of this stuff and they all called me and Phil conspiracy theorists. But everything he ever told me would happen did happen. My sister got the vax, you know. When I wouldn't get it, she stopped visiting and told me I couldn't come over anymore. She lived up north side near the river. She was like 'you're not being socially responsible, you're risking everybody's life not taking the vax, you're supposed to care about others not just yourself.' So I'd asked what she's so scared about if the vax works. She didn't get it. It's like she lost her damn mind." Louise got up and started collecting some toys the kids had left lying about and fiddling around in the sink. She was angry and sad, Lionel could tell.

"I'd ask her if she'd obey if they started enforcing being 'socially responsible' by having to donate blood every month, or give a kidney to someone who needed it, or getting a hysterectomy or vasectomy or aborting a baby if the government says it's the socially responsible thing to do. She could never answer, she never even tried. She couldn't see that it's just about exactly the same thing as forcing a person to take a gene therapy treatment - that's what it was, that jab. She said it was like the yellow fever vaccine you have to take to travel to places like Egypt. It wasn't, not even close.

"She killed our mom, you know. She took her in for the vax two – three years ago. Mom was a healthy eighty-two. She'd go to bingo every Saturday at the Baptist Church. After Mom got her second jab, she had a heart attack and died. It was the day after I think. I only found out about it because my neighbour down the road came to say how sorry she was. She used to go to bingo with my mom. My sister didn't even tell me Mom died and I didn't get to go to the funeral cause I wasn't vaxxed so I was dirty...I think my sister's dead now too. I tried calling her a hundred times - after Phil died last fall and through the winter and she never answered." Louise snapped a drawer shut and startled Matt. He opened his eyes, so she hurried over and stroked his tousled blond hair until he fell asleep again.

"Why are you mad, Louise?" Rachel asked.

"It's OK, sweetie," Louise said, "I'm just remembering some stuff."

After lunch, the two girls fell asleep on the bed after a rousing game of don't fall in the ocean which involved walking on furniture without touching the floor. They arranged the four chairs and the coffee table strategically and were leaping from one piece of furniture to another while the adults watched. Matt wanted to play, but they told him he was too little, so he subsided on the recliner somewhat sulkily with his little arms crossed. He forgot his sulks when Rachel toppled a chair over and landed 'in the ocean' and faked swimming and drowning which made him laugh very hard.

When the girls fell asleep and Matt was playing with some Legos, Lionel resumed the conversation.

"When did the gang come? How did they manage to take over the city with the military just sitting there?"

"I don't know that. It's almost like that UN military lot were working with the gang and they divided out the city. Both of them, the soldiers and the gang, like shooting the sick people and homeless. They make a game of it. One lot is just as bad as the other. Did you notice the vultures?"

"Yeah, yes, I did. I didn't know they came this far north."

"First time this year," she responded. "Never seen them things around here before. They started showing up about a month ago. Weirdest thing. There's some bodies around, like old Tom out front, so they're well-fed. They don't even have to compete with the crows, magpies, ravens, and four-legged scavengers, there's enough for everybody. Still, considering the thousands of people that came here back last summer through the fall, there should be way more bodies. From what I can tell, more than half the houses in the city are empty, with cars in the driveway. Where's all the bodies? If they're alive, where did everybody go?"

Lionel shifted in the recliner and massaged his right arm. It was definitely feeling better. "So the gang runs the city now? Where are they holed up?"

"Yeah, they do pretty much run things. I think the military is going to pull out and leave it to them. Nobody is coming here much anymore, so no point in staying for that lot. They're holed up over in the Prestige Hotel, my mom went to the bingo there sometimes. At least I heard they were there last year. They maybe have other places now, there's a lot of them."

"Where is that hotel?"

"I dunno, maybe two klicks from here, a ways south. Why?" She eyed him curiously.

"I have to get my stuff back. I have a plan, but I have to see the place." Lionel did not share his burgeoning concern for the missing children, or the seed of a plan that was growing in his mind.

Louise then went to a drawer in the small buffet in the corner of the basement and pulled out something so precious, Lionel wanted to kiss her - a map of Prince George! Lionel and Louise stood by the table where the map was laid out. Looking at it, Lionel realized that three days ago he'd been so close to getting out of the city. Only a few blocks down the street from where he'd parked the Caravan was the eastbound leg of the highway that would have taken him out of the city. If he'd only known and if the kids had only not gone into that restaurant… he shook his head irritably and shifted his gaze to where Louise was pointing.

"Look," she said, "the hotel is just down there, yeah, that's about two klicks. I don't have a car, so you have to walk. Think you can do it? I think you're nuts, though. Didn't they beat you up bad enough? You want more trouble?"

"I'll check it out," he said quietly, "I have an idea."

There was a tiny sliver of moon in the quiet night sky when Lionel set out wearing Louise's husband's jacket and carrying a small flashlight. The jacket was black and had a black hood allowing Lionel to blend more easily into the dark. Breathing the cool spring air, Lionel's mind filled with a sense of heightened optimism about his chances. He carried his 9 mm in the pocket but hoped he wouldn't need to use it. He felt a piercing sense of wellness, his limbs were moving smoothly and in spite of his colourful bruises, he was healing well and strong again.

The walk was not long, he was soon approaching the hotel. It was brightly lit, but Lionel could tell that most of the windows were boarded up. It was easy to see why the gang would choose this place. It was away from other buildings and had an extensive fenced parking lot all around it with plenty of room for the many vehicles parked in front and the black helicopter that sat silently in the back. It was also on a highway that was relatively clear, so getting around for the gang members was easy.

As he circled around, Lionel puzzled about the presence of the helicopter. Was it the same one he'd seen at the hospital? It was certainly odd. Black with no insignia just like the one at the hospital.

It occurred to Lionel to check the parking lot for school buses since Louise had mentioned that children had been collected that way. There were no buses here, but that didn't mean anything.

Scanning the back of the hotel, Lionel found what he was seeking. Satisfied, he headed back to Louise's place.

The next morning, over a breakfast of waffles and jam, Lionel told Louise what he needed. "You're amazingly resourceful," he said, swallowing the last of his coffee. "Any suggestions as to where I can get a large party-sized percolator, enough vodka to fill it and a large quantity of red pepper? Oh, I'll need goggles as well."

"You're sure you want to do this?" Louise queried. "It's really dangerous going into the lair of the monster."

"Are there any guns anywhere else?" Again, he chose not to mention his suspicion that the missing kids might be in the hotel.

"I guess not," Louise said getting to her feet from the breakfast table. She fetched a couple of waffles from the toaster and placed them on the plate. "Not since that damn prime minister sent the UN army in to collect all the guns from everybody. They went door to door and anybody who looked remotely like they might have some, they searched the entire house. They even had a reward campaign for people to turn in others if they suspected they owned guns." She sat down again and savagely finished her waffle.

"Then I guess it's my only option since I know for a fact they have my guns," Lionel said. He put his fork and knife on his plate and took Abi's plate as well. She'd eaten just one waffle very tidily and was finished.

Louise wiped Matt's jammy face. Matt scrunched up his face as though that would help. Rachel took another waffle and piled a generous amount of jam on it.

"Young lady, I don't know where you put all that food, you're such a skinny little thing," Louise said to Rachel, then turned to Lionel. "OK, fine. That Save-On-Foods probably has red pepper, I can't see it being an item people would be dying to steal. You'll probably find goggles in the sports store if swim goggles will do. Vodka... vodka... hmmm, I don't know about that. I know someone who used to make moonshine. Would that work?"

"I'm sure it would, can we check with this person?" Lionel asked, then, "any leads on the percolator?"

"I'm pretty sure the Inn not far from here would have one, we'd have to go check. What you going to make with all that?" Louise asked curiously.

Lionel laughed. "Back in my high school days, my friend George and I..." he paused, remembering what a good friend George had once been, "we got into some shenanigans. It was a grade 11 science experiment he thought up. We only made a small amount, but it was lethal. It's pepper spray," Lionel explained. "We used my mom's percolator. Needless to say, it was useless after that. When my dad found out... well, let's just say that sitting down wasn't comfortable for a couple of days."

"You was raised right," Louise adjudicated.

The man who used to make moonshine wasn't around and his store of bottled moonshine was looted. They found a plastic barrel of the stuff in the basement, though, so Lionel had more than enough for his project.

By evening, all the required materials were collected. Lionel retreated to the garage and began cooking up his mixture by the light of a shuttered lantern. He was eager to get his plan going and didn't want to waste any more time.

The following morning, he wanted mineral oil and some fire extinguishers. They found the mineral oil in the paint store as well as a few fire extinguishers. A further search in London Drugs and some of the other stores in the mall and Lionel had eight fire extinguishers of varying sizes. He also found a bicycle pump with a gauge.

By the end of that day, Lionel had filled and pressurized his fire extinguishers with his concoction. He had barely thought about his injuries all day. His right arm was still tender and his bruises still dark and colourful, but he felt ready.

Lionel left when full dark fell, with Rachel beside him. Abi and Matt wanted to go, but when Lionel told them it was scary, they reluctantly stopped asking. Rachel was wearing a dark hoodie Lionel found for her during his searches for materials the previous day. It was too big, but it would have to do. Lionel's 9 mm was in his pocket again.

"Where are we going, Lionel?" Rachel asked as she skipped along beside him in the dark. The moon was only a sliver in the sky, and they were cautiously moving on the grass beside the sidewalks.

"You're going to have to be very brave and very quiet," Lionel told her, then he stopped abruptly and hunkered down, drawing her close with his hands gently on her two arms. "Rachel," his voice was just a murmur, "I need you to go inside the place where the gang is staying, open a door for me and let me in. You have to do exactly what I tell you to do without question or argument. You have to be really, really careful nobody sees you. Do you understand me? It can be dangerous, so don't take any chances. I don't want to lose you."

Rachel nodded her head in the dark, then suddenly Lionel felt her two skinny little arms around his neck in a tight hug. "You know I can do that, don't worry!"

They continued their quick walk hand in hand.

At the Prestige Hotel, Lionel went around to the back of the very large building. Only a few of the windows in the back were lit up and there was no illumination in the parking lot. The black helicopter was gone.

Lionel silently boosted Rachel up over the fence onto a dumpster that was pushed up against it. A couple of feral cats scattered as Lionel noiselessly landed beside the little girl. He scanned the area and jumped off the dumpster in the small space at the back where there was the least amount of garbage then held up his arms. Rachel jumped into them and he set her on the ground. Holding hands, two shadows moved along the fence periphery to the point where it intersected most closely with the building.

"OK," Lionel said in a whisper, "do you see that set of two windows in the middle there?"

Rachel squinted, then nodded.

"Those windows are broken and boarded up, but the middle board in the window closest to us is missing. I'm going to finish taking out the pieces of glass," he put on his gloves as he spoke, "and boost you through. It's dark, so nobody is there. I think it's the janitor's room. Here's a small flashlight, just use it if you're absolutely sure nobody is around." He put it in the front pocket of her hoodie.

"What you need to do is find a way to that door closest to us - do you see it? It's recessed into the back. Open it and let me in. I'll be nearby. When I get in, you're going to come out and go back to the same dumpster where we got into the parking lot.

Wait behind it. Listen to me Rachel, don't let anybody see you - ever! If I'm not back when it starts - just STARTS - to get light out, head back to Louise's house. Don't wait for me! Do not wait until it's light out, if I'm not back, go back home as quick as you can. Do you understand me? Please repeat."

"Don't worry, OK, um, you want me to go in, find this door nearest us, open it, and let you in, go out and wait by the dumpster, um, leave before it's light out if you don't come back. Got it! Can I go now?" Rachel was nearly dancing with excitement.

They noiselessly approached the building. Sounds of loud thumping music, yelling and laughter emanated dimly from a distance somewhere inside the hotel.

Boosting Rachel through the gap in the window boards was quickly done. She landed lightly in the dark room and stood for a few moments listening for sounds indicating anybody was nearby. Lionel stood anxiously by the window until he was sure there was no outcry and crept to the outside of the recessed door. Flattening himself against the wall, he settled down to wait. He found himself praying for her safety and asking himself why he would involve a small child in this undertaking.

Minutes passed. Then more time. His anxiety grew. He wished he had a watch so he could know what time it was. He crept back to the window Rachel had gone through and stood listening. A few vehicles roared away down the highway next to the hotel, then a few arrived. No sound near the window. Where was she?

It may have been an hour or just ten minutes since Rachel went into the hotel, when a crashing noise erupted inside the hotel, not far from the window. Some voices shouted and there was more crashing, then a gunshot. If Lionel had been able to get through the door, he would have barrelled in there to find her, but there was no way for him to get in. He rushed back to the window and tried to pry the bottom board off without success. He went to the second window that didn't have any boards missing and succeeded in getting one side of the bottom board off. He was preparing to wrench off the second side even though he risked rousing the gang with the noise when he heard a hiss from the far side of the building.

"Lionel, hey, Lionel, I'm over here!"

It was Rachel, and she was by the far door, not the one he had told her to come out.

He had her in his arms in moments and hugged her until she squeaked. "What happened? Never mind, you can tell me later, I'm glad you're OK."

"I told you I could do it. Lionel, my shoe's in the door. Put me down please."

Rachel squirmed out of his arms and went to the door and opened it. She put her blue running shoe back on. "If you go straight down that hallway," she whispered pointing inside, "there's a big room where there's a whole bunch of people. You should go the other way."

"Rachel, go to the dumpster and wait. Don't let anybody see you." Lionel gave her a pat on the head, entered the hotel and closed the door.

C H A P T E R   1 6

Fighting Back

I prefer dangerous freedom over peaceful slavery.

~ Thomas Jefferson

If you want total security, go to prison. There you're fed, clothed, given medical care and so on. The only thing lacking... is freedom.

~ Dwight D. Eisenhower

Rachel found the wait by the dumpster very hard to take. After what seemed like an eternity several vehicles roared through the back parking lot where she was hiding.

There was a lot of shouting and some gunshots, which startled her, however, when they roared off around to the front and down the highway, Rachel felt relieved. At least it had nothing to do with Lionel.

Another eternity passed. Feral cats pursued rats near her hiding place, startling her again. The sliver of moon moved across the starry sky. Where was Lionel? She began to hop in place, it was cold and getting colder. Finally, Rachel hunkered down and wrapped her thin arms around her legs, bowed her head to her arms and decided to pray to Jesus for her new dad.

"Psst, Rachel, are you there?" Rachel leapt to her feet and dashed to throw her arms around Lionel's waist.

"Ohhh, I thought you'd NEVER come!" she whispered and almost felt like crying.

Lionel chuckled quietly, "It's only been a couple of hours, not much more than that. Come on, let's go home."

He boosted her onto the dumpster, and they were soon on their way home. Rachel skipped along beside Lionel with her hand in his.

"Tell me what happened when you went inside," he said.

Rachel needed no encouragement to tell him about feeling her way through the storeroom in the dark, her tiny flashlight illuminating shelves and strange shapes that looked like hunched up people, then getting to the door to find there were gang members in the hallway nearby.

"It was a guy and a girl and they were doing icky grown-up stuff. I thought I could sneak by them after I waited a while 'cause they were busy doing stuff and making noise. But they were right beside the door and I was afraid they might see it open – I was being careful and only peaking through a crack, that's why I saw them. Anyways, I waited a long time and almost came back to the window to tell you about it. Then I heard another guy shouting and calling the girl bad names and telling the guy – the one with the girl – he was going to kill him. They started to fight and people were punching and swearing and banging around and crying then somebody shot somebody. It got quiet after a bit so I opened the door a little wider. There was a guy lying on the floor – I think he was dead – and the girl was down the hall on the floor crying. It was where I was supposed to go to let you in so I couldn't go that way. That's why I decided to go to the other door."

Lionel's hand tightened on Rachel's as she triumphantly finished her narrative. "You are so brave," he said. "How did you know about the room where all the people are? You missed that part in your story."

Rachel looked sideways up at him. "Please don't be mad, I just wanted to see where all the noise was coming from and I was really, really careful." Noting, in the increasing light of the early morning, his tightened lips, she hurried on. "It was safe because all the lights in the hall are broken so it was really dark there and I'm dark and wearing dark clothes, so it was safe. Really, nobody saw me."

Lionel sighed and refrained from commenting as they had arrived back at Louise's home.

He had found the solution to his dilemma. He was also armed with what he knew to be the janitor's master key for all the rooms. It had taken some time to find causing Rachel no small anxiety. He was prepared to make his move the following night. They had to be ready to flee the town after he collected his belongings from the thieves. *But I need to check for the kids. If there are kids in the hotel, I will have to come up with some other plan.* Lionel had been hoping to check the premises during his current excursion, but there were too many people roaming the halls and standing around in groups after the fight and the killing Rachel had witnessed. Unarmed – or basically unarmed having only two bullets and not even a knife, he didn't stand a chance. *Maybe I should have brought the pepper spray with me tonight. No, I don't have a vehicle yet and if I got chased by some gang members, they might get MY kids. I have to be properly prepared; it will have to be tomorrow night. At least I have a weapon now. My pepper spray will protect me – I hope.*

Over breakfast that was late because Lionel and Rachel had done some sleeping in, Lionel invited Louise to come with them.

"We're leaving after I get our stuff back; we may have to leave quickly. I'm taking the kids with me tonight. I'd like it if you came with us. I don't like the idea of leaving you here."

Louise shook her head. "Sorry, I thought about it last night, but I don't think I should. There's still people around that need my help. I think I should just stay and do my part."

Rachel got up from the table and ran around it to grasp the woman's hand. "Please come with us, Louise. We love you!"

Abi joined her, throwing her arms around Louise's neck. "Please, Louise, we love you!"

Louise sighed, hugged the little girls and Matt, who came to echo, "Pease Louise!"

"I can't," she said, raising her eyes significantly to Lionel, "you know why." She then addressed the children, squeezing them tightly, "I love you too." A couple of days before, Louise had confided to Lionel away from the children that she had started treatment for breast cancer before the China virus pandemic and was pretty sure her days were numbered.

Lionel sighed. "I respect that. Kids, Louise has made up her mind." He turned back to the woman. "OK, today, I need to collect enough food for a couple of days and find a functional vehicle. Do you have any suggestions?"

"It's going to be easier now," Louise answered, "while you were in the garage yesterday making up that brew of yours, you didn't notice, but most of the UN vehicles left the city. There was probably more than 30 army jeeps and vans that left. A whole bunch of them gang members started roaring up and down the road, honking after they were gone. Me and the kids, we watched them go from behind the hedge along the highway in the morning. Right, kids?"

All three of them nodded solemnly at her words.

"Getting a vehicle is easy. There's thousands back of the hospital - well, maybe hundreds, but there's lots. There is probably at least one person that left the keys in their car - unless you know how to hotwire a car."

Lionel grinned through his beard. "I'm a doctor, not a car thief."

Louise nodded, "Anyways, you don't have to worry about food, I can fill up whatever vehicle you choose with food. Me and Rachel went out and she taught me a thing or two about how to break into houses." Louise poked Rachel, who still had her arm around her neck, in the ribs. "First time I ever congratulated a kid for knowing how to break and enter."

Lionel smiled at Rachel. "Yes, she's really good at that," he said.

It was a cloudy day with incipient showers. Lionel cautiously made his way to the hospital, slinking along beside the stores and behind bushes when he could and making a dash across roads after careful checking.

Sure enough, there were no jeeps around the hospital and no sign of the army anywhere at all. They had even taken down their orange mesh fencing. Five motorcycles roared down the boulevard when he was making his way around the hospital. He pulled out the 9 mm and threw himself onto the long grass behind a bush until they passed.

Laying on the damp shaggy lawn of the abandoned hospital, he levelled his gun at the motorcycles, thinking how nice it would be to give them some of their own medicine. Maybe blow out a couple of tires. *Nah, that's dumb, I need my last two bullets for self-defence, and I sure don't need those guys coming after me!* When the noise of the bikes faded into the distance, he resumed his careful movement to the back of the hospital.

What he saw back there was a veritable densely packed parking lot. There were rows and rows of abandoned vehicles. He made a quick estimation and calculated that there had to be at least five hundred. He whistled quietly under his breath. Where were all the people who owned those cars? What had happened to them?

Many of the vehicles were loaded with personal belongings. Some of the trucks were hauling loaded trailers.

Tarps had flown off trailers and boxes of personal items and furniture were deteriorating from likely more than a year of exposure to the elements. Here and there he saw a small group of vultures or other scavengers cleaning up remains, some human, some animal. But there were not nearly enough bodies to explain where all the people had gone.

Lionel started down the first row of cars, trying doors to see if any were unlocked. It started to drizzle slightly, so he pulled the black hood over his head. He found a few unlocked car doors, but the drivers had brought their keys with them, or at least he wasn't able to find the keys. By the time he was on the eleventh row of cars, Lionel was reviewing the movies he had seen where the car thief would pull something loose under the steering wheel or ignition and join two wires to start the engine. *Will I have to develop a new skill?* he wondered. He poked experimentally under the ignition of a few vehicles. Nothing obvious occurred to him, even after he pulled out a clump of wires under the steering of an older F150. There were certainly no red and white or black and white wires that said, "join me to jump-start your engine."

He was more than halfway through the cars, searching a green GMC truck when the motorcycles roared back down the road. They were accompanied by a car Lionel knew all too well, the black car with the horns on the grill. Ducking behind the green truck, Lionel eased his way to the front to see which way they were going. He wanted to know if they were heading to the Prestige Hotel. He ran down the aisle between the cars to see if they turned right or left at the intersection. When they made a right turn, Lionel smiled grimly, "See you tonight, guys," then resumed his search.

He got lucky with a Honda CR-V. The passenger door opened easily, and when he checked the usual places people hide keys, the fob fell into his hands from where it was tucked up above the visor.

He climbed into the driver's side and started the engine. The motor whirred a bit, then started. "Good old dependable Honda," Lionel muttered, patting the dash. He had already located two jerry cans of gas in the trailer of one truck. They were both full.

Lionel collected the gas cans, and carefully wended his way through the city using the mental picture of the map to help him make his plans for departure. He finalized that evening's escape route then got back to Louise's without incident and parked the vehicle at the back of the house, taking care to circle around the desiccated partially eaten remains of old Tom.

They spent the next hour loading up the car. Lionel carefully nestled his fire extinguishers into a large gym bag Louise had scrounged up for him and placed it gingerly in the very back near the rear door after checking to be sure all the pins were secure. They worked together to load the food and other goods into the back seat.

Mid-afternoon, the car loaded and ready to go, Lionel went into the bathroom and carefully removed the black thread he'd used for his sutures. He would have a scar on his forehead and cheek, but the hair on his head would hide the huge healing scar on his scalp. His bruises had reached the pinnacle of colourfulness, purple and green and yellow. His right eye was fully functional and there was just a residual tenderness in his right elbow.

"Louise," he announced when he came out of the bathroom, "I have to go check something out at the hospital. I want to know where everybody went."

"You're a real glutton for punishment, aren't you," Louise said, shaking her head. "Don't worry, me and the kids will be fine. Just don't get yourself into trouble again."

Carrying the 9 mm in his pocket and a long-armed crowbar he found in Louise's garage, Lionel headed back to the hospital. There was a steady rain falling by then. He headed cautiously to the back of the building. He had spotted the rear unloading bay that morning and figured it would be easiest to break into and not be seen by someone on the road.

It was a simple matter to break the unloading bay lock. He bashed it a couple of times with the crowbar, then used it to pry the door open. The smell that wafted out once he opened the door was worse than anything Lionel had ever smelled before. He was used to smelling human and animal remains since he had started his trek to Calgary. This was much worse.

The first sight that greeted Lionel as he carefully stepped into the dimness of the big medical supply storage room was appalling. There were fresh bodies of more than 20 people dressed in scrubs. It looked like they'd all been recently shot in the back of the head and just left there.

But the dreadful odour was not coming from them. There were more than 30 bins lined up along one wall. Lionel was carefully stepping around the bodies of the dead healthcare workers to go check the bins when suddenly he heard whooping and hollering and occasional crashes somewhere inside the hospital. Evidently, the gang had clued in to the possibility of finding opiates and other fun medications in the hospital now the army was gone and had come to collect.

Undeterred, though keeping his ears open for any approach by an investigative thug, Lionel pulled the little flashlight he had brought with him and shone it into the first foul-smelling bin. He had found what had happened to so many people. Gagging, Lionel continued down the row of bins. Every single one of them contained partly decomposed bodies. Each bin looked like it could hold at least 25 or 30 bodies. Every one of the bins was full. Lionel bent over and threw up everything he'd eaten for lunch. Standing up again, wiping his filthy mouth with his sleeve, he determined to press on. Were there any children here? He had to know.

At the last bin, gasping and nauseated, he lingered, scanning the decaying human corpses with the flashlight.

When he got back to Louise's after making a long circuitous route to avoid the gang members that were still running through the hospital looking for euphoria-inducing treasures, he told her what he found.

"All the bodies were naked or dressed in hospital gowns," he concluded after recounting his perilous venture. "Some looked like there had been an attempt to provide medical help. I saw IVs in some of the hands. Limbs were missing on others from recent amputations, and there was evidence of growths and deformities on a few."

Lionel sat for some time, still fighting the rage and nausea that was threatening to overwhelm him. Finally, he looked up at Louise, his face sombre, "I didn't find any bodies of children."

There were tearful farewells, the children hugging Louise and reaffirming their love for her and pleas for her to come with them. She remained firm in her decision not to go. It was full dark now, still drizzling slightly. Lionel was grateful for the clouds and rain; it would help him be that much more invisible in the dark. Before starting the car, he turned to the children.

"I am going to do something very dangerous now. I need you all to listen carefully to what I'm going to say. I am driving you to a dark road on the other side of the river. I'm going to leave you there and go away. I'm leaving this little flashlight with you. You will have to go under the blue blanket I have here and hide if you're scared and want to turn on the flashlight. Nobody must see you or the light of the flashlight. You can sleep if you want but only talk in whispers. I have to go do something that might take a couple of hours. When I come back, I'm going to knock on the window like this." Lionel modelled the knock, four knocks, pause, two more knocks. "That's just to let you know it's me so you won't be scared. Can I trust you to follow my instructions exactly?"

Three pairs of worried eyes gazed back at him. The heads of the two girls nodded and Matt stuck his thumb in his mouth.

Rachel's voice was subdued, "Lionel, will you get hurt like you did before? That was so scary."

Lionel reached over and squeezed her shoulder gently, "I got hurt before because I acted without thinking and I wasn't ready. I'm ready this time. You know I have a really good weapon in the back of the car that will keep bad people from hurting me. You saw that bag, right?"

When Rachel nodded, he continued. "When I stop the car, everybody has to go pee in the grass. You can't get out of the car after I leave because I will lock the car and you mustn't unlock the doors. Whatever you do, don't get out of the car. No matter what you hear, don't make a sound. If you see anything, get under the blanket quickly and quietly. I will be back as soon as I can but it's best if you just go to sleep because the time will go by faster."

The heads nodded again. Lionel cleared his throat. He needed to let them know that this was the plan, but it may change. "There's something else. I may have to help some kids. If I find kids that need help, it might take longer. You need to trust me that I will come back as quickly as possible, but I *will* come back. You know where the food is that we packed. If the sun comes up and I'm still not here, eat something, but stay hidden. *Do not* let anybody see you. Ever. Do you understand?"

"You promise you'll come back, right?" It was Abi this time, eyes wide and anxious.

"I know!" Rachel said, "let's ask Jesus to protect Lionel and us."

"That's a wonderful idea, Rachel!" Lionel felt again his inadequacies as a parent. *I prayed and have been praying all day, but I never thought to include the children in those prayers. I have to do better if I'm going to be a dad to these kids.* Lionel reached out his arms and clasped the children in them. They all offered up simple prayers for protection with Matt lisping his "amen" after Lionel and the girls made their amens.

Lionel started the car but kept the headlights off. He drove carefully down the road, made a couple of turns, then stopped the car. He switched off the interior light, got out, opened the hatchback door, removed the large hockey bag of fire extinguishers, and concealed it behind a bush. He got back into the car and wended his way carefully with the headlights still off through the city and across the Yellowhead Highway bridge. Almost immediately, he turned down a side road and then pulled the car off the road into a dense stand of trees.

The children all obediently climbed out in the mosquito-ey night and peed. He hunkered down and gave them all a hug, repeating his instructions briefly in a quiet whisper. Another quick hug and he got them to climb back into the Honda and he locked the door.

Lionel hurried to a cloth carport by a house nearby where he had found a Volvo that morning. He had located the keys by breaking into the house. He made his way back to the spot where he'd concealed his gym bag, loaded it into the trunk and drove, with headlights off, as close as he dared to the hotel.

The sounds of partying were even louder than last night. "Enjoying your psychopharmaceuticals?" he muttered, carefully placing his bag full of fire extinguishers on the ground in a shadowy corner of the parking lot and checking that his handgun was readily available in the back of his jeans. Pulling out a finely honed ice pick formerly owned by the moonshine brewer, he started creeping slowly from one vehicle to the next, stabbing the tires. There were nearly sixty vehicles including several motorcycles, and Lionel figured on it taking at least an hour. He had flattened the tires of maybe 25 of the vehicles when a rowdy group slouched their way to the row of cars where he was working. Lionel immediately dropped to the ground and rolled under a nearby jeep.

"Pater said 'do the patrol', that's BS, there ain't nobody around dares interfere with us," a loud voice announced almost on top of Lionel.

"You shouldn't ought to talk like that, somebody might tell Pater." It was a quieter, more timorous voice. A loud slapping sound reached Lionel's ears.

"Who gonna tell him? YOU? You muffa, I kill you!" A tone from a key fob went off for a car whose tires Lionel had just stabbed. Lionel rolled across the pavement into the darkness under another vehicle a little further away and waited to see if there would be an alarm raised.

"Sheeit! Feckin tire's flat!" the louder voice swore. "You got the keys for your crappy Mustang on you? Gonna have to take your car, but I'm drivin'!"

Lionel breathed a sigh of relief; they hadn't noticed that the tires of all the cars beside that one were also flat.

"Sure, Banta." Footsteps faded towards the far side of the lot that Lionel had still not reached.

Lionel continued his mission, stabbing tires fast and hard and moving on. His back was getting tired from the crouched position and he had to keep switching hands with the pick because his right arm tired quickly.

Soon, there were only the four vehicles by the hotel that didn't have flat tires. Lionel considered flattening their tires too, but a single figure sitting on the hood of one of the vehicles smoking a joint changed his mind. It was time to act.

Lionel crept quickly and carefully back to where he'd left his hockey bag. Keeping to the shadows as much as possible, he went around to the back of the hotel to the small door that was used for garbage disposal. He had jammed the lock on his last visit here and, sure enough, nobody had noticed. Probably because nobody disposed of garbage regularly.

Inside the foul-smelling hotel, in the hallway lit only by a single unbroken light at the far end, Lionel found his way to the janitor's room where Rachel had first entered. He placed the gym bag in the dark room by the door, removing one fire extinguisher.

He slid silently down the dark corridor to the stairs and dashed up to the top floor, taking two steps at a time. Using the janitor's master key, he began methodically to search all the rooms. Most were unlocked and in shambles, evidence of frequent use by uncaring, unwashed tenants.

Even here, on the top floor of the hotel, Lionel could feel the vibrations of sound coming from the party room on the main floor. The smells of rotting food, sex, drugs and vomit in these rooms, the thought of the cacophony and wickedness below, and even memories of the witch of Hazelton, reminded Lionel of the world in the days of Noah. As the narrow beam of his flashlight preceded him from room to room, he recited the words he remembered from the book of Genesis:

"Then the Lord saw that the wickedness of man was great in the earth, and that every intent of the thoughts of his heart was only evil continually. The earth also was corrupt before God, and the earth was filled with violence. So God looked upon the earth, and indeed it was corrupt; for all flesh had corrupted their way on the earth. (Gen.6:5,11-12 NKJV)"

If God chooses to destroy the world really soon, I would not be surprised. This den of iniquity shows how degraded some humans have become. It is only the mercy of God that He has not destroyed this world with fire.

The tedium of his slow progress from room to room was causing Lionel severe irritation and anxiety. *This is taking too long, there are too many rooms in this hotel. I calculated 30 minutes for each floor and I'm only a little over half done this top floor and it's been nearly an hour! I have to find the kids soon if they're here!*

It was in the second last room of the top floor that Lionel found the woman. She was lying sprawled on the filthy bed, lumpy limbs splayed out, completely inert.

Initially he thought she was dead, however the narrow powerful beam of the flashlight passing over her face caused her to raise one chunky arm to shield her eyes.

"Wha... who's there? That you, Wilddawg?" her words were slurred. She struggled to sit up, dried bits of crusted vomit detaching from the fat of her neck and tumbling to the foul bedding.

Lionel paused at the door, indecisive and revolted. He kept the flashlight trained on her, appearing only as a tall dark figure to the sozzled woman.

His pause gave her time to get up from the bed. "I'm sorry, I'm sorry, Wilddawg, please don't be mad..." She extended her arms and began to stagger towards Lionel.

He found his voice; his words were harsh with disgust. "I'm not this Wilddawg person. Go back and sit down."

"Who...who are you?" She complied to his order, stumbling backwards and collapsing heavily onto the bed.

He ignored her question and asked his own. "Are there any children in the hotel?"

"Children? Whaddaya mean, children?" her voice squeaked. She was still under the influence of whatever intoxicant she had taken and was still slurring and sluggish.

"The gang collected kids in school buses. Where are those children?"

The woman's heavy head sagged on the thick neck. Pudgy fingers tipped with peeling black nail polish rubbed at the small eyes sunken in the swollen flesh of her face. "I...I remember that. Yeah, the children..." There was a long pause. "Who'd you say you are? Why you wanna know that?"

"I didn't say. I want to know what you did with the children. Where are they?" Lionel swept the room with the flashlight. Spotting a small overflowing trash can, he set his fire extinguisher on the floor by the door and strode quickly over to it. The woman cowered away from his rapidly moving figure as he dumped the trash and went to the foul-smelling bathroom. Feces and urine and other undefinable human waste were in the bathtub as well as blocking the toilet and Lionel had to swallow back his desire to gag as he ran water into the trash can and went back into the bedroom. He tossed the cold water in the face of the cringing woman.

"I asked you if there are any children in the hotel. Answer me now!"

Roused from her stupor by the splash of icy water, her response was clear. "You bastard! I gonna tell Wilddawg what you done. Who you think you are?"

"Just answer my question and I'll leave you alone." Lionel had returned to the door and retrieved his fire extinguisher.

"There ain't no kids here, you sumabitch, Pater sold 'em all to those army guys. Git the feck outta here or Wilddawg gonna kill you!"

"Thank you." Lionel opened the door, brought the bottom of the fire extinguisher sharply down on the door handle breaking it off. She'd be hard-pressed to find a way to reopen the heavy door and he hoped it would delay her being able to sound the alarm about his uninvited presence in the hotel. Having to touch the woman in order to tie her up was something Lionel could not imagine doing.

Loping rapidly down the nearest stairwell to the main floor, Lionel quickly found his way back to the janitor supply room to retrieve the gym bag with the other fire extinguishers and then to his goal. As expected, most of the gang was ensconced in the large conference room where the gang boss, whom Lionel now had reason to believe was named Pater, held court. Lionel had no cause to move quietly now, a huge sound system was blaring and the walls and floors vibrated to the thumping beat of the music. He was also grateful for the habitual vandalism of the gang since many of the lights in the hallway were broken leaving it mostly unlit.

There were two doors to the huge conference room. Lionel was prepared for that. He wound a heavy chain around the two door handles of the first entrance securing it effectively unless somebody went out and unwound the chain from outside. He slipped the long arm crowbar from the hockey bag, prepared for possible close-up conflict and bent to pick up the hockey bag he had deposited in an alcove by the second set of doors.

Suddenly, a group of men burst through the double doors. All five were armed.

Abandoning the hockey bag, Lionel swung around, lowering the heavy steel bar. He had been spotted. "God, help me!" he breathed. He would not escape now and had to engage.

"What the feck is wrong with those mu'ffukin doors?" then, "Hey, you agin! Gonna git…" It was the big man with the spider tattoo Lionel had met previously. Lionel was pleased to note that he still sported a discoloured eye from their first encounter.

Not allowing him to finish his sentence, Lionel stepped out of the alcove and swung the heavy crowbar at Spider Tattoo. Its weight was very similar to the metal bar that was used against him just a few days ago. His distinct advantage was that he had an excellent knowledge of anatomy and muscles to back it. His first blow felled his former antagonist when it hit his right arm with precision snapping the humerus. The large man screamed and dropped the SKS semi-auto he was carrying. Lionel's second blow followed almost immediately, striking the man in the right knee, and shattering it. He was down, but the other four men were on him.

Lionel felt a knife slash him in the side as he slammed his elbow into the knife-wielding man's nose. Another man fumbled a semi-auto handgun from the back of his jeans, chambered a bullet and attempted to aim it at him. Lionel seized a third man who was coming at him with a knife and threw him at the gun-wielder. The gun went off, the bullet striking that man in the belly. Lionel was already on the gun-wielder, both fists going as the fifth man dove at him. Lionel seized the gun wielder's hand, pointed the gun at the fifth man in mid-dive. The bullet hit the fifth man in the left eye but didn't stop his forward movement. He was large and heavy, and even if he was dead, he still threw Lionel across the hall. Lionel slid across the floor with the heavy man after him. He shoved off the dead weight and saw the man with the smashed and bleeding nose head to the doorway of the conference room to raise the alarm.

The heavy crowbar Lionel had brought with him was within arm's reach. He seized it and, from his position on the floor, whipped it at the man. It spun through the air and struck him in the back of the head. The man dropped like a stone.

The man with the gun still had it in his hand. He pointed it at Lionel and squeezed the trigger. Lionel rolled across the floor, feeling a bullet shatter the painted concrete right by his shoulder. He pulled his 9 mm from the back of his pants and squeezed the trigger in the gunman's general direction using his last two bullets, but as he was rolling across the floor, he found himself up against Spider Tattoo who had been determinedly crawling towards him and was bent on having his revenge. Spider Tattoo's huge left hand grabbed Lionel by the throat.

"You sumbitch," he snarled, "I gonna kill you this time." His thick fingers tightened on Lionel's throat, collapsing his adam's apple and cutting off his air supply. Lionel grappled at the beefy fingers on his windpipe, and he felt everything start to go dark. He tried flipping his body into a position to kick Spider Tattoo since they were both on the floor head-to-head, then he arched his body and managed to get his left leg under him. It gave him enough leverage to throw himself onto the man. Spider Tattoo didn't release his grip on Lionel's throat but now Lionel had the advantage. Retrieving his 9 mm from the floor, he slammed the butt of the gun repeatedly onto the man's face, breaking his nose and several teeth. He only stopped when the thick fingers on his throat loosened, and the hand flopped to the floor.

Suddenly remembering the gun wielder, gasping and sucking in air, Lionel leapt to his feet, off the unconscious Spider Tattoo. The gunman was down, clutching at one shoulder with blood oozing profusely from between his fingers. A wave of nausea suddenly overwhelmed Lionel and he sank to his knees in the dimly lit hallway.

"I'm sorry," he said to the man who was losing consciousness. He gazed around him at the carnage in the hall. Those men were all injured or dead because of him. *But life is so cheap, now. They fight and kill each other randomly, like that man that Rachel saw killed.* He remembered how David had been beleaguered by his enemies and had to fight and kill so many. *He was blessed by God. God called him a man after his own heart. God, am I doing this battle for You?* Suddenly, in the dark solitude, he heard the words Louise had spoken. *We're in a war and it's the worst kind of war 'cause nobody realizes we're being attacked, not by enemies from outside, but by enemies inside our gates. We're fighting a war and we can't back down. We gotta never comply.*

The pounding, vibrating cacophony from inside the room continued while Lionel's thumping heart gradually slowed to the tempo of the beat and his mind churned. *Guns, there's guns here. I can take these guns. Maybe I won't find my pack, but I'll have these guns.* He rejected regretful thoughts of his radio, Janet's diary and the little butterfly. *I have to protect the kids; that's my priority right now.*

Wiping his hair back from his perspiring forehead, Lionel scooped up the Sig Sauer from the floor and tucked it into the front of his pants where he could reach it easily. A quick search of the bodies found another full clip of rounds for the gun, and he tucked it into a pocket. He found an extended magazine for the SKS next to the owner. His own 9 mm went into the back of his pants. He also collected the switchblade that still had some of his own blood on it then scooped up the Russian SKS. It was already loaded with a clip that looked like it held at least 30 rounds. Lionel slung it by its strap onto his back, picked up his gym bag of fire extinguishers and slung it by its strap over his left shoulder. All this took less than a minute.

Suddenly, as he was preparing to leave, he saw a lumpy female figure rushing towards him from the dimness at the end of the hall. Her small piggy eyes were starting from her swollen face, fat arms rotating wildly, heavy feet pounding the floor. She was madly screaming unintelligible garbled sounds mixed in with the names of Maddawg and Pater. Her headlong dash was like that of a rhinoceros in full rout. It was the woman from upstairs that he had believed to be safely sequestered in her room.

Lionel stepped back abruptly. *I can't stop her! She's huge – and disgusting! I am NOT going to shoot a woman, I have to get out of here!*

The chunky woman barrelled through the bodies littered on the floor, slid on a pool of blood and charged through the swinging double doors of the conference room just two metres from Lionel. Her shriek increased in volume, if that was even possible. "Paaaaaaaater, Paaaaaaaaater, PAAAAAAAATTTTTEEEEEERRRR!"

Lionel risked a glance through the wildly swinging door. A trick of the rotating, pulsing multicoloured light at that precise moment illuminated the very thing he had penetrated this den of evil to find: his bag! It was the glare of the lurid light on the solar panel at the top of the bag that had caught his eye. *It looks intact! My bag! Maybe my radio is still there! The diary, my medicine pouch! I need those things! OK, that's it. I'm going in. No need to kill anybody, just spray 'em, so spray I will!*

He donned his gloves and goggles from the side pocket of the gym bag and pulled the heavy bandana he had tied around his neck up over his nose and mouth.

Standing just on the threshold within the open door, Lionel was not at all surprised that nobody had heard the screaming woman or the gunshots just beyond. The entire hellish scene pulsated and vibrated with the dissonant cacophony pouring from the speakers around the room. The darkness in the vast chamber throbbed with flashing strobe lights and disco balls casting multi-coloured beams erratically through the smoke-fogged murk. In the lurid light gyrating figures pounded the air, gleaming green, purple, blue, red, green, purple, blue, red. Here and there, bodies reclined or writhed together on sofas or mattresses that were hauled into the room. In the very centre of the strobing darkness and bedlam, there was a large round bed mounded with pillows. By the bed was a huge shadow of a man, maybe twice Lionel's size looming over the wildly gesticulating fat woman who had so precipitously entered the room. It was Pater, Lionel was sure of that, and his bag was within less than a metre of him. The enormous man suddenly swung one massive arm, knocking the woman to the litter-strewn floor.

As the first cry of alarm was breaking out in the room with figures scrambling to their feet or grabbing for abandoned weapons, Lionel slipped the pin off the first fire extinguisher and pressed the lever. The fiery liquid poured from the nozzle arching more than two metres in front of him. He swept the area on all sides, moving steadily towards the centre of the chamber to his goal. Screams erupted, people clawed at their faces and frantically scrambled to get away from the peppery searing fluid. Lionel threw aside the first fire extinguisher and pulled a second one from his bag. He resumed his advance. People who did not get hit with the fiery spray were also screaming and rubbing their eyes. The pepper was volatilizing into the already unwholesome air.

The huge figure by the bed yanked an automatic weapon from the mound of pillows as Lionel approached, spraying his noxious pepper-laden mist steadily around him. The massive man shoved a magazine into his weapon and turned towards Lionel, then the pepper fumes reached him. Blinded, with the tears gushing from his eyes, he began strafing the room indiscriminately.

More shrieks and cries rose up. Lionel was within a few metres of his objective and continued to advance, crouching low and trying to stay out of range of the rounds spitting out of Pater's weapon. A bullet pinged off the fire extinguisher in Lionel's hands, knocking it to one side. Lionel pulled out his fourth fire extinguisher and slid the pin out. Pater was still roaring and now he was pointing his lethal automatic rifle straight at Lionel even though it was evident he couldn't see anything through his streaming inflamed eyes.

Suddenly behind Lionel, a fire erupted in the doorway. It roared its hungry way along the track of the alcohol-based fluid pouring from the nozzle of Lionel's fire extinguishers.

This was not part of the plan.

The room filled with smoke. Somewhere in the bedlam, the sound system got disconnected and the pulsating music was replaced with a cacophony of screams and wails as people turned into human torches with the filthy furnishings, pillows and drapes fueling the flames.

The only exit that Lionel had not chained shut was now blocked by the roaring inferno. Pater had stopped shooting when his throne caught fire. Toxic smoke and malignant flames raced to devour everything and everyone in their path.

Gasping with horror at the inferno he had unwittingly caused, Lionel wrenched the hockey bag off his shoulder. He dropped it and dove for his backpack. Scooping it up, he sped to the far side of the conference room through the debris of writhing bodies to the row of external windows. He couldn't remember if they were boarded up like the ones in the back. He had to take his chance.

Lionel seized a metal chair from a corner nearby and heaved it at the window with all his strength. The glass shattered and fresh air poured into the room.

Oxygen was exactly what the fire wanted. Lionel had to get out of there but the barrier he had feared present was indeed hindering his exit. He kicked savagely at the wood. It cracked. He kicked again, panting through his bandana as a cloud of toxic smoke poured toward him. He had to get out now! Another savage kick and one side of the plywood ripped loose. Lionel backed up and threw himself against the barrier knocking his goggles to one side.

Three screaming female figures ran towards him, beating at the live sparks on their clothing and in their hair, leapt through the opening and fled, still wailing, and disappeared. Lionel looked around into the inferno.

"Come outside this way!" he shouted into the roaring flames, cacophony of destruction, and screams. A whoosh of air from the broken pane, the flames took power, rising to the ceiling and roiling towards him. He turned and plunged out the window, a monstrous searing dragon of fire after him. Vibrant hues of orange, red, and yellow surged towards the night sky, licking at the air with a voracious hunger. A tsunami of searing heat followed by smoke, thick and black erupted from the shattered window.

But he was out!

He scooped his pack up off the ragged grass realizing he still had the Sig Sauer and the Russian SKS.

A series of explosions resounded in the conference room. All the windows blasted outwards spraying shards of glass and pieces of wood like projectiles. Lionel turned from the conflagration into a small group of tattooed gang members who were gathering.

The gangsters were stunned at his sudden appearance, leaping through the inferno to the damp grass like a bolt from hell. They gaped at him for a few moments before realizing that he was not one of them. Lionel had only moments to react. He pulled the Sig Sauer out and fired randomly in the direction of the men as he sprinted toward the parking lot and the disabled vehicles.

A volley of shots went off aimed in his direction, coming dangerously close to Lionel's zig-zagging figure. The entire building seemed to be burning now.

Arriving at the first row of vehicles, Lionel ducked down behind them. Staying low, he slid carefully to one side to peer toward the enormous inferno. Gasping in horror, he realized there was no way to save anybody in the building. Had anybody managed to exit out the back? Then he remembered the chains around the second door to the conference room. He expelled his breath with a groan and reached up to wipe sweat from his forehead. Only those three people that had exited before him likely survived. His glove came away black from the ash of the fire. It was falling thickly now, even the roof was in flames.

He tore his eyes from the hellish vision when a bullet pinged off a car nearby.

"I seen him! C'mon!" a voice shouted.

Lionel's hands tightened on the handgun. He had to move - now! There were five armed men out there and they were looking for him!

A sixth man skittered back to the agitated group. "That fucka flattened all the tires!" he was bellowing furiously.

"Not mine, he didn't." Lionel recognized the speaker as the driver of the horned car, the scarred man missing one ear, whom he had encountered before.

"Git that fucka!" the scarred man roared. The gang members loosed another volley of shots where they had last seen Lionel with their automatic weapons. Two men began raining bullets in his direction while plunging down the row of cars where he was hiding. Lionel scrambled, crouching low to the next row.

The scarred man leapt into the horned car and the powerful motor thundered to life. The other men dove through the doors into the car's interior. Revving the engine furiously, the driver slammed the armoured vehicle into the parked cars. The plough-shaped grille guard shoved the cars to either side clearing the way through the centre. The passengers had the windows down and the barrels of several automatic weapons were hailing bullets to either side, aiming to mow Lionel down.

Lionel ducked down and broke into a run. Bullets smashed into the vehicles behind and beside him. His mind raced. *What can I do now? I have to stop their advance! Perhaps a fire again?*

Using the Sig Sauer, he shot out the gas tanks of the vehicles as he scuttled through the parking lot. Gas began pooling on the broken pavement behind him. The roaring horned car was getting closer, this was taking too long. He dropped the pack and fumbled in a small pocket with his left hand. His right hand still held the Sig and he managed to shoot out the gas tank of one more car as bullets peppered the car right next to him and one zinged through his hair. A strong odour of spilled gas rose into the air from the growing puddles of fuel under and next to the vehicles in the path of the roaring monster coming up behind him. Just before he ducked down behind a lifted RAM with oversized tires, he flipped the burning lighter towards the nearest pool of gas, whispering a prayer.

There was a moment when Lionel thought the lighter had gone out or he had missed his aim. Multiple rounds continued to pour from the muzzles of the weapons and the driver of the horned car swerved toward Lionel. Suddenly there was a swoosh of flame and the car next to the pursuing vehicle exploded. The explosion set off the other cars. A whole series of blasts split the night and Lionel set off at a run without looking back. Shrapnel flew in all directions and the entire parking lot was an inferno of detonations. The armoured car continued its forward movement, but it was on fire now. Only inertia kept it moving towards Lionel. He was by the fence and could go no further. He dove to one side as the vehicle struck the fence and blew up.

Lionel pulled himself upright, automatically brushing dirt and mould off his clothes. Panting, heart racing, he almost staggered where he stood. Tongues of flames were brilliantly visible through even the upper-floor windows of the Prestige Hotel. The entire parking lot was a sea of fire and more vehicles exploded into the night.

Lionel ripped the filthy gloves off his hands and slowly removed the heavy bandana from around his neck. Wondering vaguely when he'd lost the goggles, he sank to the damp grass.

What had he done? He was a doctor, he had dedicated his life to saving people. Yet now, in a violent act of self-preservation and in order to retrieve some stolen property, he had killed - how many? All those souls snuffed out because of him. *O God!* The vision of the human torches in the darkness, the screaming and the wails - everything re-ignited in his churning mind. He crouched in the wet grass until the shuddering and panting stopped. It took a long time and it was only thoughts of the children waiting expectantly in the car that got him moving.

Afterword

Tendrils of light were appearing on the horizon when Lionel got back to the car. Though his eyeballs were still seared with the horrific sights of that night, seeing the sleeping children calmed his troubled mind.

Matt and Abi were sound asleep and only Rachel was awake and alert. He gave his special knock and Rachel, who was sitting in the driver's seat, flung the door open and jumped into his arms.

"Lionel, oh, I was so scared you wouldn't come back! Lionel, you smell like fire and ... what's that weird smell?" Rachel sneezed, though she didn't release her grip on his neck.

Lionel squeezed her back, her small thin form in his arms a balm to the anguish in his mind.

Lionel turned his face from the little sneezing girl. "Hey, careful where you're sneezing, kid," he said. He realized that even though most of the volatile mixture was gone from his clothes, there was still pepper. He gently unwrapped Rachel's arms from his neck. "Get in the car under the blanket, Rachel, it's cold out here."

He took off his jacket and banged it a few times on a nearby tree. Rachel had not returned to the car, she stood in the dimness of the early dawn and looked at him. "You're bleeding," she said after a few moments of inspection.

"Gee, Rachel, you have cat eyes! Don't worry, it's nothing." He looked longingly at the pack on the grass by the car. Inspection of its contents would wait until daylight. It was time to move. He could already tell that the solar generator panel was still in place with his .308 rifle on the side. He permitted himself a small feeling of happiness that none of the gang had been interested in his gun since it was a repeater, not auto. For them, their weapons were for mayhem and murder, not hunting for food.

He heaved the pack into the back of the Honda and left his jacket there as well.

They were soon heading east towards the rising sun leaving Prince George behind them.

About the Author

Simone Georges has been a teacher for more than 30 years. She was born in Montreal, lived in Quebec and later in Ontario until 2007 when she undertook a great adventure and became a vice-principal in a school in Kuwait.

She spent the next seven years in various roles in Kuwait and did a lot of travelling. She married a charming young Syrian man during that adventure and ended up bringing him back to Canada. They settled in Alberta. Their marriage lasted 12 years, and they remain good friends though they have gone their separate ways.

She is now pursuing the dream of country living. She has a homestead with lots of animals, a big garden, and tons of fresh air and silence – all conducive to fulfilling her REAL dream of writing.

Stay tuned, there's a lot more coming!